# BENEATH THE SURFACE

## A NOVEL BY
## TREY EVERETT

Black Rose Writing | Texas

First printing

This is a work of fiction. Names, characters, businesses, places, events, and incidents are either the products of the author's imagination or used in a fictitious manner. Any resemblance to actual persons, living or dead, or actual events is purely coincidental.

ISBN: 978-1-68433-833-7
PUBLISHED BY BLACK ROSE WRITING
www.blackrosewriting.com

Printed in the United States of America
Suggested Retail Price (SRP) $18.95

*Beneath the Surface* is printed in Baskerville

*As a planet-friendly publisher, Black Rose Writing does its best to eliminate unnecessary waste to reduce paper usage and energy costs, while never compromising the reading experience. As a result, the final word count vs. page count may not meet common expectations.

*For the Thirst Project, and the ThinkTank.*

# BENEATH THE SURFACE

"It is an interesting biological fact that all of us have in our veins the exact same percentage of salt in our blood that exists in the ocean, and, therefore, we have salt in our blood, in our sweat, in our tears. We are tied to the ocean. And when we go back to the sea - whether it is to sail or to watch it - we are going back from whence we came."

JOHN F. KENNEDY, 1962.

# CHAPTER 1
## MICAH

The ballroom clatters with the faint clinking of expensive china, and the kind of hushed whispers of people who know they should not be talking. They know their conversations can wait, but they do not care. Normally it would bother me, the obvious lack of interest by the exact people I was supposed to be captivating, but not tonight. I am honestly not sure I even notice. I am singularly focused on my hope for the outcome of the evening's event. An intense focus I do not typically experience, but one I am sure I will be proud of when I look back on this moment. Maybe tomorrow I will let myself feel the pride I deserve. Right now, I am too focused to feel anything. Too focused to hear the chatter or the dinnerware clinking.

I walk up the small, two-set staircase and take a few steps onto the makeshift stage. Looking out at the not quite rude, not quite disinterested crowd, I turn my glance down towards the small, plastic remote of a wireless projector in my left hand. It had taken me almost a month to find a projector powerful enough and with the appropriate number of lumens to display my presentation in high definition so I could try and keep the audience's attention in such a large conference hall. Time well spent; I suppose. A plain black slide displays a large, bold word in white text on a massive screen behind me:

WATER.

I will always hate public speaking. It has made me feel sick to my stomach from grade school, all the way through both of my graduate degrees. Speech classes were my absolute least favorite of any required course. I can feel my index finger start to pick at the dried skin at the end of my right thumb. A familiar and comforting, but perhaps nasty habit I have had since I was a child. Sort of an anxious tic, I suppose, like shaking your leg or biting your nails. Since my childhood, I have gone through many seasons of painful scabs on the ends of my fingers from this odd, but soothing, form of self-mutilation.

"You handle stress so well, Micah," classmates, then colleagues, would say. *That's because I'm butchering the tips of my fingers,* I would think in response. I give my hand a small amount of my focus and slip it into my pocket to avoid making myself bleed on stage. With my stomach in my throat and sweat starting to bead on my forehead, I take a large, drawn out breath. I feel the oxygen hit my brain. I am ready to speak.

"As of today, our planet's population has reached over 7.8 billion people," I begin. "Of those almost eight billion people, roughly one billion do not have access to safe, clean drinking water." From underneath the podium I am standing next to, I grab a plastic water bottle I had hidden from the audience. The water inside the bottle was dark and cloudy. Not quite brown—tan or khaki, perhaps. Water that is not safe, nor clean, but effective. I simply set it down on top of the podium, and I feel the previously distracted audience's whispers start to die out. The energy in the ballroom shifts towards me. I was starting to win the battle for their attention, and I was just getting started.

"Updated estimates show that around six thousand children die every single day from preventable, water-related illnesses and diseases. A lack of access to proper hygiene, sanitation, or even having to drink water like this," I reference the plastic bottle. "That's about one child every 14 seconds." I click the projector remote in my left hand, and on the screen a timer starts counting down from fourteen... *thirteen*...

*twelve… eleven.* I intentionally ignore it, knowing damn well every other person in that ballroom cannot do the same. The weight of each person's realization is palpable in the room, so I sit with it for a brief moment. I let them grapple with the understanding of what I just shared, combined with what they are looking at. This timer will eventually hit zero, and if what I have just said is true, a child somewhere in the world will have died. "What happens then?" They will think. "Will the timer simply reset and start again?"

"Building just one freshwater well in communities lacking this precious resource can provide enough safe drinking water to all of the people living near it, every one of them." The timer continues ticking down, and just before it hits zero…

*Click.*

I move onto the next slide.

An uncomfortable sigh washes across the crowd. I hear no chatter now. No clinking of expensive silverware or champagne glasses and, whether they want to be or not, they are listening.

The next slide is a bright contrast of color compared to the black and white despair of the fourteen-second timer. A child in a striped orange T-shirt smiles as fresh water pours over his hands. Another child in cutoff jean shorts celebrates similarly over the flow of clean water pouring out of a handmade well in their village in Eastern Africa. Their smiles are electric, brilliant. The joy in their eyes physically fills the room. The joy of ignoring wet clothes and feeling the cool splash of water on your face in oppressive heat. The kind of joy you know is part of real, authentic happiness, a happy life. A life we all take for granted.

*Click.* I move to the next slide.

A few images now sit on the same screen. A dam full of water, next to the same dam with none. A luscious riverbank full of green life and a rushing tide, next to a deer standing in the same riverbed, now dry and brown. Recognizable tourist locations in California full of life, then the same locations covered in dirt and dust.

"In 2011, our country saw the beginning of the worst drought we've ever experienced in recorded history. Over a decade later," next slide with more before and after images, "we're nowhere near," next slide, "solving this crisis." One more slide for effect, "Until now."

The crowd now sees the logo of Cark Strategies Incorporated. Simple red text and a blue line running along the bottom edge. With different words, you would probably think it belonged on a sign lining Main Street during election season. "Vote Jennings, US Representative," or something similar.

"Cark Strategies Inc," I explain, "is a tech start-up founded in late 2016 with the intention of…" I read along as the next slide adds: *"Designing Technology for a New Tomorrow."* I feel it coming, and try to stop it, but a slight smirk cracks the side of my lips. I had hesitated about the timing of that anecdote, but sometimes theatrics pay off. We will see soon enough if I was right.

"Their founder, Jason Cark, and I have been working tirelessly over the last eighteen months to find the solution. The solution to our world's greatest threat that's right here at home." I again click onto the next slide. A *Google Maps* image of, "Alaska, more specifically the Gulf of Alaska." I click the remote again, and the slide zooms in slightly to a better view of a tiny island off of the coast in the Alaskan Gulf labeled *Kodiak Island.*

"Over the last four to six months, we've been monitoring a strange phenomenon occurring in areas near the eastern coast of Kodiak Island in the Alaskan Gulf."

A new slide shows new terrain images on the projection screen. Drought worn wildlife, brown and dead, with dried up reservoirs. "Large, hard hit areas of the island have somehow begun rejuvenating themselves, restoring themselves." I click to the next slide and my audience sees the same area from the same vantage point, but now full of a luscious green landscape with exotic flowers. Animals drink from the refilled pond. "It's as if portions of the island have somehow tapped directly into a pure water source. A clean, fresh water source effecting this side of the island specifically. In short, we think the island has, and we think we've found it."

In a matter of a few impactful moments, the crowd has made the journey from disinterested to concerned. Now, they even seem slightly impressed. I know without question the imagery and implications are why, but I do not care. These photographs literally showcase death being given new life. It is impressive, and like I said, theatrics work. Images are more interesting than words anyway. The screen displays the island again, Kodiak Island, in the gulf. I continue, noticing my newfound momentum.

"About two-hundred miles off the coast of Kodiak Island, we've discovered what appears to be a blue hole." I zoom in to a spot of the ocean on the left side of the slide to reveal a noticeably dark, circular blemish on the ocean floor. "I'll let you all Google what a 'blue hole' is later but think of it as an underwater sinkhole. A source of natural, fresh water in the middle of a saltwater world. The Pacific Ocean."

I click back to the Cark Strategies, Inc. pseudo-political logo, tagline and all, "Designing Technology for a New Tomorrow." Something about the phrase "for a new tomorrow" makes my stomach turn. The idea of a company taking something so idealistic and using it to convince the public they are a force of altruism, while simultaneously stripping, mining, and destroying the very Earth they are creating technology to protect is sickening.

"I have spent countless hours studying the water patterns and abnormalities in the oceanic currents of this particular region of the gulf. I believe that located within this blue hole is a system of natural jet streams pumping potentially hundreds of millions of gallons of freshwater into the sea. The Pacific Ocean's very own freshwater well." I can tell these old, rich, now listening patrons are eating up every word. Let them feast.

"So. The question I'm sure you're all wondering is, 'How does all of this relate to those two, cute kids from that village in Eastern Africa?'" The crowd laughs, and I know I have them right where I want them. "I believe that if we can tap into just one of these freshwater jet streams, we could potentially provide enough fresh, clean, and safe drinking water for our entire planet. All eight billion of us."

At the sight of a new slide showing an animated graphic of clean water being extracted from the blue hole's ocean floor and pumped into containers on a cartoon boat labeled, "Clean," the crowd erupts into applause. I let myself smile, just a little. The applause feels good, and I welcome it. I earned it. After a moment, though, I know the work is not done and I raise a hand, quieting the crowd.

"Not so quick, everyone," I say laughing through my words, "hold on." They join me in a brief, and slightly uncomfortable outbreak of laughter. They know exactly what is coming now. I seize the opportunity to throw in a little humor, "Come on, now. You know I wouldn't be hosting this event if we had it *all* figured out," I say as we all politely chuckle. "With Cark Strategies, Inc., Jason and I have put together a team of the world's most skilled deep sea divers, and we have developed some of the most advanced technology ever created to achieve this goal, but we need your help." I pause for a moment. The truth is I *do not* need their help. I am the foremost leader in my field. I am a decorated scholar, and a tenured University professor. I have won awards for my research, and my ability to solve massive world problems. *I do not need their help.* Not even a little bit. I need something else from them. They know what it is, too. "If I'm being completely honest, really, I just need your money." It is not every day such an intense level of honesty can win over a large group of wealthy people, but this seems to be one of those days. The audience laughs again. I laugh with them, relieved this obviously intentional moment of humor seems to have landed with my target audience.

"Look, I've done the research. I've done the preparation. I've crunched the numbers, then I crunched them again. This is a discovery with the potential to literally save our world. The question is: do you want to be a part of that? Join me. Let's make history. Thank you."

I instinctively hold my hand in the air, half waving a grateful farewell, half begging the crowd for their praise and adoration. They give me exactly what I want. An immediate, and prolonged standing ovation. I pump my fist in the air one more time, really soaking it in. I feel like Freddie Mercury just before his signature "ey-yo" call and response. They love me. For a brief moment, I take my glance to the edge of the curtain behind me on my left. I see Sarah clapping. Sarah—my biggest supporter and cheerleader, the love of my life, the inspiration for my work and research, my wife. I smile at her, and she is almost jumping up and down. I give a quick wink before I pump my fist into the air one more time, like a true rock star. She blows me a kiss.

I walk off the small stage, and Sarah immediately jumps into my arms and embraces me. She wraps her arms around me and squeezes hard. She is not crying, but there are tears in her eyes as she kisses my cheek and whispers with a soft tone, "I'm so proud of you."

I remove my lavalier mic and battery pack before I make my way out onto the ballroom floor. I am almost immediately swarmed by potential donors innocently questioning my numbers and ideas, as if they would be able to find my tell if I was fabricating anything. I take their questions seriously and with reverence, regardless. *It's all part of the gig,* I tell myself. Few things in this life are as frustratingly tedious as explaining the science of water purification to someone whose only true experience with water is deciding between still and sparkling while they wait for their cocktail at a 3 Michelin Star rated steakhouse.

Sarah and I finally arrive home after what feels like years of questions and answers. With heavy arms, I toss my apartment keys down, and they hit the kitchen counter with a loud clank. Sarah hurries past me into the pantry. She is so excitable when she feels like something went well, especially if it was something she was nervous about. She was definitely nervous about tonight. Truthfully, I am not entirely sure why. The only expectation I held for her was to show up, smile, and look beautiful, which she fulfilled flawlessly and effortlessly. *God, she is so good. She is so good to me. We're good together.*

Sarah hesitates before turning around with an impish grin, holding a bottle of 2006 Screaming Eagle Cabernet Sauvignon I had won at a charity auction last August.

"I thought we were saving that," I say smiling.

"We were." Sarah smirks back.

The 2006 Screaming Eagle Cabernet Sauvignon can retail today for around $3,000, so we had promised we would save it for a special occasion. Since I had won it for just under $400, she decided tonight was special enough.

"Do you think it went all right?" I watch Sarah grab two coffee mugs, and pop open this brilliantly expensive bottle of wine. The irony of drinking even a $400 bottle of wine out of two water stained, porcelain, diner mugs is lost on both of us.

"Micah, you were electric. It was incredible. Your timing, your delivery, your message, your sincerity. You were amazing. They loved it." *God, she is so good.* She hands me a mug of wine which would likely have cost us $85 at a restaurant.

"Let's hope so." I say, less than convinced.

Sarah sets down her cup, and pulls herself close to me. She wraps her arms around me and pushes her forehead into my chest. She does this so I know she means business. Some of our most intimate and important moments have started with Sarah pushing her forehead into my chest.

"If this opportunity is for you, it—"

"...Will not pass me. I know, I know," I say, interrupting.

Through my dress shirt and heavy coat, I can feel her mouth turn into a snarky smile. I have heard her say that phrase a hundred million times, and each time is as annoying as the first. She knows, too, because as soon as I feel her grin through my layers, it just gets bigger. The humorous annoyance in my voice tells her exactly how right she is. "You're right. You're always right. It's infuriating." I feel her smile grow even still. I kiss the top of her head. *Goddamnit, she is so good.*

"What will be, will be," she says, pulling away from my chest just enough to look at me. She grabs her mug again, and hoists it into the air, presenting it to me, "To history." I grab my mug, and meet the two together with a soft, dull clunk.

"To history," I say back, matching her smile.

I understand few things in this life less than I understand how I have managed to get this woman to not only love me, but to continue to love me for all this time.

*Cheers, my darling.*

The buzz of my cell phone vibrating abruptly takes us both out of what had sincerely become a very sweet moment. While neither of us know for certain who it is, we likely have the same guess. My mom, potential donors with more questions, my mom, Jason, maybe my mom. It was probably my mom. I flip my phone over on the counter to see the screen, and who is calling…

"It's him, isn't it?" Sarah looks to me.

Jason Cark.

*Why is Jason already calling?* It feels like we just got home and walked in the door. I shoot a quick glance at my watch and see that we have already been home for about forty-five minutes. Neither of us have any idea how. I know Jason either has amazing news or terrible news, and there is only one way to find out.

Sarah walks around the counter and sits down on a bar stool, putting her hand on mine. I pick up my phone, take a breath and tap the green "answer" button. I wait a moment and tap the microphone icon switching the audio to speaker phone so we can both hear him.

"Jason, how's it going?" I feel an underlying quiver in my voice. I do not know if Jason can hear it, or notice it, but I would bet my life that my wife can. She squeezes my hand slightly. Maybe out of support and solidarity for the moment, or maybe she is just trying to stop her own nervous trembling.

"Micah. Hi. Are you home?" Jason's tone gives nothing away.

"Yeah, Sarah and I just walked in a few minutes ago," I lied.

"Am I on speaker...?"

"Yessir, she's right here." I look at Sarah, who cracks a small smile and looks back at me with her beautiful, kind eyes. She has always liked Jason. She has overheard hours of our conversations preparing for tonight, and I think she can tell how truly invested in me Jason is, and has been from the start. He believes in me, and that fact made her trust him, immediately. She leans over the counter and holds her head near the phone's speaker.

"Hi Jason!"

"Oh, hi Sarah... Hey—uh—Micah, would you mind taking me off speaker for a moment?" I immediately take my hand away from Sarah's grasp, and switch the phone to its normal speaker. I hold it up to my ear, and turn my back to Sarah, unintentionally cutting her off from the conversation. Or maybe it was intentional. Maybe that quick decision was my way of protecting her. I look to the ground.

"What's up, Jason? What's going on? ... I ... I don't understand... Well, how much *did* we raise?" Sarah must have known Jason's answer to my question, because I hear her stand up, and feel her wrap her arms around me from behind. Her forehead presses into my back. Only now, I do not feel a smile.

# CHAPTER 2
# MICAH

There is no traffic this morning. I do not see anyone else on the freeway at all, actually, but I had not noticed until right now. Hopefully, what would typically take me forty-five minutes to an hour would only take me around twenty minutes today. Twenty-five minutes if I catch a lot of stoplights in the blocks leading up to my destination. The fact there is no traffic feels odd for a Thursday. Mainly because of this particular freeway, and especially at this particular time of the morning. I am not complaining, but it does seem strange. *Thank you for no traffic*, I think, not sure who I am directing thought at. Sometimes, you have to force yourself to acknowledge when the little things go right. Life can be too hard and complicated to not appreciate zero traffic at 9:19 A.M. on a Thursday morning. I find myself thinking maybe I am the last car to pass by before the awful accident happens, causing congestion and a freeway closure lasting for hours. Maybe today, the universe was waiting for me to pass by before the nightmare of rush hour begins. It is a nice thought.

I normally would have a podcast, or The Beatles playing while I am behind the wheel, but I keep the car silent for this drive. After last night, it has been one of those mornings where nothing suffices. Podcasts all seem repetitive, my music playlists monotonous. Instead, I just crack the window, and focus on the sound of the wind rushing through it. The loud *whoosh* sort of calms my overwhelming nerves. I could really use a cigarette right now.

Just one nice, long drag of a filtered Marlboro 100. A guilty pleasure, obviously, but a necessity in times like this. I had picked up the disgusting, but undeniably cool, habit from my father. Rarely was he ever seen in public, or at home, without a Marlboro 100 attached to his lips. I can vividly see the deep red, almost maroon and gold label of the packaging. The backpack and beach towel I had been given for Christmas because of the amount of rewards points he was able to accumulate over the course of my childhood. "Marlboro bucks," I think they were called. I remember thinking it was so cool that my older sister and I had literal swag from a cigarette conglomerate. I started smoking when I was probably twelve years old. Successfully hiding it from my family, especially my father, who would have abruptly, and decisively ended that habit had he known. Around six months ago, Sarah had asked me to try giving them up.

"Just for six months," she essentially begged me. "Just to see if you can survive without them for *six months*. You can literally do anything for six months. It's only six months." Much to my own disappointment, I agreed to her terms, but good lord, how nice does a single drag sound right now. Goddamn nice, is the answer. Sarah always has had my best interest at the forefront of her mind, even before her own. I should feel some level of shame because that thoughtfulness or foresight is a gift I do not reciprocate. I feel it and recognize it—Sarah is easily the most important person to me in my entire life. I have just never been good at going out of my way to make sure her smallest needs are anticipated, or even met. I just rest, knowing they are. *She is so good.*

I tighten my grip on the steering wheel, its soft rubber coating gives way to the pressure of my fingers. Naturally, I push in harder, almost changing the direction of the car. I lighten my grip, ensuring I stay in my lane. Thank God there is no one else on the freeway. I resist the temptation to dig the tips of my fingers into the steering wheel's pigmented vinyl resin, as I have before, leaving dark grey slivers of the not quite rubber, not quite foam material underneath my clean fingernails. I tell myself to just try to focus on the sound. *Whoosh*, the sound of the wind through the crack of the window. I open the window slightly farther, letting the wind brush my face. *There you go, Micah. Focus.*

I park in the lot around the corner from the cafe, as I typically do. The obviously self-run business who owns the lot charges me ten dollars to park here, but realistically I would pay twenty if they wanted. I have met Jason here a handful of times, and every time it seems increasingly more and more impossible to actually get into the parking lot of this bustling, hipster-filled-coffeehouse-turned-brunch-cafe, much less actually find a spot once you make it in. Truthfully, I do not even know why Jason always insists on meeting here. It has never seemed much his speed. It is the kind of restaurant you are not supposed to call a restaurant. This type of cafe prides itself on its different flavors of bottomless mimosas. The type of place displaying a printout of the recent BuzzFeed article highlighting their "Mango-Crazy Mimosa," in BuzzFeed's *"Top Ten Mimosas You Don't Want to Miss..." or pay for*, I add sarcastically in my head. This type of place understands I am only going to order a drip coffee, black, and they will still charge me $4 for it.

I take my time walking down the sidewalk from where I parked towards the cafe. I was expecting outside to be colder than it is today. I am definitely dressed poorly for this temperature. I think to slow my pace down the sidewalk to avoid being a sweaty, disgusting mess when I meet with Jason. This thought, of course, is just a simple distraction from the thing I do not want to think about yet. The reason for this meeting to begin with: the fact we raised next to nothing at our fundraiser last night.

*How in the hell did we raise so little?* Our audience had an average income of $850,000 a year, and I had them eating out of the palm of my hand. How did we raise basically nothing? Or, more realistically, we likely lost money hosting such a large crowd. *How did I let this happen?*

I feel beads of sweat pool on forehead as my heart rate increases. Not from the heat, or walking, but from the knowledge of raising next to nothing from over one-hundred and seventy-four people watching my fourteen-second timer expire, and not feeling compelled enough to give something, or anything at all. *Fucking rich, entitled, piece of shit white people.*

*Stop. This is on me. This is my fault.*

I am so in my head I do not realize I have walked into an intersection crosswalk while the "no walk" sign is on. Tires screech, and I hold my breath, expecting the worst. You never fully realize how loud car horns are until one is blaring in your ears from six feet away. Funny, I thought my heart rate was already raised. I jump back onto the sidewalk, giving my best *I'm so sorry* hand gestures to the rightfully pissed off driver of the midnight blue Dodge Ram. I am just glad at least one of us was paying attention.

*OK, get it together, Micah.* I exhale deeply and shake the tension out of my hands. I cannot be this scattered when I am talking to Jason. He will definitely notice. He always does.

"Micah, you have to relax." I can hear him already. "You're doing good work; you just have to relax." *You fucking relax, Jason.* The light goes green and I look both ways twice, like a six-year-old, Honor Roll student. As if it makes a difference now.

All right, I need to figure this out before I walk into this conversation blind. We needed to raise roughly three million dollars for our "Series A," or first phase of project funding. The fundraising estimations for last night's event had us raising around five and a half million dollars. I catch myself laughing a little at the irony of walking into this meeting expecting to have raised over five million dollars, when in reality, we may have lost money.

A five and a half million dollar "Series A" funding would have absolutely rocketed us into a six and a half million dollar goal for our "Series B." Achieving a full "Series B" fundraising goal would have almost put us at twelve million dollars in total raised funds, triggering our ability to easily raise the final three million dollars, our "Series C," hitting our ultimate goal of funding needed for this project… fifteen million dollars.

Instead, we essentially raised *zero* dollars at our initial, "Series A" fundraiser, and now the founder and Chief Executive Officer of the only organization officially supporting this effort wants to drink overpriced drip coffee at a loud, crowded coffeehouse in the middle of the exceptionally terrible Arts District downtown… *great.*

I finally find my way to the front door. It is famously covered in stickers and flyers declaring a multitude of stances and opinions. The premier sticker on the door immediately catching your attention displays, in large red text, "TUCK FRUMP." The real shame of it is I doubt any of these angsty, early twenty-somethings working here even vote. I can make that assumption, because if they did vote, there would not have been a need for the manufacturing of that sort of sticker. No one would have given a shit about Donald Trump beyond his dumb, little reality show. I push my way through the door, and I am almost immediately run over by a struggling-singer-turned-server carrying an entire tray of avocado toast.

"Sorry!" The sweet, young waitress calls out as she passes me. Every single time I have entered into this cafe, the first words I typically hear are "I'm" and "sorry," usually from someone on the staff. A handful of customers wait for their tables, causing the entire entry way of this place to feel like the floor of a punk rock concert. Shoulder to shoulder with strangers, all uncontrollably swaying with each other; we do not know each other, but we're undeniably in this together.

I shift my gaze to the dining area of the restaurant. If this meeting is anything like every one of our other meetings here, Jason is already sitting somewhere, undoubtedly enjoying his second cup of overpriced pour-over. I think a part of him gets a small thrill out of sitting at a table by himself in this incredibly busy place, slowly sipping a cup of coffee. The glares of large groups of trendy twenty-somethings waiting for a table to open up, as he raises his mug, only seems to slow him down more. I guess it is the little things with Jason, too.

We make eye contact from across the restaurant, Jason sitting in the same booth he always manages to sit in. I swear to God, he probably has to get to this place two hours before our meeting to ensure he gets his booth, and his medium roast. He does not overtly react to seeing me. Instead, he simply raises his mug slightly higher, away from his lips, before immediately moving it back to take another slow, cautious slurp. Much to the chagrin of the throngs of waiting people I am now forcing my way through.

The walk to his table is maybe fifteen feet, but it feels like a thousand miles today. I have always been the type to prepare, to be ready, and to anticipate, I just do not get that luxury today. I am sitting down into this conversation genuinely, and completely, blind.

"Morning, Jason," I say as we shake hands, and I slowly lower myself into the booth. The cushion, too soft, folds under my weight deeper than I feel like it should. Less of an indictment on my current health, more an indictment to the need for new booth cushions, an expense in which the owner likely sees little to no value. Jason holds a single finger towards me, of the "give me just one moment" variety, while his mouth begs that last drop of drip to roll in. He sets the white, slightly cracked, porcelain mug down softly onto the table.

"Micah, it's nice to see you." His demeanor and tone shockingly… normal. He is always so able to hold his emotional cards close his chest.

I am settled, sunken, but comfortable in the booth now. My elbows fully resting on the table, hands clinched together at my chin to keep my fingers from picking the skin completely off of themselves. Rubbing my left thumb on my right, consciously making the effort to stay focused on the conversation about to take place. I slightly nod, acknowledging his greeting. My silence speaks volumes.

"I'm going to get right into it," he says, getting his grip on the Band-Aid he is inevitably about to rip off. See, now that phrase is one I can get behind, *just rip the Band-Aid off.* "I meant what I said yesterday afternoon. I believe in this project. I hope you know that. I wouldn't have spent so much of my own time and money with you on this if that wasn't the case."

"I know, Jason." I reply, dry and guarded. My tone tells Jason to cut the shit, tell me what I came to hear. He sees straight through my tough guy routine and presses his index finger down with each emphasized word, something I know he only does for dramatic effect.

"I believe in what we're trying to do here," he continues, "but unfortunately we're at a point where we need to recognize the reality of situation. Money *talks*, Micah. Money *shouts*. You know you're on the brink of something great…"

"Something world changing." I genuinely correct him.

"…world changing. Groundbreaking. I know that, too. I really do. But *they* need to know it." *They?* I hope Jason cannot hear my thoughts. "You need something *concrete*," he continues. "Something *tangible*… Something to show these rich, frickin' conservative types that this great '*something*' we're after is more than just a pipe dream."

"A pipe dream?" I catch myself from snapping back too loud. I can feel my face get warm, and the pressure of the blood flowing through me rise. I have a tendency to work myself up when I feel upset. I am working on it. My interjections do not even remotely slow Jason down from making the point he obviously came here to make.

"I need something *real*, and something... tangible, physical. Something they *have* to invest in. Not words they can just walk away from to 'think about it.' Something they don't need to discuss with their investment partners about. You gave them something they *want* to invest in, now show them something they *need* to invest in." His emphasis is intentional and, unfortunately for me, effective. He uses the same index finger to garner the attention of our waitress who promptly fills up his cup. She asks if I would like some as well.

"Sure," I say to her. "Jason, I don't want to sound like a total dick, but wasn't your name and the partnership with your company supposed to be enough to do that?"

"Yes, it was. But it didn't. And I am confident my ego is probably going to need some time to recover from that sobering truth." While there are a lot of character attributes that Jason probably lacks, sincerity has never been one of them. He means this; he feels hurt. Disappointed.

"What else can I do? You've seen the data we've pulled."

"Micah, look at me," a simple demand. "I believe you. I believe in you. I believe in what you want to do." He pauses for a moment. The pregnant pause of a potential buyer before submitting their initial offer on a home they know they cannot afford. "And that's why I'm willing to make you a deal."

Jason, coffee in his left hand, uses his right hand to grab a small glass of tap water sitting on the table. He pauses for a moment and looks at the glass. He delicately rotates the cup in his hand before he carefully slides it towards me across the flat surface. He does not say a word as he moves the glass closer and closer to my side of the table. He lets go, and rests back into his booth cushion, sips his coffee. "If you can get me one glass of the water we both know is there," one more pause, another effective fermata. You have got to hand it to him, he performs well when he is trying to be convincing. "...I'll put in the fifteen million myself."

I stare at the glass, its contents lightly sloshing from side to side. The water eventually settles and becomes still again. A single drop rolls from the edge to meet its family back towards the middle of the glass. It glistens in the sun shining through the window. I bring my gaze back to Jason who locks eyes with me.

"All fifteen million?" *Not likely,* I assume.

"All fifteen million," he says without hesitating or breaking eyes.

"All three Series funding goals..." Skepticism drips from my lips like drool during a fantastic nap. Jason leans in.

"I will give you all of the financing in one installment. One, single direct payment, from me to you. The entire project, complete fifteen-million-dollar funding. No third party, no outside bank, no financier, or fundraising black-tie bullshit. I'll do it myself." At this point, I start trying to talk myself out of believing him. A facetious attempt at calming me after the embarrassing setback of last night's absolute failure. *He's serious. Holy shit, he is serious. Is he serious?*

"I just need concrete proof to persuade the Board to support it, and not remove me from my own frickin' company. Numbers don't impress them a whole heck of a lot." He takes the glass of water back. Holds it up in his hand. "This, however... this would impress the fuck out of them." While I still try to convince myself he is joking, I do not say a word. Of all of the awful, disappointing, and frustrating ways this conversation has already played out in my mind, this version has not. This conversation was legitimately never one of the options at hand. That fact kept me sitting silently across from him.

"Listen, Micah..." again with his same sincerity, "you have all of the software we've been creating for months. You have all of the equipment we've spent tens of thousands of dollars designing and developing." *State of the art* equipment we have spent thousands of dollars designing and developing. *Groundbreaking* software and equipment. *Do not sell us short, Jason.* "If you can get there, and get that glass of water... I can get you the funding. I swear on my life." I feel the weight of the moment almost collapse my chest. *We're so close.*

"That's a ..." I have some slight trouble really finding the right word, "that's quite the offer, Jason." *Smooth, Micah, well said.* "That only leaves travel expenses, transport expenses, lodging, meals, a team for chrissake… I mean there's no way I can get the team we were discussing, and that's assuming I can even get there at all…" The amount of "what-if's" are piling up faster in my mind than my mouth can form the words.

Jason surreptitiously takes a large gulp of water before he slides the empty glass back across the table to my side.

"I just need one, Micah."

Exhausted and already stressed out at the idea of what this will take to accomplish, "I just don't see how…"

"Just one glass, one… single… glass." He intentionally adds the slight pause between the words. Again, Jason is quite the showman. "Go get me that water, Micah."

"Even if I were able to call in every favor I've ever been owed, I just— I don't understand. Why wasn't this on the table until now?" I know Jason. He is methodical and brilliant, and he is never spent a dime of his own money if he does not have to. "Why don't we just scrap things for now, and try to start the fundraising up again in a few months? It just seems more practical."

Jason takes a moment, and again twirls the empty glass in his fingertips. I can tell something else is on his mind, and he knows I am onto him. I tilt my head and look to him more intently. "Why now? Why your own money, and why now, Jason?"

I hear Jason exhale. He looks down at the table, smirking.

"OK, listen…" Jason lowers his tone, and leans in. "Everything I'm about to tell you is completely off the record. Do you understand?" I do not respond at first, I just stare back at him. "Micah, I need you to acknowledge what I'm saying. This is not to be spoken of again, to anyone, do you understand?"

"Yes. I understand." *What is going on?* I think.

Jason takes out his cell phone and opens up his photos application. He scrolls through a few screens before selecting a video, and then slides his phone across the table. He does not say anything, just motions for me to discretely look at the image displayed on his device. It is a video.

I tap the "play" icon at the bottom of the screen and watch as unexplainable happens on the device's screen. It is a short video, and it looks like it was shot in a laboratory of some kind. A plastic bin sits on a steel table, and inside the plastic bin is what looks like a rock. Two people in full lab attire with gloves and masks stand over the rock in the plastic bin. They speak to each other, but the audio is muffled, and it is too loud inside of this cafe to hear anything anyway.

"A few months ago, I was contacted by a government agency, and they showed me this video." While Jason speaks, I watch one of the laboratory technicians hold a small vial of liquid over the rock, and very carefully squeezes until a single drop of the liquid starts to build at the tip of the dropper.

A single drop falls from the technician's hands, and splashes onto the surface of the rock. The rock begins to jitter uncontrollably around the plastic bin the moment the liquid hits it, and before I can figure out what I am seeing, the rock splits in half and multiplies. I watch the rock split itself in half, and then I see two identical rocks in the same plastic bin. Both perfectly still. Unrecognizable voices on the video seem excited at the outcome. Then the video stops.

"What the fuck was that?" I feel stunned, and wildly confused.

"Our military thinks it's discovered an organism living in ocean rock that has the ability to multiply whatever material it comes in contact with. Solid, liquid, energy, doesn't matter."

"How?"

"They don't know. That's what they want me to figure out. If I can test this organism, figure out how it works, they think we can use it to solve a … whole host of issues our nation faces."

"I don't understand," I hand Jason his phone back. "What this has to do with us?"

"Micah, they discovered the organism in the Gulf of Alaska." I try my best to put the pieces of this puzzle together, but I am just not following. Seeing the confusion still in my eyes, Jason tries his best to rephrase. "They discovered this organism in the rock bedding of the ocean floor in the Gulf of Alaska. The rock bedding that very likely lines the wall of the Blue Hole that you need to get to."

"Jason, I just—I don't get it."

"Micah, you get to the Blue Hole. You pierce the rock. You extract the water you need. You bring me enough samples of this organism so that my company can run tests. We both win. You get your full funding, and I get a Defense Contract that will fund my company for the next three thousand years."

"How am I supposed to not only bring home water, but now also with—"

"Micah, I already altered the filtration system we developed to separate this organism from whatever water samples you get from the ground. You don't have to change anything about your logistics. Or your plan. Or your approach. And most importantly, you don't have to tell anyone. You don't have to do anything but bring the water home in the tank you have it stored in. Once I get that, I can have my team extract the organism out of the filtration system itself. That's it. You just... you absolutely have to keep this between us. No one—absolutely no one can know that this is part of what you're doing there. I'm talking, even if shit hits the fan, and every falls apart... your lips are sealed. Airtight. Understand?"

I start to understand his words, but I cannot shake the undeniable guilt I immediately feel.

"Jason, I... I don't know if..."

"Micah, think about the good you can do with this. Think of what we can accomplish with clean water. And think of the world of possibilities we can discover with the work I'll be able to do. I just need those samples."

"It just seems odd that I have to keep this private."

"I promise, it's just a formality. Just until the ink dries. At that point, I'd obviously make it worth your while too."

"Jason, what the hell? Are you trying to buy my *silence?*" I ask, a little offended, and caught off guard.

"God, no, Micah, I'm trying to pay you for a job I'm hiring you to do." I do not say anything. I do not know what there is to say. "Just think about it, Micah. I just need a glass of water to fund your project..."

"Our project," I correct him.

"Yes, our project. I just need a glass of water to fund our project. And if we can do that... We might *really* be able to change the world. Think about it, OK?"

# CHAPTER 3
# SARAH

She knows today means everything, and just how sick to his stomach Micah feels over it. Comparing the two of them, side by side, she also knows Micah is by far the concerned one; the anxious one in the dynamic of their relationship. He constantly worries and takes things so hard and personal. He just cares so much, he truly wants to make a difference, and he is just arrogant enough to know he can. She could tell in the first five minutes of meeting him.

She woke up this morning a little earlier than normal to make a small, but adequate breakfast for him to enjoy before heading out to meet with Jason. She also put on a pot of coffee because she knows how incensed Micah gets having to pay four dollars for a cup of drip coffee. The thought of Micah getting worked up thinking about it puts a slight, but protruding snicker on her face. "If I can take even the slightest pressure off his morning, it will have been worth it," she thinks, almost convincing herself.

They have only been in their apartment for a few months, but she already feels very comfortable, and was able to easily create a morning routine in their new space. Before they sold their home of three years, she could not even remember what drawer they decided to keep the forks in. To Sarah, a woman's place is not in the kitchen. It is in the House or the Senate. Not to suggest that Sarah does not enjoy the little things married life brings her, like cooking, or grocery shopping and picking out furniture, and of course, if it was for Micah, she would spend the rest of her life attached to the kitchen cupboard. He would never want that outcome, though, and she knows it. *He is so good.*

Their black, 12-cup Mr. Coffee machine sputters the last few drops of a light roast, pennies at a time, as Sarah grabs an eco-friendly, reusable coffee mug from their pantry and sets it on the counter. Micah had casually mentioned getting a Keurig over the holidays, but he must have sensed Sarah's aversion to it, because after only a potful of attempts, he let the idea go.

In her peripheral vision, her eyes catch a slight tinge of smoke floating up from the crack and sizzle of a few eggs scrambling in the pan. *Oh, shit,* she thinks. She cannot burn the eggs, not today! She always burns the eggs, she cannot this morning... just not *this* morning.

"Oh, please, please, please, please, please!" She says aloud to herself, in a muffled whisper. She assumes he is awake by now, but even still. Knowing Micah, he is sitting on the side of their bed, elbows creating depressions in his knees, fingers rubbing his temples. She knows he feels overwhelmed by the thought of meeting with Jason today. *Why did last night have to go so poorly?* She finds her mind stuck on how unfair this outcome is.

She carefully picks up the non-stick pan of maybe-burned-eggs and brings it towards the other side of the kitchen, hovering it over the sink. She gears herself up to attempt to flip them without flinging wet egg all over everything. She knows this part is completely unnecessary to the integrity of the meal, but sometimes the little things bring a small speck of joy to a routine.

With a quick exhale, and a "you can do this" silent mantra spoken, she flicks her wrist...

The flat, not-at-all-burned egg pancake soars from the pan, performing one, perfect, one-hundred- and eighty-degree rotation almost in slow motion. It softly, and gently lands back in the pan. She nailed it.

She hears the imaginary crowd roar with approval, chanting her name as the judges all individually hold up signs giving her... no, declaring her a perfect ten score.

Her smile beams, and she holds back laughter at how silly and irrelevant this moment actually is, her perfect egg flip. She takes the moment as an omen. Today is going to be a good day. Today *is* a good day.

She hears a soft rustling in their bedroom and assumes it must be Micah. Most likely picking what tie goes best with his mood, but also is not a solid black. *Cautious, but optimistic.* That mantra is what she always encourages him to be. "Be cautious but hold out hope. If this opportunity is for you, it will not pass you." She repeats this phrase to herself a hundred times a day, and probably to Micah twice as often. Without missing a beat, he almost always immediately smiles when the mantra finishes falling from her lips. She always wonders about the origin of that smile, but she never thinks it significant enough to ask.

Sarah hurries to place the eggs with some fresh sliced avocado onto a small, ceramic dinner plate. Topping the achievement off by pouring a healthy amount of coffee into the reusable traveler, she pops the silicone lid onto the to-go mug just as Micah opens the bedroom door and walks towards her standing there in the kitchen.

Sarah notices something is off about his walk. While she cannot quite articulate what, she can sense something is different. He walks straight towards her.

"I made some eggs," she says. Micah does not slow, and comes right up to her, sliding his arms around her, resting his head onto her shoulder. She hesitates, but gives in, returning the gesture. "What's wrong, bubbas?"

"Oh, nothing. Just everything." He responds, and she laughs.

*Thank God, he's all right,* Sarah immediately thinks, sighing relief. "I know you are in a hurry, but I made some eggs for you to scarf down before you head out," Sarah reveals as Micah gathers his things, and closes his bag. "...And some coffee because I know how much you hate paying..." Micah stops packing his bag, and slightly drops his head. The extremely slight movement causes Sarah to stop mid-sentence.

"Micah... Micah, what is it?" Her tone shifts from concerned spouse, to inquisitive partner. A playful and curious tone you would take with a toddler whose face is covered in red and purple washable, unscented marker.

"I just…" The tone in his voice is anything but playful or curious. Instinctively, she moves towards him. "I just don't know how today is going to go, and I'm nervous. That's it."

She walks up directly behind him, puts her arms around his chest, and presses her forehead into his back. Sarah had developed this loving habit in their early days of dating. While she normally attaches herself forehead to chest, certain times call for a forehead to back attachment. A variation crafted for a moment just as this.

"It will be OK, Micah. If this opportunity is for you…"

"I know," he responds. Micah has only ever interrupted Sarah a handful of times as she repeats that ideology out loud. Usually, so he can finish the sentence for her with a smile from ear to ear, but not this time.

Sarah lifts her forehead from his back, and stares into his army-green, canvas jacket. She can sense something is not right, his anxiety palpable. Any possible thing she can say in this moment vacates her mind. Sarah always has the perfect words to say, but at this exact moment of need, she cannot think of a single one.

Before she has a chance to form a proper response, Micah shifts his body. Not turning to face her. Not to wrap his arms around her and kiss her on the forehead. Not to look her in the eyes, saying silently, "Everything is going to be all right." Instead, she watches as he begins stepping towards his keys resting on the laminate countertop. She pushes her eyebrows together, disappointed, and completely lost on what to do now. She just stands there. *This is a new feeling,* she thinks.

"Thank you for making me breakfast, I'm sorry I can't stay to eat it. I'm just already sort of running behind…"

*No, you aren't,* she thinks. Micah is not supposed to meet Jason until nine forty-five. Micah has plenty of time. "I just want to make sure that I'm ready for whatever he has planned to discuss." Sarah nods, knowing he is not looking. She typically excels in moments such as this; being the type to put her foot down and give whatever is coming at her all of her might. A familiar Shakespeare quote pops into her head, as she decidedly turns towards Micah with a supportive smile.

"I completely understand," she lies. "Really, it's so OK. Go, I don't want you to stress at all about being on time." Micah slightly exhales, half not buying what she is selling, half completely taken aback by how gracious and beautiful she is.

"Sarah..." he starts.

"Babe, please go... Really, I absolutely understand." She cracks a sarcastic smile, "I'll eat the eggs." She tops it off with a wink making Micah unintentionally let out a tiny laugh.

"Thank you." He puts his hands on her shoulders and kisses her forehead. "Thank you, you gorgeous girl."

"It's going to be all right. I promise."

"Yes, ma'am," he says as he brushes her cheek with his thumb, just ever so gently. Micah smiles wryly, and leaves.

Immediately, her confidence and charm melts away. She investigates every crevice of her brain trying to decide how to interpret that interaction. Metaphorically looking herself in the mirror, asking, "Really, what on earth was that?" They are supposed to be a team and take these challenges head on together. Side by side. It is supposed to be them against the world. That interaction was the opposite of what they had agreed on so many years ago. That exchange was Micah heading into the storm and leaving Sarah on the sidelines. *How could he have done that so easily?* She pushes her mind deeper down. *What does that mean for their future? What does that mean for their life together? Their marriage? Their family?* A million outcomes race through her mind in an instant.

"Jesus, Sarah, slow down." She says out loud to herself, standing alone in their living room. "You cannot go from peaceful, marital bliss to running away in despair in forty-five seconds. He stood his ground, spoke his mind, and told me exactly what was happening. Nothing less, nothing more, and that is fine." She shakes her head, and anxiously laughs to herself. They *are* still partners. They *are* still a team. He is just going to get more information from the person who has said information. *Chill out,* she thinks, chastising her psyche.

Besides, Sarah has a million and one things to do today, the last thing she needs to be focusing on was a non-existent, marital cataclysm. Her sister Charlie would be on her way soon with their quarterly results, and next quarters' financial projections and goals. In the midst of Micah pressing deeper into this research and project development, Sarah had tried incredibly hard to create independent work, but in the same field. That idea manifested in the creation of this small but mighty non-profit designed to raise and spread awareness of the terrible water crisis the world is facing. "Mariner's Way" was starting to gain traction within the non-profit sector, simultaneously, as the rumblings grew within the community about how potentially groundbreaking Micah's research could be.

While the two were admittedly independent of each other, the entire community knew they were connected, and would sooner or later meld into one organization. Truthfully, they could not have planned this course better if they tried. The way both movements were gaining simultaneous momentum was like something out of a movie's montage sequence. They had built up, and were leading to, this perfect moment of coming together, and combining their work and passions. It really was special.

Charlie arrives at Sarah's home a little past nine in the morning, and they waste no time, jumping immediately into the business discussion. Budgets, phases, ideas, blue sky goals, roadblocks, motivators, and stressors. Sarah cannot help but feel a twinge of guilt as her conversation with Charlie turns to the previous quarter's successes. Her mind unavoidably distorts the thought of her and Micah both putting so much time, energy, and soul into their two, individual projects. To see hers blossom into this beautiful venture while watching Micah's continuing to falter is becoming increasingly difficult. Obviously, Sarah knows he wants her to soar as high as she can, and she knows he is genuine in that desire, but it is impossible to ignore the discrepancies. It has become especially difficult as of 11 P.M. last night. Her organization's third quarter results will just be further proof, validating the story her mind tells her, no matter how detrimental to her own joy it is.

"Sarah, you can't compare the two. You're in two different situations. Don't martyr our success because of his…" Sarah shoots Charlie a glare only a sister can. *Do not finish that sentence, Charlie. Don't do it.*

"I'm just saying that it isn't fair to your success, and I guarantee Micah doesn't want that for you either." Charlie says defensively.

Again, responding internally, Sarah thinks, *god, Charlie, don't put words in Micah's mouth.* Sarah knows her sister is right, though. Micah's entire project could drop out from underneath his feet, and he still would not miss a beat if Sarah needed something, anything, for her organization. A pleasant hit of dopamine from her mind tells her, *God, he is so good. We are such a good team.*

"I know, I know. I'm just trying to be sensitive." Sarah qualifies.

They finish their work around half past ten in the morning. Charlie, being the work horse she always has been, heads straight back to the office after leaving Sarah's home. Sarah quickly packs her purse, still needing to run a few errands before Micah's meeting ends. Typical things: grocery store, Target, returning a pair of jeans to Nordstrom Rack.

Once back home, she puts away groceries, and hears her phone vibrate on the countertop. Sarah lift her phone up, and sees the word *Mom*. She had debated letting it go to voicemail, but knowing her mother, her phone would ring two or three more times in a row. She might as well pick it up.

"Hello?" Like any daughter would, Sarah loves her mother. She just does not like her much if she was being honest. A woman who means well, but constantly feels the need to inject herself into any situation. The type of person who stays at the scene of an accident just to see if she can tell her point of view on the local Nightly News. She means well, but just comes on way too strong.

As Sarah had expected, her mother just wants to ask about what was happening with Micah. She then proceeds to retell her daughter a story she has told her daughter a hundred times before. The story of her childhood friend who invested everything in a small accounting firm and ended up losing it all. She was able to utilize this story to fit any archetype mold. She meant for it to be an inspiring tale of, "If you can fail at something you hate, you might as well go all in on something you love." After this morning, it just comes off callous and cold. Another incoming call interrupts the conversation.

The call is coming from Micah.

"Hey mom, listen, I'm going to have to let you go." Getting herself off of the phone with her mother is almost as difficult as talking herself into answering it to begin with.

"Yes, I promise. Of course. Yes, I promise. OK, OK, I love you too."

As quickly as she can, she hangs up on her mom, and answers Micah's call.

"How did it go?" She does not give him a chance to say anything before jumping right in. She had no interest in wasting any more time without knowing the answer.

"Do I not get a hello? Hi, I love you?" She can hear his smile through the phone.

"Hello, hi, I love you. What happened? How did it go?" She hears Micah laugh on the other end, which definitely comes as a welcome contrast to her interpretation of his demeanor from earlier that morning. She feels a wave of calm creeping in with the sound of his familiar laugh.

"Are you still out? Or are you home?" He asks her, still evading her question.

"I just walked in the door maybe fifteen minutes ago. Are you on your way?" Her words coming quick, with sharper consonants than normal.

"I should be there in about half an hour. I'm just leaving that terrible coffee place I hate that Jason picks every time."

"The place with the over-priced drip? And the sea of twenty-something's in tattered jean jackets?"

"That's the one."

"Doesn't sound familiar." Micah laughs at that joke too. *Oh, he's back,* she thinks, *thank God, he is back.*

"Stay home, if you can. We need to—uh, talk about something when I get there."

"A good something?" Nervous to ask, she almost persuades her brain not to, but curiosity prevails.

"You literally can't wait half an hour?" His smirk audible.

"Why would I if I don't *have* to?"

"Oh, well, fair enough, I guess. It's not necessarily a *good* something, not necessarily a *bad* something. Just *something*… unexpected…I guess. I guess you'll just have to wait to see what I mean… I guess."

"I love you, I guess." She lets out a small, sarcastic laugh. She always points out when he repeats himself from nerves.

"I love you too, Sarah. I'll see you soon."

Sarah.

He rarely uses her name, which she can imagine might sound strange for a married couple, but it is true. Usually, Sarah's name is reserved for special reasons. *That could be a good sign,* she thinks.

Immediately, she jumps into a nervous cleaning frenzy. She organizes the counter, then re-organizes it. She wonders what he and Jason could have talked about, and how they could have resolved this situation. Going through different scenarios, the chance of there being a good outcome was admittedly not good. His voice, though, on the phone, sounded positive. Happy, even. Excited, or motivated. A stark contrast to the voice apologizing for being so cold this morning. She wonders to herself, *that has to be a good thing, right? A wonderful thing, but…how?*

Regardless, he sounded normal again, and he was on his way home. She would find out soon, and everything would be fine.

As the door handle jiggles, and the sound of a key's ridges pushing through the lock space crunch loudly, Sarah sits on the edge of their couch, facing directly towards the door. Micah pushes the door open, sees her sitting there, silent, and still. He stands in the doorway. For a moment, they just stare at each other. Sarah with a nervous look on her face. Micah with a clever, taciturn grin on his.

"Well, Hi, Mrs. Day."

"Mr. Day," Sarah anxiously stands, keeping her feet planted exactly where they were on their living room floor. Micah raises an eyebrow at her visible nervousness and plops his bag on the floor. He shuts the door behind him, and he walks over to his wife.

They embrace next to their couch, forehead to chest, as they had hours before. With her mouth pressed against his shirt, Sarah murmurs, "So how did it go?" Micah immediately bursts into a loud laughter. Not trying to be funny, this takes Sarah completely by surprise, she cannot help but smile.

"I'm serious, Micah, how did it go? Come on, tell me!"

Micah pulls her down to sit on the couch with him, holding her hands.

"We aren't dead in the water. Pun not exactly intended."

"I don't know what that means, sweetheart. You're going to have to be a little more…"

"Jason is going to fund our entire project. That's if I can figure out how to get us there and bring back enough water to show his Board of

Directors so they don't vote him out of his own company for giving me fifteen million dollars." He inhales a deep breath. "Us," he corrects himself, "for giving *us* fifteen million dollars."

Sarah sits in complete disbelief. Her brain a mess, she can only muster, "Holy shit." She almost lets her excitement take over before the realism comes flooding back into her mind.

"Micah, how are we supposed to figure out how to..."

He shushes her and kisses her forehead.

"I can figure this out. I will figure this out. This opportunity is for us. We can't pass it."

"That's not the way you're supposed to say that," Sarah smirks.

"Right now, it's perfect." He kisses her again.

# CHAPTER 4
## MICAH

After my meeting with Jason, and discussing *almost* all of the details with Sarah, I immediately got to work figuring out how to make this happen. All-in-all, it took me a little over three full weeks to figure out most of the vital details of this trip. Who would be coordinating the team I needed; what exactly our processes would look like; how we would transport all of the equipment to the middle-of-nowhere-Alaskan-Gulf; and, most importantly, how in the hell we would pay for it all.

I was actually able to figure out the majority of this fairly easily. All but the final piece I knew we needed for any of it to work. It is a funny thing: making deals. Constantly stretching the truth, ever so slightly, about what you already have in place. A lot of my conversations were beginning to look incredibly similar.

"I need your help in this specific thing," I would always start.

"But how, and why, and what?" They would reply.

"Well, I already have *this person* doing *this favor* so I can accomplish *this goal* using *this thing*. So, now I need to you to let me use *this thing*, so I can go to *this place* and accomplish *this goal*." I would continue.

"But I need to know more information so I can make myself feel like I'm truly a part of what you're doing." They would respond.

People love to feel like they have been a part of something meaningful. It is why, regardless of the quality of a performance, we always give a standing ovation. It does not matter if the play is absolute garbage, we want the actors to know we were there for every line of it. "We were there, and you couldn't have done this without us." We stand, and we clap. It is why everyone who receives an award inevitably says, "I couldn't have done this without you."

"I need your help. I truly can't do this without you," I would finish with every single person. That plea was always the hook, line, and sinker. And so far, it has worked every time.

Sarah had accompanied me to quite a few of these meetings. She did not have to, but she wanted to. She is good is those very specific ways. She knows by being present she can, without saying a word, insinuate that Mariner's Way would be assisting with some of the funding. An utter and complete falsehood. It would if it could, but even as successful as her organization has been of late, there is no way it could bare this type of financial commitment. I would not want them to anyway. I would not want her to. Whatever the reason, Sarah framing this perceived backing in these meetings seemed to work.

Between the two of us, we had managed to coordinate flights to and from Alaska, ferry service from the coast to the project site, food and drink for a week for a crew of 5, a remarkably modest stipend for said crew, and an emergency fund to pull from just in case, all without spending a penny ourselves. I do not care who you are, that amount of work is impressive to accomplish inn just twenty-four days. The last, and most essential, piece of this puzzle we had yet to secure was somewhere to actually perform the task at hand. We needed a boat. We needed a Big, Motherfucking Boat.

Looking back over the last few weeks of pulling all of these pieces together, I start to realize maybe the boat should have been the first thing in place. It was, after all, the first piece I knew how to acquire. I think a part of me hoped it would be a sure thing, so I had not bothered scheduling the conversation yet. Honestly, I had not thought all of this would move so quickly. I had only been at this for a couple of weeks. How on Earth was I supposed to know everyone would be so willing to help?

The crowd gives a "Standing O." Cheering and playing their role. I can't do this without you. *Ah, there it is. I should have seen it coming.*

In my mind, and dominating my thoughts, there was only one real, viable option for the Big Motherfucking Boat. Early in our marriage, I was teaching a course on marine organisms and ecosystems at a nearby University. Our Dean of Admissions was this jolly, older man who would always stop by my classroom, "Just sayin' hiya!" He was nice enough, and good lord, was he consistent. Every single day, between one forty and one forty-five in the afternoon, he would pop in. "Just sayin' hiya!" One holiday season, he popped in with an envelope. It was an invitation to he and his wife's annual holiday party. "If you can't make it, no worries at all, but Norah and I wanted to invite and you and your wife at the very least."

"That's just so kind. We'll do our best to be there." I replied.

Sarah ended up traveling to visit family in Philadelphia the week of the event, but I, home alone, having no plans, felt a little obligated to at least make an appearance. Sarah has spent every holiday season since reminding me of the time I got to party on a boat, while she ate terrible soup at her Aunt Sharon's house. In fairness, I had no idea the party would be on the largest yacht I have ever seen.

"The Tethys," appropriately named after the Titan Goddess of the primal font of fresh water who nourishes the entire planet. She was the wife of Oceanus, the Titan God of the Earth-circling, freshwater stream, and the mother of Potamoi, the Titan God of rivers. Not only was this a bad ass name for a Big, Mothering Fucking boat, but an insanely appropriate title for the vessel with which I would later seek to alter the trajectory of human history.

The Tethys was a one hundred and eighty-three-foot-long Mega-Yacht. The jolly owner had installed a full kitchen, and six individual and fully furnished cabins. He had taken up diving as a hobby in his waning professional years, so he was gradually upgrading it to be his full-time home and base camp, which, conveniently, is exactly what I needed it to be for about a week. I needed to persuade him to give it to me first, though. For free.

I had finally gotten up the nerve to reach out, asking if he wanted to grab lunch on Tuesday. I have never reached out to him to make any type of plans together before, and I was definitely not known as the pop-by-his-office, "Just sayin' hiya!" type. Naturally, his initial response was hesitant.

"Is everything all right?" Concern was not a response I had anticipated, and it definitely caught me by surprise.

"Of course. It's just been what… three or four years since I left the university? You haven't popped into my office in a while." He chuckled, genuinely. "It would be nice to catch up." I hated myself for not just telling him up front my real motive for wanting to buy him an overpriced salad.

"Well, what the hey. Let's do it. Tuesday it is. Say, around noon?"

"Perfect. I'll see you then." Hook, line, sinker.

I let him decide where to meet, citing a desire to not inconvenience him with a long commute to, what I hoped would be a short, lunch. Not to mention, I did not care where we met, I just needed to ask him a single question.

He chose a small vegan restaurant about ten minutes from my former campus, where he still taught. I had completely forgotten he was vegan at all, if I even knew in the first place. No, I did know. I remember now there was no meat in any of the hors d'oeuvres at his mega-yacht holiday party. I think it is strange to keep ideals like personal dietary restrictions for a large gathering, and always assume it is more appropriate to have options for everyone. Maybe it is just me, but I am pretty sure all of the other hungry people would have agreed. I should have left that party astonished at his amazing boat, but instead I left hungry.

He was already there when I arrived, which was fine with me. *Let's make this quick,* I thought. I smiled wide when we made eye-contact, and made my way towards the booth he was seated in.

"Well, I'll be darned. Micah, it's so fantastic to see ya!" I do not know if I ever noticed his proclivity to such clean speech. I always knew I felt like I had a terrible mouth around him, but I guess I never put stock in really noticing his obvious choice in particular words. Darn, heck, etc.

"So great to see you! How the hell," ah, damnit, "have you been?" I was trying to match his tone.

"To be perfectly frank, I have been just wonderful. You know Norah just retired last spring. She's just been so happy."

"I'd imagine your big day is coming up too then, yeah?"

"Me? Oh, I don't know. I could have retired three years ago. I just really love teaching so much, ya know? I can't see myself just playing golf every day and watching The Wheel."

"Sure sounds nice to me." It does sort of sound nice. No expectations, no goals, or initiatives. No fundraisers, no deadlines, or Boards. It really does sort of sound nice.

We make painful small talk for just about another twenty-five to thirty minutes, giving us just enough time to finish our appetizers, order a second round of cocktails, and place our main lunch orders. I ordered Eggplant Braciole with a Sicilian-style, green pepper sauce. It was honestly kind of incredible. I do not have anything against vegan food. Realistically, I believe we should all be vegan. Our planet would certainly thank us a few years from now. However, something about the perfect cut of a fatty, bone-in ribeye steak will always make the agonizing apocalypse we are undoubtedly racing towards worth it.

"So, what are you up to these days, Micah?"

*Finally.*

"Funny you should bring that up. I'm doing extremely well." *Well, extremely stressed, under-funded, and in desperate need of your giant boat-toy.* "I've actually been focused more in the non-profit sector since I left the university."

"Oh, I've always had such a heart for a good cause."

"That's great to hear." *Another good sign for me, hopefully.*

"Are you working on anything exciting?"

I need to play this carefully. I cannot just come out with my favor; it is a gigantic ask. I need to set it up, and frame it in a way where he feels compelled to help. Give him some of the glory when he offers his ability to help. In Jason's own words, make him think it was his idea to help me.

"Actually, I am, yes. Have you heard of Cark Strategies?"

"I have not, not at all."

"It's no mind. Cark Strategies is this really amazing a tech start-up from up north. I've been working with their founder on this really exciting project." Exciting and terrifying. Exciting, and terrifying, and completely impossible without your Big, Motherfucking Boat.

I explain it all. The data, the research, the software development, the manufacturing of one-of-a-kind hardware for the actual water extraction, the fundraiser failure, the Jason proposition. I walk him through literally everything except the military component. He is captivated by it all. It must be so overwhelming to hear all at once.

"Micah, this is amazing. That sounds like an absolutely tremendous opportunity. How are you feeling? You must be feeling so... pardon my terrible phrasing, but... underwater..." *Smooth, friend. Smooth.*

"Yeah, it's been a bit of a wild ride, if I can speak frankly. It's happening really quickly."

"I can imagine. Putting this together so fast has to be costing you a fortune. How are you affording it? If you don't mind me asking."

"Well, I'm not," I laugh, awkwardly, but honestly. "I've called in every favor I have ever had, and some I'm not sure I did."

"I see. What do you still need to... do?

"Well, I have secured travel, food, equipment, a team..."

"Wow, that's just incredible." *Here goes nothing.*

"Thank you. Basically, everything is ready in place... but one last piece." The weight that sentence held in this particular moment was uncomfortably palpable. In that one, single sentence, the genuine enthusiasm of this entire conversation was completely vacuumed out. In an instant, he knew exactly why I popped in on him, out of nowhere, after four years without "Just sayin' hiya!"

"I see." He was utterly deflated. Tragically, it was a feeling he was all too familiar with. This conversation was obviously not the first time someone feigned friendship for favor. I could read every change of his face, but I was already here, and I needed his Big, Motherfucking Boat.

"The only piece left to this insane puzzle is a... like some sort of vessel to house us for about a week of tests. A big boat." I hate myself. I feel gross, and shameful, but this is for everything. Sure, I could have just asked on our phone call, but being so forward would have been worse, right? "Hey, I know we haven't spoken in four years, sort of intentionally on my part, but could I maybe borrow your big ass yacht for a science experiment?" That proposition would have definitely been worse... right?

"Micah, please just speak straight with me, did you reach out after four years to ask if you can use The Tethys for this project?" *Yes, you are goddamn right I did.*

From here I am presented two options. The first, deny to the death. "No way! How could you think that? I wanted to see my old friend. I had completely forgotten about your massive, perfect for this project boat."

Or option number two.

I lean in.

"Honestly, yes." He looks caught off guard. He was fully expecting option one, and I think a part of me was too. "Look, I know how terrible that probably sounds, but I have no one else to turn to for this. It's a very specific need, and you have a very specific resolution; a specific, and tangible resolution. I am sorry if you feel that I am taking advantage of the circumstance, if that is what you feel I've done, but speaking very plainly, I cannot do this without you, and without your help."

It is true, all of it. At least now it is off my chest, and out of my head. It actually took some of the weight off the situation too. I was completely honest, and he knew it. It was real. My need is valid, and there now, out in the open.

"I see." If there is one thing he is excellent at, it is hiding his inner monologue from his face. I would be terrified to be the last man standing in a poker game with this guy. Instead of continuing on, I decide to leave my peace sitting there on the table like an extra basket of rolls you forgot you asked the waiter for. It is just sitting there untouched.

"Well, Micah, I would be remiss to not mention the true disappointment I feel right now, in this moment." *I hate this,* I think, cringing at disgust for myself. He is someone with the keen ability to beautifully articulate their emotions, knowing every word they speak is one hundred percent, completely justified, and I'm on the receiving end. "I was rather looking forward to catching up with my old friend, and I feel terribly mislead with the formalities, and what I truly believed was a genuine interest to reconnect." I remain silent. I could push back. *You don't understand, I really did want to…* eh. It would all be bullshit. I just wanted his Big Motherfucking Boat. "That being said, it puts me in rather an odd predicament. You see that, yes? Say 'yes' to your request, and I completely invalidate my own value in terms of what I know I offer as a friend. Say 'no,' and I completely decimate your potential to change the course of history."

"I'm sorry to put you in this position. I just don't know what else to do."

"I understand." Silence again fills the space. "I'm having a brand-new communications system installed next week, so The Tethys is not of much use to me until then. I would be happy to let you use her for your testing."

*Holy shit. I got it.*

*I got the Big, Motherfucking Boat.*

I try desperately to contain the absolute joy pulsating through my veins. "While you're on the water though, you should know you will be in almost complete darkness. Since the new comms aren't in yet, you'll only be able to notify the authorities if something were to go wrong, and even that connection will be wildly unreliable. It's been recommended to leave docked until the system is installed, as a safety precaution for anyone on-board. It's only fair you should know that."

"I understand. Thank you so much. Thank you." I hold back tears. I had no idea how the conversation would end after it began. This scenario is the best case. "Thank you, truly."

"You are welcome, Micah. You are welcome. I would never intentionally stand in the way of human progress." I wipe a single tear from my eye, successfully holding the rest back. He clears his throat, about to say something more. He hesitates slightly in picking the words, in which he puts such value. "This favor is conditional, of course. It does come with a slightly unfortunate request of you, I'm afraid."

"What is it? Anything, really, I will do anything."

"After your week aboard my yacht, and you've accomplished what you are there to do, I do ask that you completely eliminate any communication with me moving forward."

*Oh.*

I was not expecting that response.

"It's become abundantly clear to me why you've decided to keep my contact information, and I'm simply not interested in keeping people in my life that use other people that way. I always thought of you as a friend, Micah. I guess, I just always thought you felt the same."

*You misunderstand, I absolutely consider you a friend, this situation is just crazy, I promise I will be a better friend...*

"Understood." I say.

I believe you can do things you will regret, and I believe you can say things you will regret, but I do not for one single second believe you will regret doing whatever you can to get the things you believe in. I believe that sentiment with every ounce of my being. I will never regret asking this favor of this man. I would, however, regret it for the rest of my life had I not.

# CHAPTER 5
# MICAH

I feel Sarah take my hand as we sit side by side in the back seat of an Uber Black on the way to Los Angeles International Airport. We are officially on our way to Alaska. Today will be one of, if not, the longest travel days either of us have ever experienced.

There are not any direct flights to Kodiak Island, so we essentially have to make several stops on the way, starting in Anchorage. A flight, then a car, then a helicopter, then another car, then a boat, and then we arrive. Trying to save as much cost as possible, our would be five-and-a-half-hour non-stop flight from Los Angeles to Anchorage actually has three stops over the course of twenty-seven hours, gate to gate. From there, we take a short helicopter flight for about an hour to Kodiak Island. From Kodiak, we will take a ferry to our research sight. The ferry, plus all of our other travels, makes our aggregate travel time just eclipse thirty-four total hours. I close my eyes and choose to enjoy it.

Helicopters are unbelievably loud. The roaring sound from the propeller of a helicopter is indescribable. I feel Sarah's hand on my thigh squeeze tightly as the chopper takes a sharp left turn. She has never been very comfortable flying. She does fly, obviously. It is not a debilitating anxiety, but she would always prefer driving when possible. The helicopter levels out, and her grip on my leg loosens slightly. I look to her, and she instinctively smiles at me. I know today has not only been physically exhausting to her, but emotionally draining as well. She is strong to the point of madness sometimes. I speak to her through the microphone in our headgear radio.

"Are you OK?" She nods, lying. Still smiling, I just smile back. Realistically, I know she is fine. I can tell because her hand is definitely still gripping my knee. "We're almost there, babe." She nods again, still smiling.

Being in a helicopter, overlooking untouched wilderness, is a completely different experience than being thirty-seven thousand feet in the air over-looking the vastness of the earth. From a helicopter, you can almost make out the branches of the individual trees, instead of just seeing a mass gathering of green through a sixteen-by-eleven-inch window.

Just as I am losing myself to my own thought, I see a massive hawk leap from the tip of one of those trees. Its powerful wings smoothly cutting through the sky away from the forest. A moment I would have surely missed from a Boeing 747. I point the hawk out to Sarah who is captivated by its fluid wings. I have to admit, it is breathtaking. We are looking at a portion of our world very rarely seen by human eyes. Even more rarely touched by human hands.

We fly farther over the Alaskan wilderness for what seems like a lifetime, through trees, birds, and unending rivers. At one point we see a small gathering of elk at a rushing river drinking water from the steady stream. The larger one lifts its head to look towards our chopper just in time to make eye contact with me. I have no idea if it was actually looking at me, but with zero evidence to the contrary, and no one to contest my account, it is what I have decided happened. It is the story I will tell at dinner parties anyway. "And just before we fly over this family of elk, the alpha male elk turns it head, and literally makes eye contact with me. I swear to God, it was life-changing."

More trees, and mountains; streams, and wildlife. Finally, a tiny blip appears on the horizon. It is an airport. Sarah grips my knee again, but this time because of the excitement bubbling up, overflowing into a moment of pure joy. All of this is really happening. With almost clockwork precision, the moment the clearing appears, our pilot was speaking pilot chatter into the communication system on board.

"Two-Zero-Hotel for Kodiak, did we switch back to One-Six?" The pilot asks without any sort of emotion registering on his face. He has done this a million times before.

"Negative, Two-Zero-Hotel. Proceed to One-Zero-Zero-Seven, as scheduled." The Air Traffic Controller promptly responds. I take Sarah's hand. I exaggerate opening my eyes wide, excited, and nervous. She smiles and looks at me, beaming.

"I can't believe we are here." She says into our headgear. "I still don't understand how you were able to…" I do not even let her consider finishing that sentence.

"Didn't I tell you that everything will work out? If this opportunity is for us, it will…"

"Don't use my line against me!" She jeers through laughter.

We get closer and closer to the airport, flying straight ahead. Just by looking at it, you can tell this particular airport does not see many flights. You probably should not actually even call it an airport. It is open to private flights, but from what I could tell from a cursory search, it had been co-operated by the United States Coast Guard several years ago. I also learned the state of Alaska had renamed the small airport after the designer of the Alaskan State flag, making this airport, officially, the "Kodiak 'Benny Benson' State Airport." *Now, that is a great airport name.* Maybe Sarah and I can name our first born after this airport, named after the creator of the Alaskan State flag. *Mr. Kodiak Benny Benson State Airport Day… It does have a nice ring to it,* I think.

I again feel Sarah grip my leg tightly as our helicopter sways back and forth, leveling out as we steadily drift straight down onto our designated landing platform. One-Zero-Zero-Seven, I presume. Our pilot flicks a few switches on the main console and turns a few additional knobs before sliding his radio mic back down in front of his face and turning towards us.

"I hope the ride wasn't too bumpy, folks. Y'all have a safe trip." I never truly realized how widely used the phrase "y'all" is. I feel like, stereotypically, it is reserved for a special breed of southern person, but you really do hear people using it all over the place.

We say our *thank you so much's* and we unclip ourselves from the seat straps, which are exactly as secure as you would hope for when you climb into a helicopter. Carefully, we take our steps off of the aircraft, being helped down by some of the airport workers. I am positive the comically massive rotor blades, still spinning at such a high velocity, would turn you into vapor given the opportunity. The sheer power and volume of the blades is precisely why Sarah and I both feel like we are bending almost completely over at the waist, as to avoid the whole tragically becoming dust thing.

A man in an oversized, cheap polyester suit meets us just off the helicopter's landing platform, and shakes our hands, greeting us. He is employed by the yacht's maintenance company, and will drive us from this airport about twenty-five minutes to a dock, where we will board the small ferry that will take us the final few hours of travel to where The Tethys is currently anchored. The site of everything we are set to experience.

He helps us with our luggage, loading it into the car for us. Thank God Sarah and I have traveled together quite a bit, and we know how to maximize our luggage space, packing light even for lengthy stays. We were to be on board for just a week, so we hardly brought anything.

The drive is quick, and quiet. Sarah and I sit in complete silence as we stare out the windows in awe of the beautifully inspiring landscape of this tiny, forgotten island. The mountains and trees bursting with green, silhouetted by the setting sun. The sky an unbelievably brilliant orange, glowing off of the ocean, as the world around us slowly becomes darker and darker. Truly, it is quite a stunning sight. We arrive at the ferry dock and unload our luggage onto a smaller-than-expected boat. It was seemingly less of a ferry, and more of a small catamaran.

It was when I notice the four large, extra gasoline cans set off to the side of the boat I realize just how long this leg of the trip could be. Obviously some of that extra gasoline is just that, extra, but knowing the distance from our satellite images, and judging by the way this boat's tiny crew were nestling up, I would guess this trip will take a little longer than anticipated. Sarah and I do not mind in the slightest. We know this is the final leg of this part of our journey, and when this boat's engines cuts off, the next steps we take will be directly onto the ship acting as our home while we extract freshwater from the floor of the Pacific Ocean for the first time in human history. *Worth every fucking minute.* We decide to try and sleep a little, knowing this journey will be long, there is little for us to do, and not much to see in the darkness, beyond the edges of this small ferry. Once we are settled in, I finally rest my head back, close my eyes, and let the gentle tug of the sea lull me into a well-deserved, albeit brief, sleep.

I wake back up before Sarah. A small handful of lights on the deck allow everyone on board to move about without injuring themselves. No one explains just how dangerous the deck of a boat really can be. I can feel we are moving quickly, slicing through a calm ocean. The smell of the salt in the air fills my nose and forces me to breath in deeply again. I look deep into the horizon and see nothing. Nothing but pitch-black darkness. I can hear the waves, however, and the rushing of the water our engine cuts though. I hear Sarah rustle awake behind me, while I stare off into the empty distance.

"Are we close?" Her voice grainy, and tired.

"We should be. I think."

Sarah stands, and walks up next to me. Silently, we stare together into the abyss. *Nothing* has always had a certain level of peace to it. It is interesting holding *nothing* in your sight, realizing if you press onward you will eventually run into everything.

"I'm excited to meet everyone," she says, breaking the silence.

"I'm excited for both of us to meet everyone," I respond, laughing. "I know everyone is excited to meet us."

I look straight ahead, squinting my eyes, pushing their ability to see as far into the distance as they can, and I see the glimmer of our searchlight reflecting onto something. That faint ping of light has to be it. I point it out to Sarah and take her hand as I lead the way, walking us both to the bow of the ship.

The reflection gets more and more prominent as we get closer. Before we know it, we are shining our little spotlight onto this massive craft.

The Tethys.

It is far larger than I remember it being. I feel our engine cut off, and I welcome the immediate relief the silence brings.

"Micah, this is too much. We can't afford this…" At that moment, I realized I had only explained to Sarah I had secured a boat. I had not told her what boat, or the size, or even about my meeting with What's-His-Name. A slight panic floods over me. *We never keep secrets.* Now, I am keeping a few.

"Woah, woah," I buy myself some time, "the Dean of Admissions… owed me a favor." I lie, keeping the secret. *She doesn't know. It's OK. It's not… that big of a deal.* It is a small lie. It is not even really a lie, just sort of misleading. Nevertheless, Sarah is shocked, and a Grinch-sized smile bursts onto her face. "It's taken care of." I say, matching her smile.

"You cannot be serious, you have to be kidding!" She squeals with excitement.

"I am not kidding." *I am not kidding,* I think, *I am lying.*

Our ferry abruptly slows, and I feel Sarah press into me, concerned. The ferry continues to slow as it approaches the Big, Motherfucking Boat, pausing just long enough for Sarah and me to gather our belongings, and make our way to the other side where we off-board.

One of the ferry's deckhands hops onto the deck of The Tethys, turns back and extends his hand towards us. Sarah first, she grabs his hand, and he hoists her up onto the deck of the mega-yacht. I take his hand, and step on board next. The deckhand then jumps back on board the smaller ferry, and hands our bags to us. The captain of the ferry walks over to us and shakes my hand.

"This is where we leave you, folks. We're scheduled to come back out on Wednesday and pick you up with the others. You most likely won't be able to contact us until then with the comms mess and all, so be safe. Until then." He tips his cap.

"Thank you again, for everything." He unfastens the rope from The Tethys, and with a kick, pushes the ferry off into the open water before grabbing a metal lever and cranking it. The engine putters back to life and carries the ferry back into the darkness.

"What does he mean we won't be able to reach them?" Another minor detail I realize I had not explained to Sarah.

"Oh, shit, I'm so sorry, babe. They're repairing and replacing the communications system on board, so radio between us and the shore is going to be sort of minimal…" I lied again.

"So… we are isolated."

"No, we're not. Well, yes, and no. Sort of. The radio system just isn't super stable right now, it's still usable."

"Micah, I don't like the idea that we are stuck out here alone. What if something—"I jump in before letting her finish her thought. *It's also too late.*

"Sarah, love, everything is going to be fine. More than fine. I promise. We made it."

Forehead to chest. Embrace.

"Come on, I want to show you around a little." I guide her deeper onto the deck, leaving our bags near the edge. "It has a full kitchen and dining area, six individually furnished cabins, it's a hundred and eighty-something feet long, this thing is incredible."

"This is unreal," she musters.

"He had a hyperbaric chamber installed, for chrissake. He decided to take up diving as a hobby, I guess."

"That seems like it is a little much."

"Better safe than sorry is sort of his style."

"I guess so." I can still hear the concern in her voice.

"Come on," I say excitedly, looking down at my watch, "I want you to meet our team."

It is late, but most of them should still be awake. I walk Sarah, hand in mine, down a corridor on the main deck. Through the kitchen and down a narrow staircase towards the dining area. The door is shut, but a bright orange glow shines through a crack underneath, while muffled laughter and the sound of a radio playing some terrible top-forty pop track barrels through. It is like a group of teenage friends in their parent's basement, way past lights out, and I feel like the father about to break up the party to tell them it is bedtime. "Twenty more minutes, Dad!"

We are greeted by cheers and greetings when I push the door open. *Hey, they made it! They're here!* The dining room table is littered with poker cards, chips and coins, half-finished beer cans and water bottles, and still-lit cigars. They all stand, and hugs and handshakes are exchanged. If you did not know any better, you would think everyone in this room are great friends from lives past. After a few moments of joyous chaos, I give a general waving gesture with my right hand.

"Hi, everyone! I'm Micah. This is my wife Sarah." Sarah gives a smaller version of my greeting. I look at the shorter, older gentleman in round-wired bifocals. His beard untrimmed, but his tie done with military precision. He was waiting for us to arrive before he disheveled himself. "You must be…"

"Thomas," his smile says it all. Thomas is a brilliant man in his fifties with a slight chaotic energy to his body language. It's abundantly clear that he has very eagerly awaited this moment. "Dr. Thomas Shepherd, and it's such a pleasure to finally put a face to the name." Standing next to him is a woman with a slightly smaller frame than his. She stands close to his side, smiling as wide as he is. I make eye contact with her and extend my hand.

"And I don't believe we have…" I take my time, cutting some slack to the doctor for not immediately introducing us.

"Oh, where is my mind? Micah, I'd like to introduce my wife, Marie." We shake hands. Then Sarah does the same. "And…" Thomas continues.

A third man stands up. He is large, muscular and a complete stranger. *Jesus Christ, who is this guy?* He looks like a linebacker for the University of Southern California Trojans. His dirty blonde hair tucked back over his ears, held together with a hair tie.

"Jackson Pond, but my mates call me Jax." His thick, Australian accent makes that introduction one of the more badass introductions I have experienced in a while. I extend the same greeting.

"Jax," I say, taken aback by the stature and hand strength. "I like that. It's nice to meet you."

"Pleasure's all mine, Micah." Thomas, still bursting with excitement, cuts in.

"It's so great to finally meet you in person."

A genuine enthusiasm buzzes among the group. The five of us are about to take on the greatest threat to humankind, and we will be doing it together. The energy of that revelation is palpable in this room. I take a slight step back, commanding the space and everyone's attention. I feel Sarah's hand take the inside of my elbow, and I instinctively wrap my arm around her, pulling her close to my side.

"Well, listen, everyone," I address the room. "I'll make this quick. I can't thank you enough for being here and being a part of this. I know

you're all sacrificing something to be here for the next week, and it's..."
I search for the right words, being intentional about what I am choosing
to say. "It's just really important that you know how grateful I am..."
*wait*, "...we. It's important you know how grateful *we* are." I pull Sarah
even closer; I feel her smile at my correction. "I know we are all just
meeting, but we truly would never have made it this far without each of
you here, now."

Sarah tightens her arms around me. I can see Thomas take Marie's
hand, and Jax smiles widely. I can feel a visceral, and genuine pride among
the people in this room. We are embarking on something really special,
and everyone can physically feel it.

"All right, well." I know I do not really have anything else planned to
say, so, "before I let this get weird, I'm going to say goodnight!" Everyone
chuckles a little to themselves. "You guys get back to your game, Sarah
and I have had an insanely long day, so we are going to go get settled in."

"It was so nice to meet you guys!" Sarah interjects. It was at that
moment I realize I have completely dominated the introductions, not
deferring to her for anything she wished to add. She would have spoken
up, I suppose, if she wanted to. I take it at face value.

"Let's plan on meeting here tomorrow at seven in the morning, if that
is all right with everyone. Thomas and I can walk everyone through it all
then. Goodnight!"

"Goodnight!" Sarah echoes.

We all repeat the warm, kind greetings, this time as goodbyes.
Handshakes and hugs. Smiles and excited anticipation all around. Sarah
and I make our way back up the narrow staircase towards what will be
our home for the next seven days.

# CHAPTER 6
# MICAH

If you have ever stayed overnight in the mountains, you know the familiar feeling of struggling to sleep for the first couple of nights. Since the air is so thin, your lungs are not able to inhale to their full capacity, and your brain starts to panic. A deeply, genetically engrained survival technique. Then, what feels like every two minutes, your mind jolts back to consciousness as you gasp for air; wash, rinse, repeat.

The first night aboard a large ship set at sea is extremely similar, but in a completely different way. Our body is not gasping for air, but your brain struggles to normalize the constant rocking of the water beneath. While simultaneously being rocked to sleep like an infant, it struggles to completely release control atop what is essentially a constantly sloshing waterbed. A battle it is inherently losing.

Even after the longest day I have experienced in a very long time, I still find myself gasping for air every two minutes, the weight of the nausea causing me to constantly stir awake. Normally, this type of stirring would make me to look at a clock every few minutes to check and see how much time has passed. This sleeplessness always seems to happen when you know you have to wake up early the next morning, never when you have nothing to do the next day.

After mentally breaking myself down enough to chalk it up to excitement, anticipation, knowing I need to wake up in a few hours, and *not* becoming sick from the monotonous swells of the ocean, I give myself the advantage. I have never been a glutton for punishment, so I decide to just give in, and get up. I do not have to be gone for long, just long enough to take a lap or two around the desk. Yes, a lap or two around the deck would not hurt anything. It might even help me sleep.

Sarah is pressed into me, as closely as two people could be. I exhale, and gently lift the duvet up just enough to slide my legs out to the side of the bed. I slip myself out from underneath the covers quietly and as carefully as I can. Sarah, unlike myself, is fast asleep. Not disturbed at all by the constantly swaying motion. It is embarrassing to admit, but I have watched her sleep more times than I can count. It is not something I do on purpose, but if I wake before she does, or if I am coming to bed after she has, I always give myself a minute to watch her lay there perfectly still; a princess under the spell of a witch undisturbed by the noise of the world around her.

I look at her quiet smile of sleep. Her chest lifting and lowering, filling and collapsing with the dense saltwater air. I love the way her mouth constantly switches between being open and closed. A subconscious war in her mind unresolved for the eleven years I have known her. For a few breaths, her lips purse together, as if they are keeping her tongue and teeth from running away. Then, almost just to find out what it feels like, her lips gently part, giving her teeth and tongue their chance run away before her lips press together again. Eleven years I have known this woman. Eleven years I have watched this war of lips and teeth wage in her sleep. She is so beautiful. *God, she is so good.*

I grab my glasses, and slip on a light pair of sneakers, and head towards the door of our cabin carefully not to make too much noise. The moment I step foot out of our cabin, I almost immediately start to regain my orientation. The waves suddenly disappear, and I can actually breath again.

I make my way onto the open deck of the ship's stern. A blast of a freezing cold wind burns my nose and cheeks, and in that exact moment, I feel wide awake. *Wonderful,* I think sarcastically. I bring my scarf up over my mouth and try to breath as slowly as I can. My lungs burn from the desperately cold air, and I feel my blood begin coursing through my veins, in a failing attempt at keeping my body warm. It is freezing out here. I lean against the edge of the boat and look out into a sea of black. Any time I lean over an edge of anything, I convince myself my glasses are going to fall off my head, and crash into whatever I am leaning over. In this case, basically all of space and time, never to be seen again.

They do not, and instead I find myself staring straight down, almost a complete ninety-degrees, into absolute nothingness. I have no idea what time it is, but judging by the silence in the world, and the chill in the air, it is either very late, or very early. However you want to look at it.

I look down to where I know the surface of the water should be, but still, I see nothing. I can hear the gentle flaps and tugs of the ocean waves splashing against themselves and against the steel of our anchored ship. It is a calming, yet simultaneously, alarming sound. I remind myself we are essentially at the mercy of the sea, before I try and put the thought out of my mind. I lean back up, looking towards what I assume is the horizon, and feel the blood rush away from my head. My brain pounds for a moment, and I realize how long I was leaning completely over the rail at the waist. I take a breath and pull one of my gloves off. I reach down with my newly bare hand and touch the metal of the handrail lining the entirety of first level of the ship. It is freezing cold. The cold shocks me at first, and I jerk my hand away. After a moment of awareness, I take another breath and slowly set my bare hand back down. The metal is frigid. I feel the wind shred the top of my hand now, too. *It is horribly cold.*

The tinge of freezing metal on my fingertips floods into my brain with the same realization I have felt before. *This is real. We are here, and this is happening.* The feeling is overwhelming, if only just for a moment, until the right side of my brain instantly skims through the internal checklist of everything I have spent weeks preparing. *We are ready for this. We can do this.*

My mind goes to Jason's secret, now our secret. A slight wave of guilt floods through me, and I feel a small pit in my stomach. His words come to mind again. "You don't have to do anything different." *Then how come I cannot tell my wife?* I think.

Before the cold metal is given the opportunity to partner with the wind and steal the feeling out of my fingers, I slip my glove back on, and step away from the edge. I kept my hand out in the wild too long to avoid the dull pain I now feel in my fingertips. My heart pounds underneath each fingernail. I leisurely make my way around the side of the yacht, heading towards the bow, taking my time. My nose is starting to run a little from the cold, and I wipe my cloth glove across my face. I had almost forgotten to pack these gloves.

"I promise you it's going to be freezing at night, you will want to have these," Sarah antagonized me while we packed.

"OK, OK, I'll bring them," I complied. Now they are saving my fingers, and my nose.

The sound of the ocean was calming, yet unsettling as always, as the water stands mostly still, pitch black, in every direction. We are completely alone out here. If it would not wake everyone on board, I would scream at the top of my lungs into the void. No one would hear me. I feel tempted to, even still, I do not.

From behind me, but close, I hear a quick, rough snapping sound. I turn just in time to see a faint flash. A small spark of light that instantly disappears. I fix my gaze towards it, and again a small burst of dim light, a spark. This time, a small flame holds. It moves slowly until I hear the fizz of the flame begin destroying its way through a small amount of paper debris. Someone is awake and unknowingly standing outside with me. I keep my eyes focused on the front of the ship, and I see the familiar burn of a flame at the end of a cigarette. Whoever it is just stands at the boat's edge, staring straight into the endless ocean, a lit cigarette now at their side. I slowly make my way towards whoever the figure is. They do not hear me coming, probably trapped within the confines of their own mind; a feeling I am well acquainted with. I try to delicately clear my throat as soon as I am close enough for them to hear me.

"Ahem," I make myself known.

Thomas jumps as if he has just seen a ghost and drops his cigarette. Small embers erupt as his nasty habit smashes into the wooden planks of the deck.

"Jesus Christ, Micah, you scared the hell out of me." I cannot help but smirk a little. Thankfully, Thomas sees the humor in it, too.

"Relax, Thomas!" I quiet him and try to calm his nerves. "It's just me."

"Oh, my God, you really gave it to me. I had no idea anyone else was awake."

"I'm sorry. I wasn't expecting anyone else to be up right now either." I take another step towards him and stand just at his side. We both keep our eyes towards the sea. The empty black of the ocean completely surrounding us.

"I didn't even hear you walking up." Thomas picks his cigarette up from the deck, but promptly puts it out on the railing, his body language feigning unspoken apologies.

"It's OK. It doesn't bother me," I say, gesturing towards his vice. "I kind of enjoy the smell of it, to be honest." He takes the opened pack out of his left, inside jacket pocket, and holds it up towards me, essentially signaling for my permission to light a new one. "Oh, please," permission granted, "be my guest," I respond. Thomas slips the butt of the cigarette he had just been enjoying into the opened pack, and pulls out a new, fresh Marlboro Light.

"It's a terrible, filthy habit, to be honest. I've been trying to quit… for about four years now," he says, well-rehearsed. He adds pregnant pause, expecting a laugh, but no one ever gives it to him. "Not trying very hard, I guess." Thomas laughs awkwardly, looking for any sort of affirmation.

"Well, your secret's safe with me." I approve, so Thomas smiles, and eases out of some of his held tension.

"Mind if I enable you?" I say. Thomas whips a look to me. He definitely did not see my request coming. Neither did I, to be honest. I have not had a cigarette in at least six months. *If not now, when, I guess?* Thomas again grabs the pack and holds it out towards me. I hesitate, knowing I should not take one. I can stand here and hold a conversation without joining in the cigarette festivity. I could also just enjoy one cigarette with a new colleague. After all, it is the middle the night surrounded by and endless sea of nothing. Nobody needs to know.

I grab the pack from Thomas' hands, and slip a single, thin cigarette out, holding it gently between my index and middle fingers. I slowly slide it across my nose, smelling the packed leaves of tobacco. I exhale deeply, and Thomas can tell it has been a while. We connect stares.

"Don't tell Sarah?" I ask.

"Don't tell Marie?" He answers.

We both enjoy the moment. Two men, holding innocent secrets we both feel overly guilty about. It is an addiction. Addiction is a disease. We should not feel guilt over giving in to the temptation of an extreme addiction we have both been successfully depriving ourselves of for… *Oh, give it up,* I think to myself. We both know this is a lie. Right now, either of us seem to care.

I breathe in the cancer, and I breathe out utter relief. Smoke billows towards the sky.

"Cheers," I say, feeling actual, real relaxation for the first time in months. Thomas lights up his replacement cigarette and takes a long drag.

"Feels good, don't it?" He asks.

"Feels goddamn good." I answer.

We stand together for a few more moments in silence, staring into the blank; two men, basically strangers, if not for a series of electronic correspondence, slowly killing ourselves in the most pleasurable way possible. I have always thought there was something really special happening when two people could enjoy silence together. Much of our lives demands our constant attention these days, there is something really beautiful about giving it to nothing for a few fleeting moments.

"I really am sorry I couldn't put together a larger team for this," Thomas says, breaking the beautiful silence. "I know you were probably expecting more help." *I was.* I was not necessarily expecting an entire battalion, but at the very least, a small handful.

"It's all right," I say instead, "I understand the limitations." I had only given Thomas about a week to put together the team of people we knew we needed to accomplish this. I had ended up telling him we needed a bare minimum of three, *a bare minimum.* I guess I did it to myself.

"Marie is a brilliant diver, though. And Jax is one of my top students. He spent the last four years in the Royal Australian Navy." That bit of information is actually really nice to hear. I trust in Thomas' ability to select the right people to be a part of this, and I am confident he knows exactly how much is dependent on the success of this expedition, but there is a sense of comfort knowing Jax is used to performing at the highest level under the highest amount of scrutiny and pressure.

"Trust me," I say as I turn into the reassuring leader, "I'll take what I can get." It is the truth. With the amount of work we are trying to do, in the very small amount of time we are trying to do it in, I am shocked *anyone* is here to help to begin with. I am shocked there are any of us here at all.

"Jax was very eager to join." Thomas continues his apology tour. "He said he's been following the headlines around your campaign and your wife's organization very closely for quite some time. He jumped at the chance to offer support when I brought it up to him that you and I were beginning to work together."

"That's… that is fantastic to hear. I'm glad he's excited."

"Excited would be an understatement."

The beauty of the moment comes back again. The enjoyable and welcomed silence. Black sky, invisible sea, chopping water gently bashing the side of the boat. It is so peaceful.

"It really is an honor being able to be here and be a part of this." Thomas says, carefully putting out his second cigarette in the same spot as before. A softer, quieter tone in his voice. Even his words far calmer than before, earlier this evening. "We're all quite excited to get to work."

"We're just getting started," I say with a smile. Thomas extends his hand, and I take it. "Get some rest, Thomas. We've got an early morning."

"See you then." He walks away, leaving me standing at the boat's edge by myself. I stand, staring out; just me, the waves, and the darkness. The crushing weight of mankind's future on my shoulders.

Anytime I am asked, "If you could have a superpower, what would it be?" My answer is always I would want to be able to stop time. Mostly because of moments exactly like this. If I could freeze time right now, I would stay in this moment forever. The frozen wind blistering against my face; the horizon of black serenity, the sound of the sea. This moment is perfect. I breathe in quick and deep, knowing damn well it is going to burn my lungs. It does. I hold it in for a moment and feel my pulse in my neck before exhaling slowly. My breath promptly disappears, evaporating into the heavens.

After several more minutes of enjoying this rare scene, I decide to make my way back to my cabin and try to sleep. Since I know my alarm clock was already set, I never bother looking for the time. I would rather not know anyway.

I take my time walking back through the door of my cabin, careful not to wake Sarah. She is still laying peacefully, undisturbed, almost exactly how I left her. Her left arm stretched over my side of the mattress. *I'm definitely going to wake her up when I lay back down*, I think to myself. *I was just using the restroom, love, go back to sleep,* I can say when she asks me where I have been, half asleep, half dreaming. I take my shoes off, and quietly place them back in the cubby next to the desk I had designated as our shoe bin. I meticulously remove my scarf and my coat, placing them again where they had previously been resting on the back of the chair. If there is an art to sneaking into a bed, I might master it tonight.

Carefully, I lift Sarah's left arm, and slide myself underneath it. I place it over my side, and settle in. *She is so good.* I lay like this for several minutes, hoping not to disrupt her peaceful sleep, grazing my fingertips across the back of her hand. I am proud of us. We have come a long way.

I hold my breath as I turn a complete one-hundred and eighty degrees around. We face each other now. I can feel her breath on my chest, and I wonder if it will wake her up. I consider risking rustling her awake to pull her slightly closer to my body. I would feel a small amount of guilt waking her up, obviously, but it would be nice. She must sense our bodies are close again, because without waking, she does exactly what I was wanting to do. She moves her arm around my back and pulls her sleeping body into mine. The heat of her breath now flushing up towards my neck. *Goddamnit, I love this woman.*

I pull myself back a little so I can look at her face. I look at her calm expression, breathing slowly, perfectly still. I should tell her about the cigarette. She will smell it on my coat in the morning, anyway. I am sure would appreciate me being forthcoming about it. Honestly, it is not a big deal. I had not felt any actual guilt over it, until right now. I would never want to do anything to break her trust, even something as small and ultimately meaningless as enjoying a single cigarette with a colleague after an extremely stressful forty-eight hours of travel. Then I remember Jason's words again.

I finally find comfort in this bed, in this moment, and I hear the loud groans and creaks of our metal home as the ocean pushes and pulls it about. The gentle sways thankfully begin to lull me to sleep, my lungs seem able to breathe their full capacity. Finally, rest. I want another cigarette.

I wonder if Tethys is watching.

# CHAPTER 7
# SARAH

Before she even opens her eyes, she can sense she is alone in their cabin, sprawled out in their empty bed. She had a feeling Micah would be awake earlier than she would today, even if only by a little bit. He typically wakes up before she does on normal days, and today would be anything but a normal day. Today is important; different. She pushes her hands into the sinking mattress and forces herself to sit up, wondering if Micah slept at all last night. *Probably not,* she thinks to herself. She rubs the undisturbed sleep from her eyes, and stretches her arms high, surprised her fingertips do not quite reach the low cabin ceiling.

The clock on the wall of their small room lets her know it is only around five-fifteen in the morning. *Jesus,* Sarah thinks. Her quick math means, at most, she could have only gotten about four full hours of sleep. A strange realization considering how rested she feels. A brief scent of freshly brewed coffee finds its way to her nose as she puts the final touches on her morning stretch and pulls her legs over the side of the small bed. Regardless of how much, or rather how little, sleep she knows she got, her brain is fully aware it is time to consume some of that coffee. She forces herself out of bed.

After a quick application of her simple, but necessary-to-her-sanity self-care regimen, she slowly makes her way out of her cabin, and down the narrow hallway towards the kitchen and stairway to the crew mess room. Walking through the kitchen, she catches a glimpse of Jax starting down the stairs, steam from the fresh brewed coffee he holds lofts up and away from the glass pot. The jackrabbit on her horse track.

She follows behind him at a distance, avoiding the awkward greeting of someone you do not know quite well enough yet independently of others. Down the stairs, the door closes behind him as she hits the top of the staircase. She can hear Thomas and Marie in the crew dining room area already. Wondering if Micah is there yet, she slows her pace down the stairs, hoping she hears his voice before she walks into the small room.

Sarah pushes the down open slowly, and makes eye contact with Marie who offers a sincere, "Good morning!" Also seeing her, Thomas and Jax offer similar greetings. Jax pours and distributes the liquid gold she was after all along. He hands a cup to Marie who sits down next to Thomas at the small table. Trying to be coy and romantic, Thomas steals the first sip.

"Oh, thank you, darling," he sarcastically declares. Marie eats it up, and playfully smacks his arm. She then offers a soft, quick kiss on his cheek, primarily the kind of interaction Sarah was hoping to avoid. Jax pours another cup.

"Come on, now. It's too early for all that," Jax jests.

"Sorry, Jackson," Marie offers half-heartedly. Jax laughs a little, focuses on his pour, and offers his most recent cup to Sarah. She eagerly accepts, scanning the small room for her husband, who does not seem to be there yet. She wonders where else he could be but takes a seat.

"How'd you sleep, Sarah?" Marie politely tries to make conversation, knowing it is too early for a genuine exchange.

"Fine, actually. I think the traveling really took it out of me. As soon as my head hit the pillow, I was out." Thomas stands up as she speaks and pours a full cup for himself.

"We felt the exact same way," he adds.

The door pops open, and Micah walks into the cramped dining area. Focused, and staring at whatever it is he is holding, he makes his way into the threshold, gently sliding the door closed behind him. Sarah's smile lights the room as soon as she sees him. She obviously knew nothing was wrong, but finally seeing him puts her nerves at ease. Holding a large bundle of papers, Micah looks up and smiles at his wife. Maintaining eye contact with her as he makes his way towards the table, he cheerfully greets the rest of the room.

"Morning, everyone," he leans down, kisses Sarah on the cheek, and whispers in her ear, "morning, crazy girl." She smiles and looks down. Even after all of these years, she still feels like a girl in love. *He is so good,* she thinks to herself. Jax hands Micah a cup of the freshly brewed blonde roast. Micah sets his papers down on the table and takes a sip.

"Fuck, that's hot." Micah laughs, and breaks his focus.

"Sorry, mate, fresh cuppa," Jax laughs too.

She watches Micah take off his thin rimmed, tortoise shell frames and slide them through the top button of his shirt as he shuffles through the large stack of papers, trying to organize them as much as he can. Everyone else makes their way to the small table, using it as a sort of conference room of sorts for their makeshift morning meeting. Micah sorts the papers from the bundle he brought in with him into small packets and passes them out to the group. He addresses them all exactly as they are, members of this project. A project with a very specific, and extremely difficult to achieve goal.

"We have…" he begins, still sorting and distributing the papers, "very little money, very little support, and very little time to get this right." Sarah watches as his stack disappears before he gets to her. He leans into her as he sits, and says, "I thought we could share." She smiles softly and chooses to look beyond the thoughts immediately flooding her mind. Micah chooses each word with intention and purpose, delivering them slowly and deliberately. Sarah watches him pause for a moment after his opening sentence. He rubs his forehead, and she can tell he is nervous. She tells herself this is why he was out of their room so early; probably pacing the deck, organizing his thoughts before this moment. Printing out enough packets for everyone… except her. *Stop it, Sarah,* she thinks.

"I know you're all basically volunteering your time to be here, and like we said last night, we cannot thank you all enough for doing that… for being here," he takes Sarah's hand. "It really does mean so much more to us than any of you will ever truly understand… Really." She is reminded, and reassured, that they are in this together. They are a team. "But we have to be completely on point," he continues. "We do not have the luxury of many mulligans, if any at all. What we are trying to accomplish is… well, it's really fucking big. To be plain. And we only have one shot. So…" He pauses and looks up at all of the eyes on him. He smiles. She can tell he is nervous, but she can also see his eyes beaming with excitement, and instinctively knows that, nerves or not, he is so ready for this moment.

"Today, we go in. Tomorrow, we build. By Sunday, we'll have altered the course of human history. Does that work with everyone?" He asks facetiously, smiling all the way.

"Sounds damn good to us." Thomas proudly responds. Micah opens up the packet of information, turning to the first page, and the group follows suit. He continues.

"While I was working with Jason from Cark Strategies, we developed customized diving suits that will monitor our vitals, software that can track our oxygen and pressure levels, and vision screens that will analyze the molecular consistencies of the water within our line of sight—in real time." Sarah looks down, over his shoulder, and at his pamphlet. Images drawn in intricate detail outline all of the enhancements he and Jason's team made to existing deep diving gear.

Diagrams point to certain gear functions with specifically labeled asides explaining the software developments and upgrades. Original artist renderings show the stages of the software and hardware developments. A crude, basic sketch of their goggles analyzing the water's elemental composition, side-by-side with a still graphic of the actual, manufactured equipment performing the same task. Side by side's, before and afters.

Sarah feels impressed with the detail of the sketches, but she catches herself wondering why she has never seen these images before. These creations seem like something to be proud of and excited about; something to be celebrated. Typically, things a husband shares with a wife; things Micah normally shares with her. Shaking the thought from her mind, she comes back to the room. *She is a part of this team, she is being shown them now*, she thinks to herself. *That's all that matters.*

"That's just like Iron Man!" Jax's childlike interjection helps to snap Sarah out of her mental spiral. Micah, completely caught off guard, stares back at Jax blankly.

"...Yeah, I guess... it is kind of... sort of like Iron Man." Here was this massive, military-trained soldier, geeking out over technology Micah had a personal hand in creating and developing. A sense of pride, and amusement, washes over Sarah as she watches this silly interaction. Micah looks directly to her. His eyes asking for her permission to continue. She laughs in her head, and subtly nods to him. *It's OK, darling. He's just excited. You can keep going,* she says to him telepathically. He hears her unspoken words; she is sure of it.

"Moving on," Thomas says, awkwardly smiling. She cannot tell if he is embarrassed by Jax's innocent excitement or not. Meanwhile, Jax does not seem to notice any of it, or his simply does not care.

"Once we find the freshwater system in the bedrock, we'll align it with the CS-570 Hydraulic Pumps that Cark Strategies manufactured and drill them into place." Micah continues, flipping to another page of his pamphlet showcasing a gigantic, hydraulic pump made of saltwater resistant, reinforced steel. The massive piece of machinery that their entire project will depend on.

"These pumps were specifically created for this job, so we need to make sure we are all comfortable with how they work. The pumps will extract the freshwater, transferring it through a series of filters and into these storage tanks that we have sitting out here on the main deck," another page, another diagram, another image she has never seen before.

Sarah smiles, proud of Micah for creating this detailed document, but she still cannot seem to shake the sadness building inside of her that she has never seen any of it. She rationalizes the feeling, convincing herself maybe Jason was the one behind it, but it seems highly unlikely. Jason has always been kind and attentive to Sarah, which she appreciates, but he is definitely the type to outsource anything and everything for as little cost as possible. In this case, to Micah. And for free. Then again, he could have had one of his assistants put it together for them. The feeling brewing in the pit of her stomach, however, makes her believe that Micah did create this. He put this together from start to finish, and he never told her about any of it.

"We have space in these tanks to bring home four-hundred and forty gallons of water, but really, we only need one. We just need enough to show that it's there, and once we can get to it and get it home, everything gets fully funded, and we can come back with a full operation." Everyone nods in understanding and agreement, and Sarah feels the resentment and sadness grow. She watches Marie smile at Thomas, proud of the participation he has given that she was absolutely aware of. *Stop it,* Sarah thinks to herself, *you aren't being fair.* She chastises herself even more and tells herself to pay attention; be present.

Micah looks directly at Jax and slowly delivers, "That means more Iron Man stuff." The three men laugh in a moment of relief for Thomas, a moment of deeper excitement for Jax, and a moment of camaraderie for Micah.

"Well, what the hell are we waiting for?" Jax bellows deeply.

"For now," Micah answers him, "we take shifts scouting the currents. Jax, Thomas and I will take the first shift. Sarah and Marie, you two dive this evening. Any tech questions, or wardrobe malfunctions will go to Thomas." Micah and Thomas make brief eye contact, confirming a prior conversation they have certainly had. "You are the most versed in the gear's upgrades, yes?"

"Yes, my company was contracted by Cark Strategies to design the software, and outfit the gear we will be diving in." Sarah hears Thomas address the room, but fully understands that he is explaining this to her, and only her. She racks her brain, trying to remember hearing Thomas' name from Micah in any of their conversations leading up to now. "*Dr. Thomas Shephard,*" does not sound remotely familiar to her. Thomas is a man who has worked closely, intimately with her husband for the better part of a full calendar year, and yet they had met on board this ship as complete strangers not twelve hours prior.

"I have an emergency contact from Jason written down on this card," Sarah sees Micah hold up a small business card with some text scribbled on the back, "I'll put it in our control room. Remember, this ship is between comm system upgrades, so our connection won't be very strong or consistent. I am hoping we won't need it at all, obviously, but let's make sure we all consider this for emergencies *only.* Everyone understand?" The team nods in compliance.

The excitement in the room becomes tangible. They all understand they are moments away from beginning this insane undertaking, and they could not be more excited. Sarah, still lost in her thoughts, finds herself finally, and unfortunately, deciding why she had felt so lost all along. *It is my own fault,* she lies to herself. It was her singular focus on her *own* work. She has been so wrapped up in her own successes that she has been completing neglecting Micah's. Of course, this is not true, and somewhere deep down, she knows it is not true, but often times, moments of doubt become moments of weakness. Even for the strongest of people. *If you hadn't been so goddamn focused on yourself,* she unfairly blasts her psyche.

"We need to find the abnormal water currents," Micah pushes forward. "If we find the abnormal currents, we find the freshwater jet streams. If we find the jet streams, we find the cure. Any questions?"

The sun came out during their meeting. She remembers it was foggy when she woke up and walked into the dining room area for that small cup of life. Now, the sun reflects brightly off of the surface of the ocean. Surprisingly calm for the open sea, the yacht softly rocks back and forth.

Out on the deck, the men make their way into their underwater space suits. Sarah thinks that the diving gear looks like something from an Indie science-fiction film. All three men test their oxygen tanks and vision screens and turn on the tiniest computers she has ever seen attached to their arms and chests. Each one carrying an unbelievable amount of importance.

Marie walks Sarah into the area designated as "Ground Control," and sits in front of a large wall of monitors. Each screen displays different and crucial information. The Control Room is out on the open deck with just a wall separating it from the kitchen. Marie begins logging in to bits of software created in part by her husband. Sarah watches her booting up this massive operation with predetermined codes and usernames. Recognizing she is eager to get this project underway, and excited to be a part of this, Sarah still finds herself struggling to shake the lingering feeling that she is not, and that she has not been all along.

"Oh, sorry, Sarah, excuse me," Marie says as she reaches for a switch across the desk. For the first time, Sarah feels incredibly in the way.

Jax walks over to the three hydraulic pumps resting on the deck and braces himself to pick one up. He double checks his grip and uses all the might his legs can muster to lift it off of the ground. He struggles, but walks it to the far edge of the boat, where Thomas and Micah finish adding gear onto their suits. Jax, who is probably the only person who can single-handedly lift the pumps, takes his time in moving the other two, so all three rest at the diving edge of the yacht.

Sarah stares at the pumps, and the size of them overwhelm her. She rolls her eyes a little, thinking they look like they were stolen off of the International Space Station. Her subconscious harshly reminds her they could have been, and she likely would not have even been told.

"Hey Love, can you help us test the suit communications?" Micah shouts from the deck, again snapping her out of her thoughts.

"Of course," she calls back.

Sarah looks at the disorienting wall of screens, and Marie points out the one listed as "Diver Communications." She sees three users appear as dots on the screen, one green light for each active diver. Marie shows her how to access the equipment, allowing communication directly from the Control Room to the divers, either all simultaneously, or, "One at a time, if you select this switch." Marie explains. "So, if you wanted to speak directly to Micah, hold this down, and…" she slides the microphone over towards Sarah.

"Test," is all Sarah can think to say. "Test… Sarah for Micah." Marie and Sarah look from the screen, Micah's dot blinking green signifying activity, and turn their gazes out towards the men on the deck.

Micah enthusiastically holds a "thumbs up." He flips open a piece of gear on his left forearm, and Marie grabs Sarah's attention back towards the screen.

"Obviously a breathing apparatus won't allow them to speak back, so Thomas developed a texting alternative for us while we're down there." Micah's green blinking dot on the communications display turns to orange. "Orange means someone is typing a message."

"Got it," pops up on the display. Sarah is shocked, and takes a deep breath.

"That's amazing," she spills out. She really was impressed.

"This way," Marie continues, "we can be in contact every step of the way."

"That is really amazing, Marie. Really impressive."

"It was Thomas' idea. It turned into this really effective communication system that hasn't been utilized quite like this ever before."

Despite the obvious and expected excitement, and anxious anticipation, Sarah still cannot shake the idea she absolutely should have known about all of this. She does not understand how Micah could have kept all of this from her, and she decides it must have been intentional. You cannot be a part of the creation of this much brand new, arguably groundbreaking technology, and just casually forget to bring it up to your wife when she asks how your day was. She can feel her face growing warm with frustration. She knows she needs to calm down before she makes any more unfair assumptions based somewhat tenuously in reality. She needs to just talk to him about it. Maybe she will tomorrow, but not today. She cannot today.

# CHAPTER 8
## MICAH

Up to now, everything had been planned, organized, and easily executed, given the circumstances. The arrangements made, the favors cashed in, the gear synched and powered on, the makeshift control room up and running. Everything ready for what comes next. The part no one could plan for; entering the Epipelagic Zone of the Pacific Ocean.

Thomas, Jax and I are the first to go. The afternoon sun shining hot against my skin makes me momentarily forget how cold the air is. The water is calm, but the ship rocks gently back and forth with the current. Thomas had given me a little pushback when I initially mentioned Marie and Sarah diving together later tonight, but it is something I had to put my foot down on. His concern, he expressed, was it would be too dangerous. He was worried the currents would be too rough, as night dives are always more difficult. I casually reminded him that Marie and Sarah are the two best divers on board, and he backed down. It is the truth. I mean, sure, we are all "divers" but Marie and Sarah are actually *divers*.

We finish adding the peripheral gear to our diving suits and make ready for the moment at hand. The moment we had all been anticipating.

It is time to go beneath the surface.

Sarah and Marie walk over to us at the boat's edge while we make our final preparations. Marie touches Thomas' face and kisses him, both reminding him that he is about to change the world, and to be careful. Sarah sort of mimics the same, though I can sense a slight distraction in her eyes. A glaze of distance before she musters a smile and squeezes my hand gently. I raise an eyebrow and tilt my head to the side. She just smiles slightly and squeezes my hand again. We are all a little overwhelmed, and exhausted. I am sure it is nothing. I find rest in knowing that she would absolutely tell me if it was something more serious.

"Be safe." She mutters, cracking a small peak of another smile.

"You too," I joke. She laughs a little, which is nice to hear. Honestly, if the last thing I ever hear is Sarah's laugh, it would all have been worth it.

With a deafening whoosh of water immediately surrounding me, I enter the Pacific. My direct line of vision is filled with hundreds of thousands of tiny bubbles as my equilibrium adjusts to new pressure. I get my footing, metaphorically of course, and with a steady breath and a low heart rate, I start my descent. Thomas and Jax are quick behind me, eagerly jumping off the deck of the yacht, and straight into the future of humankind.

Once we are all submerged, I look to them both. The three of us signal to each other we are all ready to begin, oxygen secured, no snags in our diving gear, etc. After our individual gear checks and giving each other the affirming thumbs up hand symbols, we all three start to make our way into the deep.

We continue our pace into the ocean, and I envision Sarah and Marie getting comfortable back in the control room area. Sarah maybe pouring some fresh coffee for them both, while Marie monitors our oxygen levels, our depth, and our pressure per square inch. The three statistics most likely kill us the quickest.

"Steady as she goes, boys," Sarah speaks to all three of us through the communication pieces in our head gear. "Approaching our first check point." The path towards our destination is marked by three theoretical checkpoints. We physically inspect ourselves, and our diving suits four separate times during each dive. The first immediately after breach, the next at around one hundred and sixty-six feet below, again at around three-hundred feet down, and the last being the destination. *So far, so good.*

We let gravity do most of the work for us, keeping still, and steadily making our way farther and farther down until we catch our first glimpse of it. Barely visible, but there it is; the blue hole we have been looking for. The mouth of it, anyway. It is absolutely massive, and pitch-black inside. It looks like something out of a graphic novel, or maybe even a horror film. Then again, so do we. I cannot really see into it, but all of our thermal scans estimate this natural well descends hundreds of feet into the earth's lithosphere.

"All right, boys. It's now or never," we hear Sarah speaking to us again. I look over towards Thomas and Jax who both give me their thumbs up. I nod back a few times, give them the "OK" hand sign, and we enter the mouth of the blue hole. The small remnants of light from the surface completely vanish, as if someone had pulled the covers over the ocean. We are completely enveloped by darkness. We had anticipated it for the most part, but this is indescribably dark, biblically dark.

"Micah..." I hear a slight hesitation in my wife's voice. Concern. I intentionally slow my breath as to not disrupt my heart rate at this depth. "It's Sarah, I'm speaking directly to you." I keep my pace, keeping an eye on all of my visible metrics. Then she says the one thing I was pleading with God she would not say. "Something's not right."

In the control room, I imagine Sarah and Marie watching as one gauge rumbles slightly, before another begins mirroring the behavior. Sarah speaks down into the microphone, and back into my headset, "We're picking up some really rough currents at the mouth of the hole. Be careful as you get deeper, we don't have visibility into conditions inside."

*Oh my god.*

It is at this moment I realize we had not thought of this before. All of our data is based on the currents outside of the hole, at the floor of the sea, yet the most crucial part of this entire adventure is going to happen somewhere we have not been. Inside of the blue hole. *How could we have overlooked that?* It immediately felt dangerous, and I was overwhelmed with a feeling of recklessness, to not have been more thorough, or give it any actual thought.

Sarah, addressing all three of us again, says, "You're clear to initiate opticals." I look for Thomas and Jax, but I likely will not be able to actually see them until we do what she says. I reach to my head and find the small switch at my left temple. I flip it, and hear a bright, drawn out bell, not unlike tinnitus in my ears.

A bright light bursts from my headgear and into the black nothingness surrounding me. We will rely heavily on this bright, LED beam of light from the headgear Thomas' company created for us, providing just enough visibility so the three of us can, at the very least, see where we are at in this monstrous hole in the crust of the earth. I see Thomas and Jax, both within about ten to fifteen of me. We all three reach for another switch, located directly next to the first, and then we all flip it, too.

In my line of sight, numbers & metrics litter the screen of my goggles. I laugh to myself the moment I realize Jax was right. It really is like Iron Man. Comically, it is almost exactly like Iron Man. Maybe we are just really big kids. One of the pieces of information on our screens is the current depth.

Two-hundred and twenty-eight feet... two-hundred twenty-nine...

We can also watch, in real time, the pressure change as we descend. Finally, the most important piece of information—the molecular composition of the water directly in our line of sight.

$[NaCl(H_2O)5]$ changes to $H_2Fu$, then immediately turns into $Csna34$. Each grouping of letters and numbers telling us the molecules comprising the water we are submerged in. Obviously, we're looking for one particular combination. The only molecular composition I give a single fuck about: $H_2O$.

I lose myself in joy for a brief moment. This one, simple moment hits me like a ton of bricks. We are here. We are inside the blue hole, and we're doing it. It is still hard to believe, and I literally feel the pressure of the ocean on my skull.

Since Sarah and Marie from the control room can see the same view our goggles can, we rely solely on them to focus on our depth and PSI levels. This support frees our focus from those metrics to only pay attention to the molecular composition of the water we can see. The molecular data flashes quickly, and in real time, so it is admittedly difficult to clearly follow along. Only focusing on that one piece of information makes it infinitely easier. I look at our depth for a moment. According to the research I did with Jason's team, we are still quite far from our goal depth. The depth where the freshwater should be flowing into to the Pacific Ocean.

I watch Thomas as he descends, his hand grazing the rock along the wall of the blue hole, using it as a guide. *This has to stay between you and I,* Jason's words flash through my mind. Thomas hesitates, slowing his descent for a moment, and I see him notice something embedded into the side of the cavern. A large rock protruding from the wall. Its color slightly off, darker in comparison to the rest of the wall, and its shape distinctly different. I also look a little closer, and I admit, it does not look like rock at all. It looks more like something created to mimic the rock itself. A mirrored, alternate version of the texture of rock. It looks inexplicably larger, misshapen, and almost cartoonish. Thomas wades his way through the thick water pressure of our depth, and moves closer to it, as Jax and I continue deeper. I look back again to Thomas, and he is still fixated on this small boulder.

Something about this rock has completely entranced him. He gets closer and closer to it, letting the bright light from his headgear shine onto its surface. I wonder what has him so obsessed. Does he see something moving? No, that thought is preposterous, it is a rock. The idea of this object being anything *but* a rock would be impossible. In my head, my imagination shows it gently expanding, contracting, in a breathing motion. A distinct inhale, then the gentle collapse of a deep exhale. I roll my eyes, and laugh to myself, then I remember the rock in the plastic bin. I remember watching it split and multiple with my own eyes. I feel my heart rate increase. I look back at Thomas to see him carefully reach his hand towards the edge again, and just as he touches the surface…

"Thomas!" Marie shrieks. Jax and I jolt from her piercing scream into our earpieces. "Thomas, where'd you go?" I can hear panic in her voice. In my ears, I can hear Sarah and Marie frantically working in the control room. I assume Thomas' vision screen has cut to black, and they have lost sight on him. I hear them quickly check his vitals; oxygen and pressure meters going crazy, rapidly reporting false numbers.

"Marie, what happened?" I hear Sarah's calm tone. She speaks gently, but with an enormous sense of urgency.

Marie does not answer, and instead speaks into the planted microphone, "Thomas, can you hear me?" Sarah, the rock on which I build, speaks directly to Jax and me.

"Guys, Thomas' system just completely failed. Do either of you have eyes?" I can hear Marie in the background, not as steady as my wife. Truthfully, few are as steady as she is. Sarah is strong. *She is so good.* "Marie, what the hell happened?" I hear Marie respond that she does not know, she just watched his vision display cut out suddenly.

I turn around in the thick of the blackness, and just barely towards the edge of my headgear lanterns, I see Thomas floating. My lanterns glisten in the reflection of his diving suit. He is still. Surrounded by darkness. Seeing the light from my gear, he motions a thumbs up towards me. His gear is dark, but it has to be working. If it was not working, Thomas would be a compressed corpse, crushed under the weight of the current pressure per square inch. Bubbles erupt from his breathing apparatus. At the very least, I know his oxygen is still available. I start to make my way towards Thomas, and I notice Jax is already there. He is quick underwater. He wraps his arms around Thomas from behind the way a lifeguard would a flailing child.

Jax looks towards me and gives me his own thumbs up, matching the hand gesture that Thomas is still holding for anyone looking at him. They are okay.

I imagine Sarah and Marie watching the whole scene play out on the available vision screen displays in the control room. The thumbs up, the malfunctioned gear, Jax's superhero underwater speed, the second thumbs up. Sarah placing her hand on Marie's back, comforting her. She is so good in these moments.

Maintaining his hold of Thomas, Jax motions to me that they are going back to the surface. This decision is the wisest, as Thomas is completely useless down here without working gear. They start their path, ascending back towards the surface, until they disappear out of my view.

"Steady, Jax. Not too fast," I hear Sarah caution in my ears. Jax's monitors still working normally, I imagine the more appealing countdown: Two-hundred and forty-one feet... two-hundred and forty feet… two-hundred and thirty-nine feet… Confident now that Thomas is fine, and that Jax is as well, I look further into the deep. We are here for such a limited time, and we have such an important an objective. I continue my descent.

"Micah, what are you doing? Come up with them." Obviously, my decision comes much to the chagrin of my wife.

My light catches the smooth surface of the rock wall of the blue hole. Impossibly smooth for underwater stone. I notice a large, but still perfectly smooth, indenture in the wall. It looks like something had been attached to it, glued on even, then sanded down evenly. Sarah continues, "Marie and I can pick things back up later, it doesn't make sense to stay down right now."

I know her. I know she will continue to repeat the same facts in different ways until I communicate that I hear her, I understand her, and I lay out my reasons why I am choosing not to listen to her. I decide to take that exact approach.

I flip open the small keypad attached to my forearm and type a simple, "Ten minutes." In my ears, I can hear how dramatically she rolls her eyes, and I smile. This moment, I guarantee, shaking loose in her memory all the unnecessary arguments ending in my constantly repeating the exact phrase, "I hear you, I understand you, but…"

"All right, weirdo, but that's it. Talk to you in ten."

I softly glide my hand against the smooth stone surface. Despite years of research, I have zero explanation for how smooth this rock is. Then I see it. I almost missed it; it was hidden in plain sight: a hole. A perfectly round, quarter-sized hole. Right, smack in the middle of the brilliantly smooth surface of the rock wall lining this blue hole two-hundred and fifty feet beneath the surface of the Pacific Ocean. I delicately trace the edge of this small puncture in the rock with my left index finger.

I have never considered myself a risk taker, but some questions demand answers. I stick my finger in as far as it will go. Unfortunately, the only answer I get is the hole extends past the length of a grown, adult male's index finger. I try to feel around, but I only feel more stone.

I remove my finger from the hole, and small debris and sand come out with it. Ninety percent of my brain understands quite well that the ocean, and oceanic structures, are covered in geographic and geometric anomalies. The other ten percent, however, cannot shake the idea that this particular anomaly could end up holding some sort of significance. Again, images of the rock and the plastic bin flash across my mind.

I remove a small yellow rod from a strap on the side of my left leg. These plastic markers, also designed again by Thomas' company and the manufacturing team at Cark Strategies, were a brilliant addition to our scientific arsenal. A simple, plastic rod, designed to be attached to rough surfaces, digitally marking a specific location. An underwater GPS system for areas of significance. In this case, a meaningless, but weird, hole. I feel my forearms burn as I forcefully screw the marker into the hole in the rock. I have to put a little elbow grease into it, as the rock is far more solid than I anticipated. The surface gives way, and I am able to securely attach the rod. I pop a small cap off of the end, and press a button protected by a thick rubber sealant. A soft, yellow light pulses, radiating off the marker.

Knowing I have not found anything, I am currently a team of one, and it has definitely been more than ten minutes, I move my head straight up to look towards the surface before I begin my ascent back to the boat.

I only get about fifteen feet away from the marker before I notice the yellow light stops flashing. Ultimately, the light itself does not matter much. The important aspect is the GPS location can be determined. My concern, however, is if the light stopped working, the GPS could have failed too. Annoyed at our recent mechanical malfunctions, I make my way back to the marker. It only takes me a few moments to get back to it, and I inspect it thoroughly. Everything checks out.

I press the sealed button again, no response. I press it again, hearing myself ask my mom, "Did you turn it off and turn it back on?" after she calls me, explaining that her phone does not work anymore. I press it again, holding it down, and nothing happens.

Finally, I start to unscrew the marker from the rock. I feel it stick, so with one swift tug, I rip it out. Some of the rock breaks off, and dust fills the space. I click the button one more time, and the light gently pulses again. A soft, yellow light, pulsating on and off.

Deciding it has fixed itself, as technology sometimes unexplainably seems to do, I turn to screw it back into the wall. When my light shines against the rock wall, I notice a thin, black mist permeating from the cracked stone. Like smoke spilling out of the end of a cigarette, it flows artistically into the water, dissolving almost immediately. *What the hell is that?*

I scour the resources of my mind, and through all the subsequent conversations Jason and I have had trying to pinpoint what this mist could be. Nothing comes from it. I gently wave my hand through it, and it simply disappears into the water. In the countless periodicals and scientific journals I have read, I have never encountered any literature mentioning anything like this.

Well, I know there is nothing I can do to figure it out right now, and it has all but stopped, so I decide to screw the marker back into place. Slightly deeper, this time, as to not give it any reason to fail again.

Once I have put it back in place, I float next to it, staring like a plumber watching the water run after unclogging a drain. I wait a few moments to see if the light remains pulsing, which it does. Somewhat confused, but ultimately satisfied, I resume my journey back to our yacht, and to the rest of my team, who probably have not noticed any of my little experiment.

Two-hundred and forty feet…. Two-hundred and thirty-nine feet… Two-hundred and thirty-eight feet…

# CHAPTER 9
# SARAH

Thomas and Jax finally hit the surface of the water after a slow, but steady ascent. Marie was waiting at the edge of the ship, praying Thomas was OK. Sarah, believing everything was all right, is slow to make her way behind Marie, still distracted by the invasive and deceptive thought, *why didn't I know about any of this?* After helping Jax and Thomas back on board the Tethys, Sarah helps Jax in carefully removing the meticulously designed gear from his large, strong frame. Marie, hovering like a moth around a porch lamp, dodges pieces of equipment Thomas rips off of his body, without regard to the value of the gear his hands helped create.

"Thomas, would you please calm down?" Marie asks forcefully, trying to keep her voice to a hushed whisper. Sarah and Jax share a knowing glance, agreeing silently to ignore the impending conversation between Thomas and Marie.

"I am calm, I'm just frustrated." Thomas tries unsuccessfully to match her intentionally soft tone. Marie, periodically glancing over to Sarah and Jax to see if they are gawking, positions her body between them. Sarah understands the embarrassment of arguing with a spouse in public.

"Thanks for bringing him up safely," Sarah says to Jax, maybe louder than necessary, trying to avoid eavesdropping on the lover's quarrel a few feet away.

"Of course," Jax matches. He looks around, then back out to the water. "Wait, where is Micah? Did he not make it back up yet?" She picks up on a hint of concern in his voice.

"He stayed down. Just for a little bit longer," she responds, in her best reassuring tone. "He'll be up soon," she hoped. Their quiet conversation is immediately interrupted by a louder Thomas, and a more embarrassed Marie.

"I don't *know* what happened, Marie. That is the problem, clearly." With each word he makes less of an attempt to conceal his frustration. Half undressed, he fidgets with a piece of his gear attached to the left sleeve of his suit. Flipping it forcefully, the suit's power boots back up, like it was turned on for the first time. The lights shining bright with no indication of any struggle or failure. An exasperated Thomas mutters, "You've got to be kidding me."

"Well, I'm just glad you are all right." Marie tries to change the subject.

"Of course I'm all right. I have been at that depth a thousand times. The moment I throw a bunch of fancy shit on my back, I go blind."

"Fancy shit you designed." Marie snaps back, stopping Thomas is his tracks. *Good for you, Marie,* Sarah thinks, resisting the urge to snap her fingers like she is in some mid-nineties' teen movie.

"I'm sorry. I am. I shouldn't raise my voice. I'm just... tense. I'm just frustrated, Marie. I'm sorry." Thomas stares straight down, avoiding eye contact with his wife.

"I know." Marie looks over to Sarah and Jax, who apparently have abandoned their efforts to pretend they could not hear everything going on. Needless to say, they both get caught staring again. Overcome with embarrassment of Thomas' childlike outburst, Marie storms off the deck towards their cabin.

Sarah helps Jax out of the last bit of his gear, and he starts to pile it all together. He offers a fresh pot of coffee to Thomas in an attempt to change the subject and ease the tension. Thomas accepts, before Jax puts his gear away and disappears into the galley.

A loud splash startles Sarah. She turns to see Micah, breaking the surface of the water. A smile creeps across her face, as Micah makes his way towards the edge of the ship. The water's surface is far choppier than it was even just a few moments ago, causing Micah to sort of struggle to the edge of the boat. He finally reaches out, and grabs onto the metal railing.

"Here, let me help you," Sarah offers, taking a step down, gripping his arm with both of her hands.

"Thank you." Micah pulls himself on board. He kisses her cheek.

"I saw you activated a marker," Sarah asks as they start to remove his gear piece by piece. "Find something?"

"I don't think so," he replies, but his tone gives way to her implicit skepticism. Noticing something has caught Micah's stare, Sarah turns her head to look in the same direction. Thomas hastily puts away his dive suit, aggressively throwing his boots into their designated cupboard.

"What's up with him?" Micah rightfully, but almost rhetorically asks.

"He's pretty upset about what happened down there. He says everything is working just fine now."

"He would know." Micah shrugs, and casually continues removing pieces of his wardrobe.

"He's taking it pretty personally, I think."

"I mean... wouldn't you?" Sarah cannot help but concede. She knows damn well if the roles were reversed and her organization had invested thousands of dollars into a piece of equipment which then failed her in her exact moment of need, she would be taking it pretty damn personally too. "He'll calm down," Micah says reassuringly.

Sarah helps her husband out of the last bit of his exterior gear, and puts her hand on his face.

"Come on, I think Jax put some coffee on."

She really does understand how Thomas feels, and she agrees with Micah that he has every right to be upset about what happened. Something, however, does still seem off to her. There is something in Thomas' reaction, something in his tone to Marie, that she finds unsettling. A red flag she cannot unsee. Micah takes her hand, and squeezes it, breaking her focus. She looks at him, and he smiles.

"It's fine, I'm sure." He gently grazes his thumb over the soft skin of her hand. A calming technique he had learned she responds well to. "Let him vent, let him be upset, then we'll make sure he calms down, and can move on. It will be fine. Trust me." Sarah squeezes his hand back, signaling her agreement.

A short time later, as she sits at the mess table with her second cup of coffee in hand, Sarah watches the sun starting to set against an endless horizon of ocean. She feels her hand twitch a little and remembers that she had told herself not to pour this cup. *It is way too late for caffeine,* she thinks, *too much.* Still, here she finds herself with a fresh, warm cup in her twitching hand. She takes a sip.

Micah sits next to her, rustling through papers strewn about the table, but all she can focus on are the brilliant colors bouncing off the choppy surface of the water. She wonders how many people have seen the sunset before from this spot. *It couldn't be many*, she wonders as she continues to look out to sea, enjoying the vibrant colors.

It was an intriguing thought and made her smile. The idea that two people, however unknowingly, can participate in the same event no matter how far apart, and somehow become connected to one another. Even if just for that one single moment. A special thought she always keeps for herself.

Micah's elbow accidentally bumps her, and he immediately grabs her arm, rubs it softly, and apologizes.

"It's all right, Love," she says, without taking her eyes off the sunset, still wondering if in that moment she was connecting to someone, somewhere. Noticing her distraction, Micah glances out the window.

"Wow. That's breathtaking, huh?" He might have immediately gone back to his work, but Sarah smiles a long smile. In that moment, despite the chaos and stress, they are the ones connected. Unaware of what the moment would eventually come to mean to her, she smiles.

Finally breaking her stare, she looks down at the papers Micah is thumbing through. Mounds and mounds of documents filled with the printed data of the information they gathered during their first, brief dive. She catches some familiar molecular compositions on the front page. Water with sodium chloride particles, detections of hydrogen fluorine, but no fresh water. The symbol of "$H_2O$" fills the pages, but always followed by "NaCl," or "Csna." Never by itself. Never what they need. Never what they came to find.

Micah sets the pages back down on the table and takes sip of his coffee. Sarah, deciding to find a way to fill this time productively, pulls out her laptop, and opens up a notation app. She begins typing out a recap of their first, somewhat successful, dive of the trip. She had offered to take on the added responsibility of acting as the historian for the trip, as a secondary way of outlining their process moving forward.

"It's not here." She can hear the slight hint of frustration in Micah's voice. Micah has never been one to effectively hide what he is thinking when he speaks. He scours through the pages again and runs his hands through his hair. Sarah looks at the papers, and then to her husband.

"What's not?"

"Anything familiar... water... Fresh water. I have thirty-six-something pages of molecular data, and absolutely nothing we can use."

"Today is just day one, we'll find it," she hoped. "It's down there."

"I hope so." His frustration turns to defeat. If there was anything Sarah was sure of, it was her ability to prevent Micah's emotional mind from spiraling to the point of no return.

"Micah, look around you. I know it sounds cliche but look how far we've come." Micah smiles slightly from the corner of his mouth. "You got us here with literally everyone telling us 'No.'" With her fingers, she brings Micah's face up, forcing him to look towards her awaiting smile. He matches it. "We will find it..." Micah steals a kiss, interrupting her speech mid-sentence. It always makes her laugh. Any chance he gets to steal a serious moment and turn it into a funny one, he takes it.

"OK, all right," He gives in. "We'll find it." He takes another sip before diving back into his piles of data. She hears some footsteps on the stairs leading to the door of the mess area. She brings her glance up towards the door just in time to see Thomas hesitantly enter the room. He catches her eyes, clearly not expecting to see her here.

"Oh, I'm sorry. Am I... am I interrupting?" Thomas looks to Micah, who sets his coffee and papers down and rubs his eyes.

"No, come in, Thomas." Micah straightens up some of his data chaos and makes room for Thomas at the table across from him and Sarah.

"Do you… uh… do you mind if we speak in private?" Concern generously showering over his every word. Sarah cannot decide if it is because of what he wants to discuss with Micah, or the lingering embarrassment of his previous outburst on deck. She begins making a move to gather her things to leave, but she is interrupted by Micah placing his hand on her thigh, stopping her in her place.

"Whatever it is, I'm realistically going to tell my wife anyway, so it's all right. What's up, man?" Her initial reaction was one of sweet satisfaction. He would eventually tell her everything, so why should she worry? Her second thought, however, was the prevailing idea festering inside of her for hours. *Would he tell her?* Micah was yet unaware of her observations of all he had been keeping from her in the weeks and months leading up to this trip. *Or was he?*

Her racing thoughts were halted when she caught Thomas glancing over to her, awkwardly smiling. It was not the outcome he had hoped for. Sarah was not sure how to react, so she simply smiled back at him, as politely as possible. She sort of expected Thomas to push back, at least a little bit. To her surprise he went straight into the conversation he wanted to have. She was a little relieved.

"I have checked every component. I have taken the goddamn thing apart and put it back together. There is nothing wrong with my suit." Exhausted and exasperated, the weight of every word lands heavy.

"Well, that's a relief," Micah was not even looking at him.

"You don't understand, Micah. I designed the software within these suits. I ran thousands of tests at three times the depths we were this afternoon."

Micah has always had a short attention span for conversations he was not particularly invested in. This trait had always been a source of contempt for Sarah in their early days together. Micah, however, uses it strategically to diffuse potentially conflictual situations. Sarah notices how he almost immediately moves from combing through his files to fidgeting with a flashlight sitting on the table next to his papers. A welcomed distraction he most likely placed there to take his mind off the data if he felt himself getting frustrated with the lack of answers he was looking for.

"I've never experienced that type of malfunction," Thomas continues, "never. Not once."

Micah has now removed the cap of the flashlight and inspects the inside canister where normal batteries would go. This flashlight, however, has a thick, robust solid-state battery which Micah methodically removes. Carefully, meticulously removing safeguards, he exposes part of the wiring in the device itself.

"It is possible," Micah takes his time speaking, "that the ocean water…"

"No, it is not possible." Thomas' interruption is not what momentarily grabs Micah's attention. It was his confidence. Then after a moment of eye contact, and as if Thomas never had it at all, Micah's attention is immediately back on the electronic device. He begins reassembling it. While she knows full well Micah heard the intention in Thomas' voice, Sarah wonders if Micah noticed his body language. Thomas is holding himself taller and stronger than he has since he had come into her life mere hours before.

"I wanted to talk to you because I would like to use the secondary suit when I go back in." His straightforward tone absolutely catches Micah's attention. Micah stops assembling the flashlight device, and looks up towards Thomas, proudly standing still in the doorway.

"That's the only one we have. We need it for emergencies."

"Micah, I'm not comfortable going back under wearing the suit that…"

"Thomas, you just told me that your suit was fine, yes? Not sixty-seconds ago, correct?"

"Well, yes, but…"

"We cannot afford to be down an entire extra set of gear if yours is working properly, which you just confirmed it is." Micah maintains his eye contact with Thomas. A "telltale" sign you have his full attention: uninterrupted eye contact.

"Yes, I understand the concern, however…"

"I'm sorry, Thomas, but my answer is no." Thomas is visibly defeated. He drops his head, and silently exhales. A metaphorical deflating of the confidence he had worked so hard to muster before coming in and making eye contact with Sarah. A part of her wishes she had left. "You were made fully aware of the constraints we were going to be under when we arrived here, and you had my full confidence in your preparation of the hardware and software upgrades. We cannot go down a suit after day one if it is not absolutely necessary." It is difficult for Sarah to hear Micah speak in any way potentially construed as cruel, but she recognizes a power in his command of the moment, and it makes her fall in love with him all over again.

"It's too dangerous, Thomas. If your suit malfunctions down there again, we can absolutely revisit this conversation, but for now, my answer is no. I'm sorry."

Thomas nods silently in acknowledgement of Micah's decision.

"Now, we need to start getting Sarah and Marie prepped and ready. They dive in about twenty minutes."

Thomas, again saying nothing, just nods and then turns to leave the room. Micah slyly looks at Sarah, making a face that says, "oops…"

"That went well, eh?" He laughs uncomfortably for a moment, before going back to his flashlight assembly project. Sarah is stuck on Thomas' tone. It is the very real concern in his voice she cannot seem to let go of.

"What if there *is* something wrong with his suit?" She works up the courage to ask out loud.

"There's not." Micah responds quickly.

"How can you be sure?"

"Because if there were, he would've fought me harder. And he wouldn't have given in to my decision." He smirks at Sarah. She knew he was right. If Thomas truly believed the malfunction is an actual threat to his safety, there is a zero percent chance he would have let Micah push him into using faulty equipment.

Micah tinkers a little more with the flashlight before clicking it on. The light beams bright across the room. He smiles at her.

"You need to get ready."

He tosses the light to her, still shining, and she clicks it off.

# CHAPTER 10
## MICAH

I notice Sarah's distance and distraction almost immediately once we step back onto the main deck. It was either something I said or something I did, but I know her, and I know she will not actually say anything until I am finally in bed and just on the brink of falling into a deep sleep. Her eyes toggle between being locked onto the wooden planked flooring of the deck or cast out towards the endless horizon. Her body is here, but her mind is somewhere else entirely.

"I can tell there's something on your mind, but this dive isn't going to be easy. You need to focus." I try as delicately as possible to call attention to whatever it is that seems to be distracting her.

The sun is still setting, keeping the most brilliant eruption of orange and pink clouds across the Alaskan skyline. Every passing moment seems to be a little dimmer and darker than the one before. The water, taking the approaching darkness as a threat, begins chopping more quickly, and more loudly, gearing up for the epic showdown of transitioning from day to night.

I grab Sarah's gear, and walk it over to her, eyes still absently cast out towards the setting sun.

"Water looks a little rough right now, doesn't it?" I ask, breaking her lost at sea gaze.

"Huh?" She asks, even though I know she heard me. I have never understood why that response is so automatic. We hear a question, and our brain instinctively asks the person what they said, hoping they will repeat themselves even though we heard them the first time. I have never understood it. Regardless, I oblige, and repeat myself.

"I said the water looks choppier right now than it was earlier. It's rough."

"We'll be all right," Sarah says, glancing at me just for a moment before reaching for her suit.

"I know." I try to smile at her, but she is already looking back down to the deck floor, sliding her first leg into the skintight diving gear. I pull one of the flashlights out of my back pocket, and hand it over to her. "Can't be too careful, though. Especially after today. It'll be even darker down there."

Sarah takes the flashlight from me, and clicks it on and off a few times before securing to her suit with a tight strap along her left leg.

"Thanks." She is distracted. I lean in, and kiss her on the cheek, and notice she does not even try to lean in towards the kiss. *OK, then.* I sigh quietly, but hope it is enough for her to notice my disappointment, and I turn to see Thomas giving one final check of Marie's gear. I take the second flashlight from my back pocket and toss it towards the two of them.

Thomas catches it, and hands it to his wife. I can hear them discussing something in a hushed tone but cannot quite make it out. *Why is everyone so on edge?* Sarah and Marie, now both ready for their dive, walk towards the boat's edge and fix their goggles and helmets securely in place. Sarah looks back to me, and smiles. She blows me a kiss like she always does before we go separate ways. It has always been her little way of saying, "I love you," without having the worry of wearing out the words. A silent gesture so I know. I always know, anyway.

Even though it has become a habit, I cannot help but think this time it is a small way of telling me I am not crazy, and she will talk to me about what is bothering her tonight. I smile back at her, a silent "thank you" for the acknowledgement. It is amazing when you know someone so well, where so much can be said without ever actually speaking a word. *God, she is so good.*

With a large splash, the two women breach the surface of the Pacific Ocean. Thomas, Jax and I walk back across the deck into the control room, the screens already littered with data. I see Marie and Sarah's individual vision screens, already pitch black, and they have just barely begun their descent.

"It's scary when it's so dark." Jax says. The statement serving as the perfect contradiction to his intimidating stature and impressive resume. He is right though. It is terrifying.

The current seems calm under the surface, however. Far calmer than the frantic, chopping water at sea level. I can still hear the wind clipping the tips off of the tiny waves, bashing them against the side of the boat. The two continue down, and I flick on the microphone communication to speak to them both.

"All right, ladies. Go for lights."

Marie turns hers on first, shining bright beams into black nothingness, like a flashlight pointed into space in the dead of night. The beams of light revealing only the micro-organisms in their line of sight. Sarah follows suit, revealing the same, only tiny specs of life.

I pull another screen out of the mass chaos of technology displays and follow along with the two blinking dots. It is an underwater GPS tracker, showing us exactly where they are in proximity to the surface and the estimated destination point. "You're on target, steady down." Thomas' team designed this tracker specifically for this trip. It allows us to navigate for someone from the surface, which is especially useful for night dives. The three-dimensional interface is completely interactive, allowing us to bend and shift our perspective. "You're getting close, around a hundred and ten feet." They do not need me to tell them; They can see it in their head gear. I hope hearing my voice, though, keeps them calm while they relax, and let gravity pull them farther, and farther down into the deep.

The farther they dive, the stronger the currents become. Pushing and tugging at them, as they are pulled down deeper and deeper. These two women, easily the strongest divers among us, stay as steady as they can. The three of us huddled around, eyes glued to the tiny displays. Both Marie and Sarah's bodies' hold as still as possible against unfairly strong underwater ocean currents.

Steady as can be, they descend into the deep until, barely visible, we see it again: the mouth of the blue hole. Slowing their pace, they approach it cautiously.

Out of nowhere, a small, shiny creature swims directly through Marie's line of sight, and we hear a loud *"whoosh!"* through our communications system. Marie screams, bubbles erupt from her mouthpiece, and her heart rate monitor spikes. Jax, Thomas and I all simultaneously jump back in a jolt of fright as well, ending with a loud and awkward laugh. Marie was not laughing.

"Woah, woah! You're OK, Marie." I hold back a slight chuckle too. "It was a just a fish, just a fish. You're OK. You're OK." *Jesus Christ, that fish came out of nowhere.* The guys and I laugh uncomfortably, our hearts still pounding. Marie, I am sure, can feel her pulse through every inch of her body. She breathes heavy in her oxygen mask.

"Marie, listen to me, listen to my voice. You're all right. Calm down, it's OK." I try my best to level her heart rate out. When it does not work, I bend the microphone towards Thomas, and subtly clear my throat, in a "you're up, big guy," kind of way. He takes the hint and leans over to speak to his wife.

"It's OK, Marie. That spooked us, too!" The residual laughter in his voice finally calms her down.

Sarah and Marie enter into the mouth of the blue hole, nothing visible except the lights shining off the gear on their heads. It is a type of darkness you cannot fully comprehend unless you have experienced it. The closest thing I can even think of is when you go into a cave, and they turn out the lights. That moment when they tell you to open your eyes and wave your hand in front of your face. For a second, you convince yourself you have gone blind, or maybe you have even died. Then your tour guide flicks the lights back on, and the brightness overwhelms your eyes. That comparison is the closest I can think of. This darkness is blacker, even still. Worse, somehow.

"All right, you're in. Go for opticals." They both turn on their interactive headgear software. Brighter lights cut through the empty black of the water. Like before with Thomas, Jax and I, crucial information floods their line of sight. Sequences of numbers and letters, molecular compositions, pressure, depth, and oxygen levels. I talk them through the initial shock of it all, "It takes a second to get used to it, but I promise you will." Farther down into the blue hole, they continue. "You know what we're looking for. Let's go get it, ladies."

I look at Sarah's display screen, and I see the non-stop flood of information: two-hundred and seventeen feet, 117.7 PSI, and endless molecular compositions. Deeper and deeper, they are getting closer.

Thomas stands and walks over to grab his suit from before. He walks it across the deck and sits at a meeting table. He begins tinkering away at his gear, still trying by any means necessary to replicate the issues he experienced underneath. Jax looks at me, and acknowledging I am on the first shift watching the ladies.

He turns to Thomas and asks if he would like to join him in the galley and watch a football match.

"Who's playing?" Thomas asks, genuinely curious.

"Chelsea and Man U." Jax responds."Come on, it'll be fun. You can bring your suit." Thomas nods his head and follows Jax into the galley. I hear them turn on the small television in the corner of the room. I hear the static and the sound of Jax flipping through the few available channels before he finds what he is looking for. I can hear the fans in the stands, and the announcer's English accent.

While they relax and watch the match, I keep a close eye on Marie and Sarah's vitals as they continue descending into the darkness. Since we decided to take shifts at the control room desk, and this shift should not actually be too long, I expect to be here the entirety of their dive.

I do, however, start to hear the shouting and cursing coming from the crew mess, and a part of me wishes I could join them. I heard a phrase recently for the first time, the "fear of missing out," or "FOMO." Such a stupid phrase, but it rings as true as ever.

Sarah's display continues to show me a never-ending flow of information. Depth: two-hundred and thirty-eight feet... two-hundred and forty-four feet... PSI: 120.6, 124.8... I pull the small microphone back towards me, and press an input button, allowing me to speak directly to Sarah.

"Sarah, you're approaching two-hundred and fifty feet. This is just about where I left that marker."

Suddenly, I am startled by a loud, roaring crash bursting from the galley. I jerk my head, instinctively, in that direction. I hear Jax shout, "We're all right! A little help, though?" *Jesus, guys. Come on.* I look back at the monitors, then decide I should stay here, instead of helping them out with whatever they have obviously destroyed.

"Sorry boys, someone's gotta work."

"Boo!" Jax yells, and I hear Thomas laugh.

I watch Sarah continue her slowed pace. On Sarah's display screen, I see a trace of the marker I left behind—the blinking yellow light. She maneuvers her way over towards it, and I cannot help but think it seems brighter than before, stronger somehow. She gets closer, and sure enough, there it is. Right there in her line of sight. The bright, yellow light flashing off of the end of a yellow marker. She gets even closer, and I realize why the light seems so bright. Directly next to it is a second yellow marker. The lights pulsing at exactly the same time.

"What the hell," I mutter quietly to myself.

Confused, I keep watching. Sarah gets closer still, examining the second marker. *I only left one,* I think, *I told her I left one.* Then I remember the rock in the plastic bin. She flips up the shielded keypad on her forearm and begins typing. Her green dot turns orange, then a message pops on onto her display, "Two?" The text sits on her screen for just a moment, then disappears. I do not know how to respond, so I say nothing.

I watch as she shifts her focus to the second marker. The yellow light flashing brightly from the end of it, unexpectedly bright. Sarah looks down, deeper into the blue hole, and I see Marie. Much farther than Sarah is.

I watch Sarah look back at the marker. She lifts her hand towards it and touches it. I feel my heart rate rise slightly. At the exact moment her fingers touch the plastic surface, the yellow light stops flashing. One marker still pulsing, one completed dark. She leans in, taking an even closer look, and we both notice there does not seem to be a light fixture on the second marker. *That's impossible,* I think. Closer still, and we notice there are no markings at all on the second rod. No labels, or stickers; no buttons, or carabiner clips. Just a smooth, yellow surface. *This doesn't make any fucking sense.*

Still, I say nothing.

Sarah grabs at the marker, and tries to unscrew it from the rock wall to which it is embedded. It is solidly screwed in. She cannot move it at all, but she tries again.

Marie is now about thirty feet beneath Sarah now, certainly in her own world. On Marie's display screen, I see two-hundred and eighty-one feet, PSI: 139.7. Marie looks at an extremely large opening in the middle of the rocks compiling the wall of the structure. I watch Marie as she looks farther down, and the beams of light coming from her headgear shine on more openings, even larger. Two-hundred and eighty-nine feet…

Meanwhile, I watch as Sarah still tries to pry the marker from the wall. She grips the yellow marker as tightly as she is able to, and yanks hard. It does not even budge.

I hear Jax's booming voice call out to me.

"OK, we got it!" I hear he and Thomas share a laugh.

I laugh, and yell back, "Keep it down now, too! Some of us are actually trying to work up here!"

"Sorry!" He cheerfully calls back.

Sarah yanks at the marker one last time. With all the force she can muster, she completely rips it out of the wall, nearly breaking it in half. That familiar, thin black mist spills out of the rock, where the marker was screwed in. It is almost as if the rock is bleeding from a wound. My mind races, but my voice remains silent. *I should have told her. I should have told about all of this.*

I grab the mic to tell Sarah I saw the same black mist before, but just as I go to click the "speak" button, I look to Marie's display, and notice her oxygen level depleting way too fast.

*What the hell?* I think instead, letting go of the "speak" button. Marie's oxygen levels depleting at this rate should not be possible. Marie, not knowing or noticing, continues deeper and deeper into the hole. In Marie's display screen, I see the openings in the wall getting larger and larger, and increasingly covered in a black tar-like substance. For a moment, Marie stops and stares, almost like she is in a daze. I watch as she cautiously reaches her hand into one of the holes and touches the tar-like substance. She slides her fingers gently across it. The black substance immediately clings to her glove, thick and seemingly sticky. Thin clouds of black mist begin billowing around her. She takes her left hand, and scoops it into the tar, removing a literal handful from the wall. She holds it for a moment, before trying to flick her wrist to shake it off into the water, but it sticks. Clinging to her hand. She flicks her wrist again, but it remains. Harder and harder she flicks her wrist, until it finally starts to slide off her hand. Three-hundred and six feet…

"Marie," I speak directly into her communication system. "Your oxygen levels are lowering pretty quickly. Do you have a leak?" I watch as she inspects her gear. No air bubbles flowing out from her air tubing. No identifiable leak in any portion of her gear. It does not make any sense. If the oxygen was leaving at the pace our system says, there would be bubbles everywhere, and Marie would not be damn near as calm as she is right now. I watch as Marie begins to perform a self-check on her gear, and then I look back just in time to see Sarah attach the second marker to a strap on her leg.

"Hey Sarah, I'm talking directly to you. Do you have eyes on Marie? Her oxygen is leaking pretty bad, and pretty fast. She is losing a lot of air. If you can get to her, you should bring her up before it gets too low." Sarah starts typing on her arm. "I need you to go now, though, sweetheart." She could hear the change in tone in my voice. What first had been care, had quickly become concern.

A piece of text pops up onto Sarah's display. "Can't see, depth?"

"Three-hundred and six feet… About fifty feet lower than you." *Shit.* That distance is deeper than I thought. "You need to head there now, Sarah."

Then Marie's screen goes black.

# CHAPTER 11
# MICAH

Marie's display keeps cutting in and out. I get quick flashes of seeing Marie bury her arm into the tar covered hole, then nothing. Glimpses of that same black smoke billowing around her, clouding all of the space in her vision, then the screen cuts back to black.

"Come on, baby, you gotta get there." I say, trying to keep both Sarah and I calm. Sarah looks down, and I see a tiny image of Marie force her arm further into the opening. Her arm slides easily into the substance, now up to her elbow.

Her display pops back up, and I see her now reaching in, fully up to her shoulder. Back on Sarah's screen, I can see Marie gently pull her arm back out. Black tar and mist, and that smoke like substance fill the surrounding area. Her interactive lens erupts, reeling with an unintelligible amount of data. Her pressure per square inch, her depth, H2O.

*Wait.*

Her screen cuts out again. Then back on, it is relentless.

I see Marie's heart rate jump. *Water.* She just saw fresh water. She pushes her arm back into the narrow, but endless void in the rock wall of the massive blue hole. Almost as soon as she reaches her shoulder, she less carefully rips her arm back out of the hole. Creating a scooping, cup shape with her arm, she pulls a large amount of this… whatever it is from the hole, and again her surrounding space is filled with black, and cloud, and mist, and tar, and $H_2O$. Two parts of hydrogen, and one mother-fucking-part oxygen.

She found it. Marie found the fresh water.

She found $H_2O$, and none of our technology reacts to it.

None of our gear upgrades reacts. We installed software upgrades specifically designed to notify us to positive readings. Trigger points, alerts, warnings, we went out of our way to make it painfully, and abundantly clear to us.

If she had been paying attention, she would have noticed her oxygen levels had been depleting more and more—now maybe only a handful of breaths away from being completely depleted. Shame on me for trying to focus on something as trivial as breathable air three hundred plus feet below the surface of the ocean when Marie just found fresh, clean, drinkable water in the flooring of the Pacific.

Her oxygen levels continue to rapidly drop, and I can only expect her communication system is cutting between static and my frantic voice.

"Fuck—Marie—oxyg—help—Sarah…" I doubt she even hears me. I am confident all she cares about are those three letters undoubtedly showing on her vision screen.

$H_2O$.

She fucking found it. I cannot believe it. The emotion of the moment almost overtakes the fear building inside of me.

Again, I watch as she forcefully plunges her arm into the hole, tearing it out with even more force.

Cloud, tar, black, smoke, more $H_2O$.

I see her heart rate racing; she wildly digs deeper and faster.

I switch the mic to speak directly into Sarah's gear.

"Come on, Sarah, I need you to get to her faster. She's running out of air quick." Sarah knows me maybe better than I know myself. I know she can hear the panic in my voice, even though one of her favorite attributes of mine is that I do not panic… ever. This feels different, and she shows it. Maybe it is the raw excitement underneath the chaos. Marie's screen, again, cuts to black, only this time it does not return.

Helpless, I watch the screens and try to assist as much as I can with so much unfamiliar technology. I scramble, troubleshooting, restarting the communications system, bypassing plug-ins potentially confusing or disrupting the connection. However, nothing works. I try every solution I can remember from my all too brief training with Thomas and his team.

*Thomas!*

"Thomas, I need you up here, bud!" I scream behind me. Thomas must have sensed the concern in my tone because he and Jax almost immediately appeared at my side. "Sarah, I think Marie's comms are still down. Can you see her?"

Again, on the small screen displaying Sarah's line of sight, I watch her look down towards where she last saw Marie. There she is. Still farther away than I am comfortable with her being, but at least we still have a visual on her. I watch Marie, again, jerk her arm. She looks like she is struggling, and I start to feel my stomach in my fucking throat.

"Babe, I'm sorry," I beg, "I need you to hurry. I don't think Marie can hear anything I'm saying, and she's running out of air too fast..."

Thomas looks overwhelmed, struggling to catch up. He sees Marie's screen is black.

"What's going on? What happened?" He asks, his panic matching mine.

"I don't know. Her visuals are reporting data, but her feed keeps cutting in and out. I don't know if she can hear us. Thomas, she's losing oxygen fast." Thomas recognizes this is the best I am able to try and explain what is happening. He jumps right in, going straight to work. Worried, but focused. He first tries all of the maneuvers I had already tried only moments before. A "trust with validation" type of thing, I assume. Even in the midst of truly terrifying chaos, a sense of pride floods over me, making the hair stand on my arm. *I already tried that, Thomas. I tried that too.* I should say it out loud, but a part of me is also afraid of taking him out of a troubleshooting routine. Some people cannot start reciting the alphabet at H. Some people have to always start at A. I am not sure which type of person Thomas is, but now is not the time to find out.

Sarah finally makes it to Marie while Thomas plugs away at interfaces and wires.I see Sarah's depth meter reads two-hundred and eighty-one feet, with a 139 pressure rating. Two-hundred and ninety feet, with pressure at 143. I know descending at this rate is difficult, even for a diver as experienced as Sarah. On top of it all, the circumstances are extremely stressful, only adding to the difficulty.

Sarah again looks down, and on her vision display, I see Marie, still digging, still pulling, wiping the tar off of her arm and hands, again clouding the water around her. One last time, she shoves her arm into the hole, and rips it out again.

Again, I see the cloud and tar. The smoke dissipates, and in the motion of the substance, I am able to see a strong flow of water. A distinct change in the current explodes from the hole Marie had been digging in. Her vision screen cuts back in, and her interactive lens now consistently reads the precious, sought after composition. The one we came for... H2O. Just as I am realizing what I saw on her screen, it cuts to black again. *Surely not...*

Marie has no idea Sarah is now almost directly behind her. I watch Sarah reach out her arm, and grab Marie by the shoulder. Marie, completely immersed in what she was doing, jerks around, and screams. Bubbles erupt in a giant burst of wasted air.

Sitting, powerless in the control room, Jax and I watch as Thomas frantically moves around the electronics displayed before us. I see Sarah use the emergency gesture letting Marie know it is time to go. Marie seems to resist at first, motioning relentlessly to the hole, and the black tar, and the dissolving smoke like substance. Sarah forcefully grabs her by the arm, and Marie stops fighting. They finally start to head up, Marie's system still completely unresponsive.

An immediate wave of calm floods over me, though I know they are definitely not out of the dark yet, literally and figuratively speaking. I keep my eyes glued to Sarah's screen, watching them begin their ascent back to the surface. Thomas still troubleshooting, crossing off F and moving onto G.

Unexplainably, as soon as Sarah and Marie begin their ascent, all of Marie's systems immediately restore, stopping Thomas in his tracks. My mind races to comprehend what I just witnessed. The only thing I can guess is the depth combined with the confinement of the blue hole itself is tampering with our ability to maintain a connection. The chance of that reasoning being the answer still does not make any sense. Sarah's gear was fine the entire time. She was equal to Marie in depth and pressure, and her oxygen tank has not malfunctioned once. Her visual feed has also not cut out, so that resolution does not make sense. A lot of this does not make sense.

Almost the moment Marie's visuals came back to life, Thomas jumps over me, and desperately shouts into the microphone.

"Marie, thank God, can you hear me?" His panic sincere, but hopefully no longer necessary. Instinctively, and now far more calmly, I take over.

"Listen, Marie, you're losing oxygen way too fast. Sarah, you two will probably have to share your mask." I knew what I was asking. They knew what I was asking. Thomas knew what I was asking.

"That's too dangerous, Marie can make it back to the…"

"No, she can't. Her tank is too low, and we don't know where the leak is. Taking the time to find it just wastes more air. She can't make it back to the surface. They have to share," I said, decisively putting my foot down, and putting my wife's life in danger trying to save his. "I'm sorry, we don't have a choice."

In the short time we have spent together, I have noticed anytime Thomas hears something he either does not want to hear, or is given an order he does not agree with but knows he must follow, he swallows hard. A physical reaction he is convinced is internalized but is obvious to anyone paying attention. Paying attention, at least, in the way I pay attention.

Thomas looks at me, and swallows hard.

I turn back into the microphone, and talk to the women, still gradually ascending towards to surface of the Pacific Ocean.

"Take turns, one breath at a time. You are both going to be blind, but you have to pace yourselves coming back. Don't come up too quickly."

Thomas and Jax watch the display screens while I speak, silent, both having fallen in line of the chain of command. Thomas, thinking preemptively, turns to Jax.

"Suit up."

Seeing the anxiety in his eyes, Thomas gently places his hand on his friend's shoulder and continues, "Just in case." Jax immediately moves to action, assembling his diving gear.

"Be careful, you guys." I keep talking, hoping to keep them calm. "It's not a race, you're both OK. Take your time." I mute the microphone and turn to the frightened man standing to my right. "Thomas, get the decompression tank ready," I say, trying to remain calm myself. Thomas, understanding the significance of time under the circumstances, nods, and immediately rushes away. For the sake of consistency, and hoping it helps, I unmute the microphone and again speak directly to them, "Steady now. Not too fast."

I force my focus back on Sarah's display screen, watching her hold tightly to Marie. She takes a long, slow breath before she detaches her mask. She pulls the straps off from behind her head, and carefully pulls her mask off of her face. A barrage of oxygen flows into the water, flooding the display screen with air bubbles. After what feels like an eternity, Sarah's face appears in the vision display screen. Marie removes hers as well, before securing Sarah's mask onto her face, and the chaos subsides.

Two-hundred and seventy-one feet... two hundred and sixty-three feet... two-hundred and forty-eight feet... As each foot ticks off of their depth level, I find myself exhaling long and deep. It definitely did not take this long on the way down.

I stare at my wife, unmasked, now nearly two-hundred and thirty feet underwater, and I do not panic. I am honestly not even concerned. My wife is over two-hundred feet underwater without an oxygen mask, and I am not worried at all. Sarah's eyes are closed, and a pocket of air forms on her right nostril as she holds her breath. She is so strong, and so fucking courageous. Both of them, now effectively blind without masks to protect their eyes, continue taking turns with Sarah's oxygen mask. One at a time, separated only by drawn out breaths and bursts of bubbles, they gracefully drift back to the surface.

The importance of returning to the surface at a slow pace is to allow your body to pressurize back to the normal, livable pressure levels on land, which is astronomically different from anything underwater, regardless of the depth. Coming up too quickly can cause decompression sickness, or "the bends," as it is also known. Nausea, joint pain, vomiting, visual abnormalities, memory loss, and death are not even half of the list of symptoms attributed to this affliction. If Sarah and Marie do come up too quickly, we can place them into the decompression chamber below deck and allow the machine to regulate the pressure of their body, reintegrating them to what the atmosphere is like at surface level. Effectively saving their lives.

By now, Thomas would have made his way downstairs and down the narrow hallway leading to the small room at the end, separated from the majority of the other areas below the deck of The Tethys. All he would need to then do is pop open a plastic casing, and flip a switch, turning the hyperbaric chamber on. I know Thomas has done this, because I can hear the rumbling of the massive steel tank designed to specifically house and pressurize divers after coming back up to the surface too quickly.

One at a time, I watch the two ladies trade the oxygen mask. Bubbles. Sarah, peaceful and calm. Bubbles. Marie, scrunching her forehead, doing her damndest to keep it together. Bubbles, Sarah. Bubbles, Marie. Back and forth, over and over again, for what feels like a lifetime. Thomas returns from preparing for the absolute worst-case scenario and retakes his place to my right.

"How are they doing?"

"They are doing well. Surprisingly, well. Not that they aren't capable, it's just…"

"Stressful, yes, this is hard. I understand."

"Ideally, by now they're feeling more comfortable with it, though." I glance to Thomas quickly; he nods in agreement.

One-hundred and eighty-six feet… one-hundred and fifty-seven feet… Bubbles, Sarah. Bubbles, Marie. All we can do is sit, watch, and wait.

I glance over towards the deck's edge, and watch Jax make his final adjustments, ready to dive and retrieve them if he must, all of us hoping he will not actually need to. One-hundred and nine feet… Bubbles, Sarah.

"You ready, bud?" Jax nods nervously, strapping on his oxygen tank.

I turn to face Thomas, a confident resolve resting behind the concern in his eyes. I take my hand and grab his shoulder. "They're going to be fine, Thomas."

"I know," he hopes.

Eighty-two feet… Bubbles, Marie.

I stand and walk past Thomas, who instinctively follows me towards Jax at the boat's edge. I help Jax fasten the last bit of his diving gear, internally praying we will not need him to use it at all. In silence, we stand, preparing for the worst while relentlessly hoping for the best.

Forty-seven feet... Bubbles, Sarah. Bubbles, Marie.

Thirty-six feet... Bubbles, Sarah. Bubbles, Marie.

Twenty-four feet...

"I don't think they'll need the tank!" Thomas calls out, still watching them from the control room area. I take a step towards the edge, securing my footing on the step extending just off the boat, my hand tightly gripping the rail.

The water, dark and choppy, clips and claps all around us. The sun has disappeared, and the horizon has blended into one consistent shade of black. The stress of the circumstance, and the pure darkness of night makes the ocean surface seem even more rough than it has been all day. These elements combined make the next sixty-seconds the longest sixty-seconds of all of our lives. We stand, waiting for something to happen. Waiting for anything to happen. Listening for the sound of someone breaching the surface, but we hear nothing but the clip-clapping of the dark horizon.

Finally, we hear it. The loud splash we have been waiting for.

Marie and Sarah both crash through the surface of the ocean, gasping for air they can now breath in at will. Without thinking or hesitating, I immediately jump into the water, slicing my arms through the water, swimming towards them. Sarah and Marie adjust to the dark sky, using the dim lights permeating off the boat to guide their direction towards us. Between the splashes of my quick strokes, I can hear them both loudly taking in air.

"We're fine, we're all right," Sarah's voice sweeter than ever. Regardless of anything she said, I would have continued to swim straight to her. Finally, I reach her and feel the sweet relief of knowing she is, in fact, all right.

I wrap one of my arms around Sarah, and she grips my shoulders tightly. I reach my other arm out to Marie, and make sure she is all right as well. The three of us make our way back to the boat.

"We found it! We found it!" Marie keeps shouting as we make it to the boat's edge. Jax and Thomas there, waiting to help the three of us back on board. The moment Marie steps foot back onboard, she flings her arms around Thomas, holding him tight, and screams directly into his ear. "We found it!" Then, at that moment, it finally clicks. I finally realize what she is shouting. Those words: *we found it.*

The moment she let go of Thomas she sets her sights on me. Flinging those same arms around me, jumping and screaming, now directly into my ear. "Micah, we found it!"

"What do you mean we found it?" Thomas asks.

Frantically and aggressively excited, she continues, "H2O. It was everywhere! It kept popping up, and then disappearing, then popping up again. So, I kept digging! I dug deeper, and deeper, and then bam! H2O. H2O. H2O. Solid! Micah... we found it! We did it!"

She is so elated I resent the fact that I have to be the one to ruin it. I imagine this is the feeling most parents experience after their fifth grader's classmate spills the beans that Santa is just mom at midnight with a glass of cabernet, and the Carpenter's Christmas Portrait playing in the background.

"Marie..." I burst the bubble, "We have to check the data... We need a solid reading."

"Micah, I'm telling you, I promise it's there. Why would I make this up?"

"I saw the reading on your screen. I promise I did. But... Marie, we have alerts set up. Systematically, we would've been notified if the reading was accurate..." I turn to Thomas, hoping he takes the unpopular stance and affirm my information.

"It's true, Marie. I configured alerts to automatically notify us when freshwater was detected." Marie, deflated for a moment, continues her platform.

"Check the pages. They print automatically. Check them, it's there. I promise it's there!"

At about the same time, Jax walks up, halfway out of his diving gear, thankful he never had to use it. He hands Sarah a blanket and I help wrap it around her. He moves and hands the same to Marie, Thomas obliges, wrapping it around her as well.

"Let's get some tea or something, and we can take a look together, OK?" I offer a proverbial, placating olive branch.

"Tea? Pop the fucking champagne!" Marie laughs, still undeterred from my skepticism.

I lead the pack, as our entire group power walks back towards the control room. A small, industrial printer still spits out reams of information from their dive. A direct feed of the molecular compositions their headgear detected. This stream of information is specific to their visual monitors, and completely independent of our other systems. If Marie and I saw what I know we both saw, I would see it here. The pages are full of the usual suspects; depth, pressure, and oxygens levels, and finally the piece of contested content: molecular compositions.

We all stop a few feet away as the last page prints, and falls to the paper tray below, still warm. I turn back and look at them: Jax and Thomas look skeptical, Marie is beaming, and then there is Sarah. Sarah looks at me, and it is difficult at first to translate the look in her eyes. Skepticism, of course, but something else is there too. Pride. An anxious energy, hopeful and excited. Her smile lines showing as she furrows her brow and holds back a smile. She catches my stare and lets the corners of her mouth turn up softly. Just enough to tell me whatever happens, she is so proud of what we have been able to accomplish so far. The permission I need to look at the freshly printed pages.

I take a few more steps towards the printer in silence and pick up the papers. Page after page, I see all of the same compositions from our dive earlier in the afternoon. Nothing usable, nothing fresh and clean... nothing drinkable. Page after page, depths, and pressure levels... and then I see it and the blood drains from my face.

Depth: three-hundred and six feet; pressure: 150.87; molecular composition: $H_2O$.

No sodium collaborations, just straight water. Pure, clean, and drinkable fresh water. My palms immediately clam up, and I wipe them on my pants hoping to dry them. I completely forgot that my pants are still soaking wet from jumping into the water. I feel Sarah approach me from behind, and she puts her hand on my arm. Gentle, cautious, and unsure of how to interpret my reaction.

"Micah, what is it?" She asks. I just stare at those inked letters, $H_2O$.

"We found it," I say, barely audible. "We actually found it."

I turn and look at Sarah, tears welling in my eyes. She sees me and immediately she knows. I say it again anyway, louder now. "It's there. We found it."

A collective wave of excitement explodes from the group. Thomas and Marie embrace, Jax takes off in a lap around the deck, yelling and shouting with pure, absolute joy. I pick Sarah up and spin her around before holding her hard against me. I look her in the eyes, and we both begin to cry.

"You did it," she manages to push through her tears.

"We," I correct her. "We did it."

We found it. We actually found it.

# CHAPTER 12
# SARAH

They remain on the deck of the boat for an hour or so before they all retire to their respective cabins. They all know the next day the real work would begin. While they would all love to celebrate their success today, they understand tomorrow would prove to be the most important day if this entire experience. Several hours later, it is now far past three o'clock in the morning, and Sarah lays still on the bed. She has barely shut her eyes since laying down, and based on her unending thoughts, she is still quite far from being able to. Laying motionless in the small, uncomfortable bed next to her husband, Sarah stares into the ceiling resting in a makeshift Supta Baddha Konasana. Her hands intertwined, one over her heart, one over her belly button. She takes a deep breath, and lets the air drag itself back out of her lungs.

Her mind races with questions for which she has no answers. She watches these questions invisibly scroll along the walls of their cabin, continuously, without rest for her mind or body. They had now found what they came to look for, and yet she cannot figure out why she feels such a strong sense of discontent. The haunting feeling of unease pulses so hard she swears she can feel it in her temples. The familiar, dull pounding beneath her eyes she knows will turn into a headache at any moment, despite her desperate pleas with God.

Looking plainly at the truths which she has gathered and understood from her last thirty-six hours is that her husband has basically coordinated this massive undertaking completely by himself. Not only has she not been a part of the planning, she has not even been made aware of the major arrangements. This fact does not settle well in her stomach, and keeps her awake in this small, uncomfortable bed within the small, uncomfortable cabin she shares with Micah.

The small details Micah has, consciously or not, withheld from her; the debts he may have created in coordinating and scheduling this trip; the favors her marriage will owe countless individuals upon their return. At the same time, she knows none of these factors will be at all problematic if their trip proves to be the success it was beginning to shape into. *Well, not the favors and debts,* she thinks, *but the lies...* The success of this trip would never negate the lies Micah has told her to get them here. *Stop it. Omission is not deceit,* she thinks, trying desperately to believe herself.

The internal war of her mind wages on between her ears. The thoughts continue to compound onto themselves, reassuring and damning, one after the other. *He didn't overtly lie, he just didn't answer unasked questions.* She tries convincing herself if she had truly wanted to know those answers she should have asked more specific and thoughtful questions during the planning and preparation. A complete falsehood she knows she cannot escape from.

Her room is silent, except for the ticking of a small clock on the wall. She is distracted for a moment, and tries to figure out how such a small, insignificant wall clock could produce such a large sound in the ticking of a long, thin second hand. *Tick, tick, tick...*

Again, the insidious thought pervades her mind: tomorrow, without a doubt, will be the single most crucial and important day of this entire trip, and she will most likely be half asleep for it. She once again assesses her physical comfort, wondering if a different, more relaxing position would persuade her brain to finally shut off for the night. Gently turning to shift her body weight onto her side without waking Micah up from his deep, well-well-deserved sleep, she rests her hands under her face, and lets out a disappointed sigh. She thinks to herself, *this wasn't how tonight was supposed to go.*

She glances again at the bellowing clock on the wall. The hour hand sits just past the three, while the minute hand ticks quickly from the bold, black forty-eighth hash mark to the forty-ninth. She again resumes her pathetic bargains with God, promising another small penance she knows she will not fulfill, even if he keeps his end of this trivial bargain. *"Please, God, I promise, if you just let me fall asleep."*

Reluctantly moving her eyes away from the clock, she looks back to Micah. Despite the war waging within her own mind, she is not without the ability to acknowledge the very real pride she feels in him, especially after a day such as today. A day of experiencing an amalgamation of emotions most people do not experience for weeks at a time, maybe even months, maybe ever. She smiles, and welcomes the brief, joyous respite watching him. On his back, his fingers weaved together on his stomach, like the "this is the church, here is the steeple" children's hand gesture after you "open the door and see all the people." Micah always sleeps like a vampire, and anytime she cannot sleep, she will remind herself of this silly fact by watching him. It always makes her smile, and inevitably creates a sense of calm within her mind. Her very own, gently resting Lestat.

For a few fleeting moments, she watches him sleep. Earlier in their marriage, Sarah would suffer from small bouts of insomnia, and she fell in love with the habit of sometimes watching Micah sleep. The graceful rise and fall of his chest, and the sound of his breath leaving his lungs through his nostrils just before replenishing itself and starting again. She dull repetition creating a sense of peace. She realized he does not quite snore, but she would find herself describing the sound as just "heavy breathing."

"No, he doesn't snore," she would tell her best friend Rebecca just a few weeks after they began dating. "He does this… thing. This *heavy breathing* type of thing. It's hard to describe," she would say before attempting to recreate the sound for her friend, making them both laugh loudly at whatever restaurant they were eating at that day. "I don't know why, but I think it's the cutest."

This type of memory only surfaces under desperate circumstances. She wonders if that ancient interaction would have come to her mind had she not been stuck awake with these anxious thoughts. While the memory makes her smile for a moment, she almost just as quickly feels it fade away, and the cruel, relentlessness of her insomnia again declares itself at the center of her attention. Defeated, she gives in, reclining fully onto her back once more, blankly staring into the ceiling.

It has been several years since she has had the type of night she is experiencing now. She has tried multiple kinds of sleep aids but cannot stand how disoriented she always feels the following morning. She would lose hours, sometimes days, to those side effects, and she had decided she would rather lay awake all night than lose any amount of her following day to pharmaceuticals. A decision she finds herself actively second guessing, now.

It is another hour and a half before she is able to finally let her eyes delicately come together, and force her brain to use its "inside voice" so she can drift into a few precious hours of sleep before the sun rises again.

And then the sun rises again.

After a night like the night she has had, there is always an interesting moment she experiences the instance she wakes up. She spends so much of her time consumed with the idea and hope of finally falling asleep, and then in the metaphorical blink of an eye, she is inexplicably awake again. She can never pinpoint the moment she fell asleep, but now the sun is out, her mind clear of the throbbing and unshakable anxiety, and she is able to begin her day.

Typically, even after such a short amount of sleep, she is able to regain a sense of rest. Her body wakes feeling whole again. Recharged. This feeling though, is sometimes unattainable after a night of particularly terrible insomnia. In her first few conscious moments, she knows today will be one of those days. A day lacking energy and poise. The kind of day she never looks forward to. The kind of day no one ever looks forward to.

She reaches her arm to feel the other side of the bed. Empty, naturally. Micah has already left their cabin when she decides to finally acknowledge she is no longer sleeping, and not to her surprise. She knew he would be up before her this morning, assuming he was probably out of the room long before she awoke. Today is the day he had been waiting for. Today is the day he had been planning and preparing for. Today would be his day, forever, hopefully.

The air, thick with the delicious smell of breakfast being carefully made overwhelms her senses, and charmingly seduces her into finally sitting up. She stretches her arms and lets out a deep yawn, not only acknowledging, but accepting, the unfortunate fact that she was not rested at all. Slowly, she slides her legs to the edge of the bed, letting them drift down towards the floor. Keeping her eyes closed, she stretches into a sitting staff yoga pose. With her back tall, and straight, she presses her legs together, and extends them directly in front of her at a ninety-degree angle. She rests her hands just behind her hips and focuses on keeping her back as straight as possible. She imagines a tiny, invisible rope gently pulling her spine directly into the ceiling.

Since she has decided to keep her eyes shut during the entirety of this small morning stretch, she completely misses Micah silently sneaking back into their small room. She remains oblivious to his stealthy movements, creeping over to sneak up behind her, and whisper almost directly into her ear…

"Good morning."

"Oh, shit!" Sarah jerks out of her pose, turning and seeing Micah directly behind her. If she wasn't already awake, she definitely is now. "Jesus Christ, Micah! You scared the hell out of me." Micah plops his entire body onto the mattress, doubling over in the type of laughter where your body loses the ability of making any sound. His face turns red, and he lets out pure, guttural joy. She smiles and joins in with his laughs despite her best efforts to resist. She slugs him hard in the arm resting closest to her.

"Ouch," he shouts between deep, abdominal chuckling. He dramatically rubs his arm and feigns authentic pain. "I'm sorry, you just looked so peaceful I couldn't help myself."

"You jerk. That scared me," she says through her smile, her heart still racing.

Sarah erases every ounce of peaceful progress she was making to get out of bed, and lays back down, positioning herself directly next to Micah. Quietly, they look each other in the eye for a moment before Micah starts to lean in for a kiss. Sarah immediately squirms, turning her head away from his, still fighting laughter.

"No, I haven't brushed my teeth yet, I still have morning breath."

"Mmmmm," Micah starts, in his best Cookie Monster impersonation, "me love that."

Sarah laughs loudly now, no longer fighting the urge, and continues squirming as Micah tries to wrap his arms around her, subduing her. The joy they share together is loud, and obvious. After successfully pinning her arms down, and holding her close, they find themselves face to face again.

"Ready?" Micah says, raising one eyebrow. Sarah matches, raising an eyebrow of her own.

"Ready." She responds.

"One… two… three!" They quickly peck lips together, then pull their heads away again. A rehearsed morning move they had choreographed far earlier in their marriage.

Once the struggle of the morning romance was over, they quietly lay next to each other. Neither playfully resisting each other, both looking into each other's eyes. Micah pushes a piece of her hair behind her ear, and gently grazes his thumb across her cheek.

"Today's a big day," Sarah says, quietly, immediately bringing the tone of the room back to tolerable.

"It's the biggest day." Micah responds in a very even keeled tone. Even still, she can sense a simple, yet truly pure happiness about him this morning. Today is a day he has been waiting years for. He recognizes the gravity of that realization and has seemingly made the decision to be present and aware.

He quickly steals another kiss from her, and she softly laughs again.

"You ass."

"Jax made breakfast, and it looks incredible," Micah says.

"I didn't know he could cook."

In the worst Australian accent Sarah has ever heard, and certainly the first she has ever heard Micah attempt, he responds, "He's Australian. He can probably do anything."

"OK, Bert the Chimney Sweep. Was that supposed to be Australian?" Micah laughs, acknowledging his completely failed attempt of the dialect from down under. He kisses her left cheek and moves around her face to kiss her right.

"How did you sleep?" He asks, kissing her forehead, before repeating all three moves over and over again.

"Well," she lies. Knowing her real answer would do nothing but cause a drawn-out conversation with no destination, she simply continues, "Fine, I guess. I just had a terrible dream."

Micah abruptly stops his barrage of kisses, and looks her in the eyes, concerned. "Yeah? What's up? What was it about?"

Sarah has him right where she wants him. She holds back a smirk and presses forward with her story. "I dreamt that you got food poisoning and died from eating too much Australian breakfast."

Without missing a beat, Micah dramatically gasps and grabs his throat and simulates death by asphyxiation. He drops his head down and remains motionless laying next to her while she laughs and plays along. After a moment or two of fictional, playful drama, he lifts his head up and pops right back into his knowingly terrible, should-be-Australian-is-actually-Cockney accent.

"No way, mate. Would never happen. Our breakfast isn't Australian. It was bought in Alaska."

Sarah laughs, and Micah springs up out of the bed, and heads for the door. He opens it, and looks back to Sarah, who smiles in response.

"I love you. Take your time."

"I will," she responds.

Once again, she moves her legs over the edge of the bed, and resumes her staff pose, stretching her arms straight towards the ceiling. Maneuvering her head from side to side, she cracks her neck and opened her eyes, staring at the wall. Today is a big day. For her, for Micah, for their team and for their cause, and she is only half awake for it.

Finally, her brain configures the right combination of synapsis to compel her muscles into standing, and she stretches again, rubbing her eyes. Afraid to look at the clock and realize precisely how little sleep she actually got; she is struck by how silent the wall clock had become. Only a ticking shell of its previously hellish self from the night before, just hours ago. She looks at it with disapproval and walks across the room to her wardrobe. After getting dressed in an "as professional as she is willing to look" outfit while maintaining a necessary level of comfort this morning, she leaves her cabin, and makes her way towards the kitchen.

She enters just in time to see and hear the crack of an eggshell and bubbles of boiling water in a pot with Jax, the master chef, at the helm. Focused on the task at hand, Jax does not even notice her walk in. She watches what he is doing and sees a small pile of soft eggs resting on a white dish.

"Good morning, Jax," she says quietly, as to not startle him.

"Oh, morning, Sarah, I didn't see you come in. You're up early."

"It's hard to stay asleep when the kitchen smells so good. Are you poaching eggs?" Jax smiles, appreciatively. He subtly nods and tries to simultaneously accept her compliment without bragging about his ability to poach a dozen eggs effortlessly and perfectly. "That's really impressive, I never could quite get that right." She moves towards the cupboard and picks out the large bag of ground coffee. "And completely unnecessary to put yourself through, by the way." Sarah smiles so he knows she is joking.

"Unnecessary? Of course it is necessary! Today's the big day!" Jax matches her smile and raises her one.

"Yes, you are one-hundred percent right. It is. Today is the day. The biggest day, I guess." She says, glancing over at Micah who is completely absorbed with the work in his hands. He plugs away at the keyboard on his laptop, and squints at the screen because he refuses to wear his glasses in front of his computer. She assembles the makings of a large pot of drip coffee and turns the machine on before she hears the water begin percolate. She walks over to Micah, and gently sits next to him. Resting her head on his shoulder, he gently presses his down against hers, acknowledging the sweetness of the moment, yet completely unaware that she uses the brief silence to again close her eyes and rest.

"What time are we all meeting for the day?" She asks as Micah checks his watch.

"Now…ish, to be honest." Micah smiles, and closes his laptop. "I should get the others."

"Let them be. Yesterday was exciting. I'm sure everyone is a little more tired this morning than we expected." She knows she is right, and Micah knows it too.

He smirks, and gestures to Jax, "He's not." Sarah rolls her eyes without opening them, and she can feel Micah's chest pulse with subdued laughter.

"He's Australian." She sarcastically retorts, "He can do anything." She smirks, and Micah lets out a loud laugh. Jax, startled by the sound, quickly turns to face them.

"What happened?" Jax asks curiously, and sees Sarah and Micah, now both riddled with laughter. Sarah still with her eyes closed, Micah with tears filling his. Micah waves his hand side to side, signaling that Jax did not miss anything important. All the while, he laughs, wiping the tears from his eyes.

He kisses the top of her head and moves to stand up. Sarah keeps her head tilted to the side, as if it is still resting on his shoulder. Slowly, she straights it up, and opens her eyes to watch Micah walk away. As he moves past Jax, he pats him on the shoulder. "Looks great, Jax. Thanks for doing this for everyone. It's really kind." Micah gets to the door and turns back to Sarah. He smiles at her, and she returns the favor. He maintains eye contact with Sarah while he addresses them both. "I'll gather the troops." He smiles to her one more time, and then he is out the door, and heading towards Thomas and Marie's cabin.

Sarah, looking down at her hands, smiles to herself and closes her eyes again, exhausted already.

# CHAPTER 13
# MICAH

Jax and Thomas help me rig one of the large, steel hydraulic pumps onto an even larger pulley system. I make sure it is attached and secured, before the two go straight back to assembling their diving gear for today's dive. Once suspended just above the wooden deck, and the pump's weight is counterbalanced, I maneuver the massive piece of machinery over the boats edge and drop it into the water. The water's surface splashes wildly as the pump makes its grand entrance.

As Thomas checks every component on his suit three or four times, Sarah and Marie make their way out onto the deck to join us. I can sense a certain edge about Thomas today, his movements quick and calculated. He looks up to me, and I smile. He nods, acknowledging the intensity of the situation. I walk over to Jax and pat him on the back of his shoulder. Jax has easily become the most pleasant surprise of this trip so far. He is dedicated, efficient, and genuinely excited to be a part of this process. I am glad he is here.

Marie makes her way to Thomas just as he finishes tightening the last few straps of his suit. She puts her hands on either side of his face and kisses him hard on the lips. Her display of affection seems more like a showing of pride, than of concern. Something undeniably electric is in the air, and it has been missing from the two previous dives. A palpable and clear energy. Today is the day, and we all know it.

"This is it, boys." I say, an anticipated satisfaction filling my every syllable. Jax and Thomas seal their helmets into place. They adjust the valves of their oxygen filters, testing their connections and the flow of air. Jax is the first to give a thumbs up, but Thomas' hand is right behind him. The two men step out onto the ship's edge and grip the handrail before they both turn back to face our group.

Quiet, but confident, Thomas offers a muffled, "Let's make history."

Jax is the first one in, shouting loudly as he leaps from the boat's edge into the ocean. Thomas, maintaining eye contact with his wife, smiles slightly before he lets his body fall into the sea. The water splashes up well above the deck of the boat. We are all ready for this moment.

Once they both even out, and settle underneath the water, Jax takes hold of the large steel pump with both hands. Thomas, maintaining his grip on the security chain keeping the pump attached to the ship, follows several feet behind Jax. Staying a fair distance allows him to ensure the chain will not become a tangled mess during their descent to the blue hole. The location where they will drill the pump into rock wall.

The two wait for each other to be confidently in place, Jax with the pump and Thomas with the chain, before they head down into the deep. Jax gives Thomas a thumbs up, Thomas returns one of his own, and they begin their descent.

From inside the control room, I sit at the desk and watch the display screens, sipping slowly on a now cold cup of coffee. The temperature does not deter me. Sarah and Marie stand just behind me, eyes stuck on the small screen displaying both man's every move. I grab the microphone.

"Hey Jax, before you get too far, want to switch on the pump cam?" Earlier this morning I attached one of our spare cameras to the hydraulic pump so we see what was happening inside the blue hole at all times.

Jax flips the camera on and the visual feed displays on an extra small screen now at the control station. This camera view does not emit much light, but it is better than nothing. I see the small ocean organisms float by, and Jax's glove gripping the pump's handle tightly as the weight of the pump carries them farther and deeper at an almost perfect pace.

They continue sinking farther and farther down. Finally, after what feels like forever, the first checkpoint of their destination becomes visible: the mouth of the blue hole. Jax and Thomas land the edge of the monstrous opening, and Jax sets the massive pump down onto the ocean's floor, giving them a chance to rest for a moment. Once both of the men are standing on the ocean's floor, I decide to really get the work started.

"We're at just about one-hundred and eighty feet, guys. Very good start to this day. The pump needs to be pressure optimized, so go ahead and initiate your opticals now." Jax and Thomas both switch gears on their suits, and their interactive headgear boots up. Lights beam brightly from their faces, and their interactive vision lenses flare up with all the familiar information. "All right, Jax. When you're ready, let's go ahead with Function One."

On Jax's display screen, I watch him turn the pump over to its opposite side. I read the data on his screen; one-hundred and seventy-six feet, with 93.2 PSI. Jax finds a small lever on the pump, and cranks it up, pulling it tightly towards himself. The hydraulic pump's engine starts to rumble to life, and a bright light turns on, shining a green glow all across the area. It looks like a glow stick illuminating a pitch black, middle school bedroom in the middle of the night. I feel a similar level excitement if I am being really honest.

"Now the other side," I instruct as I continue watching his small display screen, my eyes glued to every movement his hands make. On the opposite side of the hydraulic pump, Jax cranks an identical lever in the opposite direction. The pump rumbles a little more aggressively, and a second beam of green light permeates through the otherwise black water. "Perfect." I wonder if they can hear my smile, or my shaking hand. "Head on down, boys. It's showtime."

Thomas pats Jax on the shoulder, and takes his place, security chain in hand. Jax, using significant force, lifts the large pump off of the floor of the ocean, and with heavy steps, he walks over towards the edge of the blue hole. Like astronauts jumping off of the surface of the moon, the two men leap, in what seems like slow motion, from the edge of the hole into the deep opening. Again, the weight of the pump perfectly pulls them farther and farther down without almost any physical effort from the men at all.

Thick black nothing all around, never mind the bright green glow surrounding them like a cosmic bubble, deep beneath the surface of the ocean. The light is just bright enough to see the rock formations along the entirety of the blue hole's structure.

I feel Sarah's hand resting on my shoulder, and she squeezes lightly. At first, I do not react, letting it rest there as I continue my relentless focus on the screens in front of us. After a moment, I realize Sarah is trying to share this moment with me and I place my hand on hers, but I keep my eyes ahead, watching every moment passing before us via these small, digital displays.

After several minutes of sitting in silence and watching Jax and Thomas continue their steady descent, I press my hands into my eyes, realizing I haven't blink. I needed to take a step away.

"Marie, would you take over for a minute?" We trade places, and she picks up where I left off. I take Sarah's hand in mine and squeeze it as I stand. She smiles at me as I walk across the deck, over towards the large storage tanks. Even in the best cast scenario, we are at least an hour or two away from actually needing them, but the nervous energy coursing through my veins compels me to start pushing them into place now. *Might as well*, I suppose.

They are heavy, but they move fairly easily with a little effort. Either I am stronger than I thought, or my adrenaline is more powerful than I had assumed it was. I position them close to the deck's opposite end, nearby the large pulley system Jax and I assembled earlier in the day. I stop for just a moment, but it was a moment long enough for the oxygen to evade my brain, and I yawn wide.

Before I even have the chance to look, I feel Sarah make her way across the deck towards me. Knowing she is watching and knowing I cannot give a real answer as to why I am already putting the storage tanks into place, I just keep moving them without looking at her. She is familiar with this "oh my God, I'm so focused I didn't even see you" routine, so it does not phase her at all anymore. She stands, statuesque for a moment before shifting her body weight from her right to her left. I am not looking at her, but I know she did because as familiar as she is with my focused routine, I am equally as familiar with her silent stance routine.

"Feeling all right?" She finally asks, her voice scratchy. The kind of scratch your voice naturally has when you have not spoken much all day. A deep, low, edgy tone. She and I both know I cannot continue my charade after she speaks to me, so I turn slowly to face her, and lean against one of the tanks. I look at her and smile. She stands, arms crossed, leaning onto her right foot. Her calm, but in control, silent stance routine.

"Of course I am. Why do you ask?" I smirk, knowing she caught my exhaustion.

"Oh, nothing, I just saw that big ol' yawn a second ago." I laugh and turn my focus back to moving the large tanks into place on the deck. "And you had an awful lot of that Australian breakfast earlier this morning, so I thought I'd check to see how you're feeling."

I stop again, and turn towards her, turning my face from a smile into a scowl, trying not to break character.

"You know," I start, hesitating and grabbing at my stomach, "now that you mention it, I think maybe I might be coming down with something…" In an attempt to play along with the bit, and hoping to change the subject, I dramatically keel over, and begin dry heaving is as dramatic fashion as I know how. Otherwise studious and mature, this kind of cheap, physical comedy always makes Sarah crack up laughing. Today is no exception. She bursts into laughter and walks towards me to push my bent over body back upright.

"Gross!" She says through her own cackling. "Stop it!" I gently kiss her on the forehead, both of us smiling, and I try again to move my focus back to the storage tanks. They are basically where they need to be now, so I look over the tubes and security chains connected to them. The chain itself rolls, letting out slack for Jax and Thomas still on their way down. Thomas, no doubt, holding on tight to the chain as they cruise at the perfect tempo through the abyss of the blue hole's dark cavern. I wrap my fingers loosely around the chain, letting the links pass my palm, each one bumping the padding on the inside of my hand. I look again to the tubing and follow it with my eyes to the start of the actual filtration system. I remember my conversation with Jason, and my heart rate rises slightly. Almost startling myself with the remembrance of my secret, I turn back to face my wife. *I should have told her.* I don't. Instead, I just turn back to the chains.

"I'm fine, I just don't think I got much rest last night. Probably slept worse than you did." I say, still just watching the chain links pass through my open hand.

"You sure you're all right?" Her tone changes, just slightly. She notices when I talk without looking at her, and it worries her. I know this emotional response from her, how observant she is, and yet I do it anyway. I do not like admitting it is a game the two of us play, but one of us always ends up losing. I take my hand away from the chain links, the metal cord still plummeting into the ocean, and I see the water pump line is not entirely attached to the filtration system connected to the storage tanks. I grab it, and snap it back into place, readying the entire pump, filter, and storage system. I turn to face Sarah. I look her in the eyes, and tell her I am fine before even speaking, but I do not know if she believes me or not.

"Yes, I promise." I crack a smile out of the side of my mouth. *No, she definitely does not believe me.* I can see it in her eyes, she knows I am holding back. She can see I am nervously finding tasks to keep myself busy. Still, she says nothing. She just stands, arms crossed at her stomach, weight shifted to her right, quietly smirking at me. "I'm just a little anxious, I guess," I say, giving the mouse a cookie. "I'll feel better when we can fill a glass."

I feign a smile and look down towards her feet. Genuinely, I just do not know what else to say, and I do not want to continue having this conversation. It could go on and on with no real point, and I would rather have those conversations with strangers, not my wife.

"Be happy when you can fill a world," she says, the mouse asking for a glass of milk.

"We," I reply. She smiles.

The moment of silence following our apt, and witty conversation is interrupted by Marie's high-pitched voice letting us know, "They're at about three-hundred feet right now." I look up towards Marie, still sitting at the control room desk, looking over back at the two of us. I turn back to Sarah. *Be happy when we can fill a world...* She is right, and I realize how silly I probably sound. I walk a step towards her and put my hands on her shoulders. She takes one of my hand's in hers and looks up to me.

"You're right. I'm sorry. I just think I feel a little stressed out today, and I don't know if I can really articulate why. I'm sorry." I say, hoping she finally believes me. She moves her head down towards my other hand, so she can rest her cheek on it. Her way of saying *thank you, I understand, and it's okay.* She believes me.

Hundreds of feet below us, Jax and Thomas continue their steady pace down. Sarah and I walk back over to Marie, and I look down to see Jax's visual display screen. They come to a stop, ending their descent at the exact spot where Marie's gear failed, but both of their suits seem to be operating normally, *thank God.* Their depth reading on the bottom left corner of Jax's display reads three-hundred and seven feet. Three-hundred and seven feet, with a pressure level of 150 PSI, and a molecular composition of H2O. Clear as day.

"I can't fucking believe it." My heart races inside of my chest, beating so loud I am convinced Sarah and Marie can both hear it. Even if they cannot, the look on my face likely sends a similar message. Nervous sweat forms on my forehead, and I put my hand through my hair.

The three of us just stare at their vision displays. Thomas and Jax are both fixated on the opening the size of a tire on a big rig, covered again in that black, tar-like substance. Jax and Thomas clear a portion of the tar away from the large opening, revealing a smooth rock surface, jackpot. Now floating at the mouth of the opening, Thomas clears away the black material, making a space to secure the pump. The familiar black cloud blooms and obscures their vision. As it subsides, Jax lifts the large hydraulic pump, and Thomas helps him guide the pump into a favorable position.

A piece of text pops up on Jax's display screen, *"Here goes."* Without even giving anyone else a chance to, I lean down, and grab the mic echoing Jax and his short quip.

"Here goes, guys. Go for drill." I feel Sarah take my hand and grip it tightly. She squeezes, as if we were the ones down there, about to install the most important piece of equipment on this mission.

Thomas, using every ounce of his strength, holds the large, steel pump in place against the rock wall of the blue hole, and Jax readies a long screw to secure the first corner. He lifts the large drill loosely dangling from his waist, and powers it on. He places the end of the drill bit into the grooves of the large screw. Gently, at first, he squeezes the trigger of the drill, and immediately sends a burst of bubbles into the water around the two men. A large, high pitched buzz pierces through our communications, causing Marie to jerk her hand over and turn the noise down. It was unexpectedly loud.

After several moments of bubbles, and that awful noise, the buzz stops. The bubbles clear, and we see the first screw safely in place, deep in the rock wall.

That thin, black mist begins seeping out of the screw's placement. Again, as if the rock is bleeding from the screw-sized wound. Jax immediately moves onto the next, opposite corner. That piercing squeal, an eruption of bubbles, chaos, then silence. The second screw securely in place.

Thomas holds the pump in place with all his might while Jax moves on to screw number three. Piercing noise, bubbles, but where the silence had come before, we all hear a loud *crack!* The silence comes, the bubbles clear, and we see a large web of fissures radiating out from the first screw.

With a loud *thunk,* the weight of the pump buckles the first screw slightly, causing the pump to drop about an inch. The wall crumbles slightly, a large piece breaks away, and the two men watch the debris drift down towards the floor of the blue hole, God only knows how many farther feet down, until it disappears from their sight. The black mist spills out of the fracture, filling the area with the thin smoke.

Even though the pump only budged about an inch, it was a miles' worth of concern for everyone. Jax stops drilling, and Thomas gently relinquishes his force from holding the pump against the wall.

"You guys all right?" I ask, making them painfully aware I was watching every moment. Thomas and Jax both carefully inspect the integrity of the remaining screws, and their placement in the rock. Jax, looking at the buckled screw, sees part of it slightly stripped when it fell, but when gripping it, and trying to shake the pump loose, he seems to feel confident it is still securely drilled into place. No major damage. We see

Jax flip his text pad up again, and a piece of text pops up on his display screen.

*"We're good."*

"Okay. Be careful down there, get that last screw in place and come on back, guys."

Sarah, Marie and I watch anxiously as Thomas again holds the pump into place, and Jax bullies in the final screw, safely securing the large, steel hydraulic pump into the rock wall of the blue hole. Another cloud of that black mist surrounds them, still spilling out of the four screw holes in the rock surface. Sarah grips my hand again.

"This is it, you guys." Jax and Thomas both click corresponding levers on either side of the large pump. The green lights turn blue and begin a synchronized, pulsing dance. "We're ready when you are," I say, my voice trembling with anticipation. Jax flips open a small, plastic cover exposing one, final lever. On his screen, we see him look towards Thomas. Thomas nods, and we see wrinkles in his eyes through his goggles. He is smiling. Jax nods in return and flicks the lever.

The blue, pulsing lights both turn a solid, bright red. The pulse becomes a bright flash. After three or four more of those bright flashes, the lights turn back into that peaceful blue, and remains solid. That small rumble becomes audible again, and the pump shakes slightly. Smaller rock debris from the wall drifts away, and some bubbles slide off the pump into the water around them.

It is working. The pump is fucking working.

"We're live." I can barely contain my excitement, and Sarah squeezes my hand again. The hardest squeeze yet. Marie jumps out of her seat, and she and Sarah share a long, celebratory embrace. "Amazing, you guys, absolutely amazing," I say into the microphone. Jax and Thomas take each other's hand, displaying their own, subdued, underwater celebration. They both give each other enthusiastic thumbs ups, knowing we are watching back on deck.

Switching places with Marie, I wrap my arms around Sarah, and twirl her quickly through the air as she laughs, tears welling in both of our eyes. Marie leans down and speaks into the microphone.

"Thomas, I'm so proud of you! Both of you! Get up here and let's celebrate!" She watches Thomas type something on his forearm and waits for the text to pop up onto his screen.

*"5 min. Wanna check stability."*

Marie laughs, not surprised, "Okay, well, make it a fast five minutes!" She then joins me and Sarah for a few moments of pure joy.

We fucking did it.

# CHAPTER 14
# MICAH

The moment Jax breaches the surface of the water his fists are already shooting directly in the air. He spits out his breathing gear, shouting into the bright orange, twilight sky. Screaming at the top of his lungs, as loud as they will allow, he flails and thrashes his arms and begins making his way back to the boat. When he makes it, I am there to help him back on board. Excited, and a little reckless, Jax almost slips back into the water, nearly pulling me in with him as I try and leverage my body weight against his to hoist him back on board. He laughs out loud, and once he has his feet securely on the deck of the boat, he throws both hands into the air, and yells out again. You can almost hear his roar echo across the endless ocean.

After jumping up and down, excitedly shouting for a few moments, and giving me a number of soaking wet bear hugs, I try and help him out of his gear. He wildly throws it off, still whooping and hollering like a frat boy after flipping the winning cup. He hugs me hard again, lifting my feet just barely off the deck, and shouts almost directly in my ear. His excitement is contagious, and I find myself shouting right back.

"You did it! You did it, Micah!" While I know his statement is created with genuinely kind intent, I immediately feel the urge to correct him.

"*We* did it, Jax. We did it!"

"It doesn't matter, it happened! Doesn't matter who did it, it's did!" I laugh, acknowledging how true it is, and make a mental note to myself not to spend time tallying the level of responsibility of everyone involved, even once things calm down. Really, if I'm being honest, *Jax* did it. He did the final dive, drilled in the final screw, and flipped the final lever. Jax technically did it. He is right, though. It honestly does not matter who did it, but it *is did*.

Sarah and Marie rush over, and we all embrace one another. All of the stress, anxiety and chaos of the day leading up to this exact minute simply disappears in this single moment of celebration. Here we are, four people, practically strangers, who have been working tirelessly towards a common goal, making countless sacrifices to *achieve* that goal, and now embracing the joy of completing one of the hardest hurdles of this experience. I recognize the beauty in this moment, and intentionally, I force myself to take a step back and be fully present, soaking it all in. I take a slow breath in through my nose, feeling the cold air pierce my throat, and I exhale, taking several, mental notes; an emotional journal entry.

*Feel the breeze, Micah,* I tell myself. *Be here, right now.* I hear the water clipping and clapping itself, brushing against the steel of the boat's hull. I look out to the horizon and see how bright the sun is as it sets along the ocean's edge. I feel how cold the air is. *Remember this moment. This is the moment* it all began. *This is the moment* everything to come will be built on. *Remember this.* I have always held the belief that life is simply decades of nothing, book-ended by five or six crucial moments. This is *my* moment. It has to be. I will make damn sure I am here for it.

I watch Marie walk back over to the control room. She watches her husband, still three hundred plus feet below the surface of the water at the hydraulic pump, monitor the large piece of machinery. It rumbles and sucks water from the opening in the rock wall, and Thomas slides his fingers gently across all of the intricate gadgetry. I can see the small hint of a smile on Marie's face, as she watches Thomas going through the mental checklist he created when finalizing the production details of this pump. He checks the pressure system and suction valves. In his vision display, I see the blue light still brightly shining against the wall next to him, and then simply disappears into the black water.

I walk over towards Marie, and I see that black smoke still seeps from the screw holes keeping the pump in place. It looks slightly different now. Before it was thin, and disappeared almost immediately, dissolving into nothing. Now, however, it appears thicker. It looks like the wax inside a lava lamp, weightlessly floating from top to bottom. It is as if the mist is turning into the tar-like substance the hole was covered with. We watch as Thomas stares at it the way a child would stare, mesmerized at the green blob of wax shifting and morphing in the lamp in his bedroom. Thomas is consumed with the curiosity of what he is looking at, when his focus is interrupted by the sound of Marie speaking into his headset.

"Thomas, get up here!" Through the shouting of his wife, and the static of wirelessly communicating through over three-hundred feet of solid ocean water, I wonder if he can hear the sounds of celebration on the deck of the boat above him. Justified celebration. I see that same joyful crinkle in Thomas' crow's feet, and we see him typing a message back.

*5 min.*

Marie and I laugh as we see the message pop onto Thomas' display screen, and she pulls the mic closer to her mouth. She flips the mic switch and makes a loud kiss sound with her lips. On the screen connected to the pump's camera, we watch Thomas blow a kiss to his wife. She blows one back knowing he cannot see, hoping he knows without needing to. Thomas is almost instantly sucked back into his focus and curiosity. We watch him meticulously check switches and levers, while periodically swiping away at the black whatever it is clouding his vision. Marie walks back over to the group, and hugs Jax.

"Nice work, ya big lug," I hear her say as she slaps him affectionally on his large, strong shoulders. I hear Jax, like the big kid his is, hug Marie back, lift her off the ground, and shout again.

"We did it! Thank you to you and Thomas for bringing me. This has been the experience of a lifetime!"

"Of more than one, I think!" She replies, and they embrace in an excited hug.

I walk back over to the large storage tanks and wait. Sarah is not far behind me, and I feel her press herself against my side from behind, her arm around my waist. I toss my arm around her shoulders, pulling her in, holding her. The two of us, standing in silence, just waiting for the part that comes next. The part we have literally been waiting for since we arrived. The most important part of anything else we have done so far; the *water* part.

The water, once extracted from the large opening in the rock wall of the blue hole, is sent through an intricate and detailed filtration system located within the pump itself. Once the water makes its way through filter, it will make the journey through the pump's tubing system, traveling over three-hundred feet towards the boat. After it makes it to the boat, the water goes through a second filtration system, where it meets maybe the most impressive piece of technology being utilized in this expedition. The part Jason added.

In a device no larger than a shoe box lies a piece of hardware allowing for the separation of the $H_2O$ from potential molecular debris contaminating it. Disease, particles, and the bacteria-sized organisms that Jason is after will be filtered out, rendering the water drinkable. It is a lot like the filter systems in place in most city water treatment facilities, it is just the size of a pair of shoes instead of a building, and it is on board with us right now. Once the water travels through that second filter system, it makes its final move up the last hose, and pours into the storage tank.

I watch with Sarah as the first drops of liquid spill into the first tank.

We pull our bodies closer together, almost in disbelief that we are watching what we are watching.

This is it.

We did it, and I cannot fucking believe it.

Sarah and I just stand there watching the water level rise in the first tank, rising unbelievably quick. The first tank is almost a quarter full, then almost half full, and the clean, drinkable water just continues pouring into the tank. The storage tanks are made of a thick, industrial, but BPA free, anti-microbial plastic, so you cannot really hear the water splashing against itself inside. Sarah and I stand so still, however, that we can almost make out the sound.

"I'm so proud of you," Sarah sort of whispers.

"Of us," I correct her again.

"Stop. None of this would have happened without you. You did this."

I am not for a second going to allow myself to believe her. The truth is I could not have accomplished anything I have so far without her, and I am honestly not sure if she realizes that simple truth. We watch as the first tank almost completely fills to the top.

While I am watching it, it occurs to me the water level has risen well above the small spout in the tank which means we can officially pour it. My eyes go wide, and I turn to Sarah, facing her straight on.

"Do you want to try it?" Her expression remains blank.

"Try what? …The water?" She realizes why my eyes are so open. I smile wide, and nod. The excitement is almost too overwhelming. Sarah throws her hands over her mouth, and shakes her head *no*. "Micah, it's yours! You have to take the first drink. You *have* to!"

"It's ours, Sarah. I want you to…"

"Are you kidding me?" She shouts, interrupting me. "It *has* to be you, Micah! It has to be!" I laugh as she proclaims her truth. Sarah never interrupts anyone. She is always careful to actively listen, and let people finish speaking before she responds. For this moment, though, she jumps on every word of mine, refusing to let me finish. Her genuine excitement is a wonderful, and beautiful change in demeanor from her normally calm, and collected aura.

Jax and Marie must have overheard our conversation, because from across the deck, I hear the large Australian voice booming to us.

"Don't pawn this off on her! It's yours, Micah!"

"Yeah, Micah! Drink the damn water!" Marie shouts immediately on Jax's toes. Sarah sprints away from me towards the kitchen, and is back in an instant. Standing a few feet away from me, she tosses me a small, plastic cup. She smirks as Jax and Marie walk up to stand next to her. I look at the cup, and then back at my team. My wife. Sarah nods, smiling at me.

"Do it." She says.

I feel my smile stretching ear to ear. This result is it. This exact result is what we have been working towards and waiting for. The moment Jason needed me to have. The moment I needed myself to have.

I take a few steps towards the tanks, water now spilling into the second tank after completing filling the first. I grab a metal lever on the full tank and pull up. I remove another plastic shield protecting the spout before looking back to Sarah one more time. She still smiles brightly at me. I smile back, then turn towards the tank, and press a small handle to the side, holding the cup under the small spout.

Jax throws both arms around Sarah and Marie, and they all watch me as I stand, staring at the tank. The tank is so full of water when I press the handle, water blasts into the plastic cup, almost knocking it out of my hand. I barely keep my grip.

Crystal clear, beautiful water floods into my cup.

I close the valve and hold the cup up to my eye level. The orange sun shines right through the clear liquid in my hand. Clean, drinkable water.

I look to the group and hold the cup up towards them. No one says a word as we all just stare at this little, stupid cup of water. This little, stupid cup of water is about to change everything.

I make eye contact with Sarah, and we just look at each other. I nod a few times, and then lift the cup up as if to say *cheers*. I close my eyes and I take a drink.

I feel the cold liquid slide down my throat, and rest in my stomach. With my eyes still closed, I can feel everyone else's gaze on me. Patiently, yet anxiously, they wait for my reaction. I open my eyes, and smile ear to ear.

"It's perfect." I say.

We all erupt in a second wave of celebration. Jax and Marie hug each and jump up and down, and Sarah walks over to me. She throws her arms around me crying, and we embrace, holding each other tight. We did it.

I think of Thomas, still over three hundred feet below, checking the pump's stability. I imagine him checking the screws' security, and the flow of the suction mechanism. He is just as much a part of this celebration whether he is here or not.

I look back towards the control room and catch a glimpse at his screen. I am close enough, where I can make out the black mist continuing to thicken as it still pours out of the rock wall lining. I see a text blurb pop on his display, but I cannot quite make out what it says. He is now almost entirely focused on the black tar floating in the water all around him. I watch as he waves his hand through it in front of his face. I squint my eyes, trying to clear my sight. It looks like a large glob of the substance attaches itself to his hand as he swipes it across through the water. With his free hand, I watch as he wipes the tar off of his other hand. It just sticks to both instead. Impossibly, it seems to be getting bigger and thicker, covering more of his hands as he tries to get it off.

*Pop!*

The sound startles me, and I turn my gaze back to Jax, as he pops open a bottle of champagne. A part of me feels bad we are not waiting for Thomas to join us, but another part of me is in full celebration mode and genuinely does not give a shit. Sarah and Marie enthusiastically coerced Jax into pouring four glasses. Thomas chose to stay when he knew he did not need to, and we are here together. This achievement is worth relishing. None of us has any plan to delay it even if we were remotely able to, which we are not.

"Jax, where the hell did you get that?" I was genuinely curious.

"It's a stowaway, I didn't want to throw it overboard. Don't tell the captain." Jax pours a little champagne into four small cups, passing them out to all of us.

After the cups are distributed, they all look to me like I have some sort of inspiring speech planned. I don't, but a lack of planned words has never stopped me from talking before.

"I don't have anything prepared to say, because if I'm being honest, I wasn't sure this moment was going to actually happen," Sarah walks to stand next to me, and takes my hand, "but regardless of all of that, here we are… and we're here together. I am so fucking proud of every one of you. From the absolute bottom of my heart and soul… thank you. Thank you, thank you, thank you." I pull Sarah closer into me and wrap my arm around her. She presses her forehead into my side… close enough. "We would not be here, and we would not be literally changing the world right here, right now, without you. So cheers."

We all raise our glasses and drink our fucking champagne.

Jax and Sarah continue talking and drinking, and I watch Marie walk over to the control room again, likely hoping to cheers her husband. I imagine she would be happy just to get an update and see him making his way back up to the surface, towards all of us. When she gets back to the desk, she sits down in the chair, and looks at his display screen. I can see he is still right there, watching the pump. I still see that thick, black mist clouding Thomas' entire line of sight. It looks even thicker… and far more intense. It seems to be building around him, clouding his vision screen entirely. I watch Marie pinch the side of her pants, and twist. She is worried. She pulls the microphone to her face, and I hear her demand that Thomas leave the spot, and head back up towards the surface.

"Thomas, come on. That's enough, now, get up here." The playful tone in her voice leaving with every word. Together, but from two different places, we watch him move down to type another message back, interrupting himself to swipe away that thick, black substance. "No, no more messages, get up here now." Marie grows more frustrated as I notice a bit of that black blob attaches to Thomas' vision lens. I watch as he tries to wipe it away, but it just smears across his goggles.

More and more that black *something* clouds his vision, until he looks like he is moving through a living room in the middle of a fire. I watch as he waves his hand through the mess, but it seems unfazed by his attempts to move it out of the way. Marie, also seeing his attempts, grows more and more concerned by what she knows neither of them can explain. Forcefully, she grabs the small microphone again, and rips it towards her mouth. No more playful demeanor, and no more kissing sounds, Marie speaks daggers into the small communication device.

"Thomas, I'm serious, the pump will be fine, get back up here, now."

I hear her raise her voice from across the deck. We all hear it, because Jax stops himself mid-sentence, and all of our attention is immediately dominated by what happens next. Jax and Sarah now join me in looking over towards Marie just in time to see her drop her glass of champagne. It crashes against the wooden deck of the boat, spilling all over the ground of the control room.

We all look up at the control panel and see Thomas' feed cut to black.

# CHAPTER 15
# SARAH

Their world goes sideways for a moment. Sarah feels like she is looking through the glass of an old, Mexican Coke bottle. Like a soldier, mere feet away from an exploding shell, her ears ring with the sound of Marie's blood curdling scream. She tries to remember the last time she heard a person scream quite like what she is hearing from Marie. The sound of an airplane engine the moment before it crashes back into the concrete runway, or perhaps it was more like the sound the craft's tires make as they squeal against the airport's tarmac. A dreadful sound, awful.

It is only a few breaths of confusion until the entire group sees it too. The moment they all realize what they are looking at, Sarah sees a blur in the shape of Micah flash past her towards Marie, sitting at the desk. She watches him bee-line straight towards Marie, carefully but forcefully. He immediately moves her to the side of the desk area, taking over full control. In one of those instances where your brain almost slows the world down to have simultaneous thoughts, Sarah wonders why Micah jumps into the mix. She knows damn well, as does every other single person on board this boat that Thomas and Marie know the system better than anyone else. The idea that Micah would be able to better handle a malfunction, any malfunction, just simply did not seem accurate. Then again, she also knew damn well one thing Micah was extremely better at than anyone else on board was exactly what she believes he is doing right now: remaining calm. Remaining absolutely calm and steady in any and all crisis situations. Something she assumes… well, something she knows is not one of Marie's many defining characteristics.

Jax is not far behind Micah, and as Micah goes to work trying to regain contact with Thomas, correcting whatever systematic error was occurring now, Jax focuses primarily on calming Marie down, and talking her off the ledge, metaphorically. That awful squeal still projects powerfully from her lungs, through her mouth, and what feels like directly into Sarah's ears. Naturally, this shriek causes Sarah to stay put, and not move anywhere closer to the rest of the group. Her world still warped from fifteen feet away, she does not need to find out what it looks like standing next to it.

The guilt of that decision eventually catches up to Sarah, and she, against her own better judgement, takes steps towards the group. With every step closer, she hears Micah punishing the switches in the remote communications, screaming into the microphone. She also hears Marie's high-pitched squeal turn into somewhat recognizable sentences.

"Goddamnit, not again!" Marie shouts, now seemingly angrier than concerned. Sarah continues approaching the desk, and looks for the small screen displaying Thomas' metrics, wondering if it still was. She finds it and sees the portion of the screen displaying those numbers is still, in fact, functioning somewhat normally. Only, Thomas' vitals are going haywire. Fluctuating maniacally between static and impossible depth and pressure readings. Level changes that defy the laws of physics in her natural world. She watches Thomas' metrics change at such a rapid pace that she decides it has to be an error in the data reporting.

It is only after a few moments of focusing in on those two pieces of data that Sarah notices they are not fluctuating at all. They are rising. Fast. They are rising too fast.

"This isn't right," Micah says, frantically trying to reboot the entire system. The task Thomas instilled in us all as a first ditch effort to fix any malfunctions. The *turn it off, and turn it back on-again* method. It is not working.

Jax now walks from Marie to Micah and begins trying to help Micah move this process along a little quicker. He grabs the microphone and does his due diligence next.

"Thomas, Thomas, can you hear me?" Jax speaks, to no avail or response. Sarah, just standing, helplessly watches the others work, and becomes aware of the feeling that she is in the way. Impeding their progress in trying to regain contact with Thomas, still hundreds of feet down. Again, she looks and focuses on his rising measurable metrics. The fact remains, he is coming back up to the surface far too quickly.

Thomas' depth monitor reads two-hundred and eighty-seven feet, then in the blink of an eye, two-hundred and seventy feet, and then just another inhale later it reads two-hundred and fifty-five feet. One single thought hits Sarah's mind and refuses to be moved. Thomas is going to die. Thomas is going to die right now.

"Jax, he's coming up too fast, go prep the chamber!" Micah commands the situation with such grace and control. His voice strong, though she knows that he is terrified, because he is thinking the same thing. Thomas is going to die. Jax, without a moment of hesitation, runs towards the direction of the room where the hyperbaric chamber rests. Marie, now sitting on her knees, watching, covers her mouth with her hands. Covering her screams, she begins to cry silently.

"That's too fast, Micah," she begs him. "That's too fast, Micah, that's too fast!"

"He's going to be fine, Marie. It's going to be fine." Sarah marvels at her husband's composure. Regardless of the chaos surrounding them, she always remains consciously impressed by his ability to remain calm, and strong.

Successfully rebooting the system, all of the screens go black, and Micah turns to console Marie while the entire system restarts.

"Thomas is going to be fine, the chamber is just a precaution."

"He's coming up too fast," she continues to repeat herself.

"Yes, he is. But we're here, and we're ready." *He is so good,* Sarah thinks.

One by one, the screens flicker back to life. One by one, the screens begin displaying normally, until they all immediately cut to black again. Then, after a lifetime in a matter of moments, the screens all begin flickering between normal function, and an error window displaying one simple, but devastating message.

*"System Failure."*

"Fuck." Micah was not prepared to see that update. Marie again shouts, now standing directly behind him

"He's coming up too fast!" Turning towards Sarah, Micah almost shoves Marie aside.

"Sarah, please get her away from here!" Then he is immediately back to step two of the emergency troubleshooting guide soaring in front of his eyes. Sarah takes Marie in her arms, but only manages to pull her a few feet away before they collapse together onto the boat's wooden deck. Sarah, arms still tightly wrapped around Marie, physically impairs her from flailing frantically. Being physically harnessed, Marie lets her voice do the flailing, loudly combining a one-two-punch of screams and cries. Loud, wailing cries.

Sarah's eyes stay focused on that one display.

She sees in a flash of data the words *two-hundred and seventeen feet,* then *System Failure.* Back and forth, over and over again; One-hundred and eighty-six feet, then System Failure, one-hundred and fifty-five feet, and then System Failure. Like a bullet fired from the short barrel of a handgun, Thomas' body flies uninterrupted to the surface. Again, the thought implants itself in the forefront of Sarah's mind. *Thomas is going to die.* She will be holding his wife as his lifeless body crashes to the surface of the ocean, and he will be dead.

"Oh, my God…" Sarah hears Micah utter under his breath, all confidence disappearing in the gravity of the situation. Without hesitating, Sarah carefully moves her hand over Marie's mouth. She can feel the hot air and spit from Marie's throat on the palm of her hand, and in almost a moment of understanding, Marie ceases her scream long enough for Sarah to wipe the saliva on her pants. She covers Marie's mouth again and repeats the process. Micah stands, helplessly watching the display flick back and forth between *System Failure,* and a number disappearing at a dangerous rate.

Sarah imagines Jax sprinting down the narrow hallway, and crashing into the door, slamming it open. The room is kept cold, and it is very small, housing only the hyperbaric chamber. No decorations, no excess furniture, just a small room, with a gigantic piece of steel machinery only there to potentially save someone's life. A task it would certainly fail at today.

*Thomas is going to die.*

She looks at Micah as he watches the screen continue their frustrating dance, and remembering a moment of emergency preparation Micah walked them all through, she thinks of how Jax would pound on a small red button "Start" attached to an interactive screen of the hyperbaric chamber, and then see it light up. Multiple fields would become visible on the display, and Jax would frantically tap the first to edit the content. Adding first the depth of the diver at the deepest, Jax would type the number "300." The second field, requesting the diver's gender, Jax would type "Male." The next field down, would likely give Jax a pause. Requesting the weight of the diver, a crucial piece of information needed for the correction of pressure to a person, Jax would hesitate.

"Oh, Christ," she imagines he would mumble to himself before hesitantly typing "Two-hundred pounds." Finally, there is a field requesting the amount of time the diver should be contained. She imagines Jax staring at the screen for only a moment, before selecting the option of "Ninety minutes." Acknowledging all of the appropriate, and editable fields have been filled in, Jax would frantically slam his open hand down on the red button once again. From the deck, Sarah can just barely hear the groan of the swinging tank door at the opposite end pop open.

The control panel of the large, life-saving tank would change to reflect the words *"Press to Begin Cycle."* The large, red button would begin flashing. This is how Jax would know the hyperbaric chamber is now prepped and ready for use. Breathing a sigh of relief, Jax would drop his head only for a moment before restarting his adrenalin burst and rushing back out of the room, mentally and physically ready for whatever would come next.

Again, Marie stops screaming just long enough to catch her breath and give Sarah a chance to wipe the spit off onto her pant leg, before repeating the back and forth. Tears stream down both of their red, flushed cheeks. Micah stands, staring at the malfunctioning displays, watching the small glimpses of Thomas' depth rising and rising. Faster and faster, he watches, just holding his hands in his hair, above his head.

"Jax," he calls out loudly as the large, Australian runs back towards him, "I need you back up here, man!" Micah rips off his thin jacket and runs towards the edge of the boat's deck. Sarah and Marie stationary, watching him, see Jax rush past them to meet Micah at the edge. Slowly, Sarah takes her hand away from Marie's mouth as her screaming subsides. Watching Micah delegate Jax, informing him of what they both need to do next, the two women listen intently.

"He is coming up way too fast, so we don't have much time. As soon as he hits the surface, we *have* to get him in that tank downstairs."

"Yes, sir," Jax responds in full military mode. The two men stand on the boat's edge, staring out into the open sea. The water clashes against itself, choppier now than it was before when Jax and Thomas began their descent. Micah exhales, as he and Jax just stare out to the water, waiting. Seconds tick like hours.

Sarah, still tightly holding Marie down on the ground, looks back over the control screens. All still flickering and alternating between the error message and Thomas' depth. She sees his body continue to rush to the surface; *eighty-nine feet,* then *sixty-five,* then *thirty-two feet.* She has the thought again; Thomas is going to die. Looking back to Micah and Jax standing at the boat's edge, Marie and Sarah watch the two men. They stand, like two statues, staring and waiting.

She wonders why Thomas' body has not hit the surface yet. She saw that Thomas' body was hauling ass through the water, and now they are all just standing there waiting. *Why are they still waiting?* She screams in her mind but does not make a sound. She can feel Marie's heartbeat against her forearm. It pounds fast, and hard, increasing its pace without hesitation.

After what feels like another entire lifetime, they all hear the force of Thomas' body crash through the surface of the water. Unsure if she actually saw it happening, the image of Thomas' body lifting above the surface enters her mind. Like an image of a shark breaching the surface, catching a seal, she swears she sees Thomas' body go airborne for a moment, before splashing back into the water.

Immediately, Micah leaps into the sea, swimming towards Thomas. His arms splitting the water at an Olympic medalist's pace. Micah slices through the ocean, and keeps his eyes fixed on his colleague; his friend's lifeless body floating just several feet ahead. Through the small clipping of waves splashing him in his face, Micah notices an alarming amount of Thomas' skin is visible. After only a few powerful strokes, Sarah sees Micah grab onto Thomas' body, only to discover he is completely naked.

Sarah hears Micah scream slightly, but does not move. She either does not move, or she cannot move, but regardless, her and Marie stay still. She looks at Jax who stares out, not reacting at all.

Pushing forward, Micah grabs his friend's naked body, and begins pedaling back towards the boat, and safety. After a moment of watching Micah start to struggle on the way back, Jax leaps into the water after them. He is a strong, powerful swimmer, and grabs the two men, pulling them quickly back to the boat.

"Come on, Thomas," Micah struggles out.

"Hang on, buddy, we've got you. Hang on." Jax pulls the two men back to the boat, avoiding eye contact. Micah, on the other hand, looks into Thomas' face. His skin blotchy. Deep, purple undertones make Thomas' skin look infected. The way a zombie would look during a pivotal episode of *The Walking Dead*. His eyes are so bloodshot, they are practically bleeding. Fixing his stare for just a moment longer, Micah realizes that Thomas' eyes *are* actually bleeding... his ears too. Taking a full inventory, Micah realizes Thomas is not conscious. At least Micah did not believe him to be.

"Let's go, Jax!" Micah shouts, trying to keep pace.

They get back to the boat, and Jax and Micah lift Thomas' lifeless body onto the boat's cold, wooden deck. Jax takes a step up, pulling Thomas' body safely onto the floor, away from the boat's edge. Micah struggles to take his first step up on board, and Jax is immediately there, holding his arm out. He helps lift Micah back on board, before Micah collapses down to his knees, breathing heavy.

By the time Micah garners the physical strength to stand back up on his own accord, they all see Jax carrying Thomas across the deck towards the room with the decompression tank. Sarah watches Micah's shoulders lift dramatically up and down, a physical exhaustion present with every deflation.

She thinks with one-hundred percent certainty seeing Thomas' bloated, purple, bleeding, naked body being carried across the boat's deck would send Marie straight back to her uncontrollable wailing, but it seems to have the opposite effect. Marie freezes, as does Sarah, as they together watch Jax carries Thomas past them. Blood from Thomas' eyes and ears dripping on the worn, wooden floor beneath them.

Marie shoots her gaze straight down to the ground, too afraid to cry any further. Sarah, fixing her stare on Thomas' blotchy appearance, realizes in that moment she is too afraid to look away. It is only a moment after Jax passes them that Micah is right there at his side, helping him carry Thomas the rest of the way.

Sarah watches as they quickly rush down the staircase into the narrow hallway, careful not the bump into anything on their way, for their sake, and for their unconscious friend's. She imagines them continuing to struggle down the narrow hallway, exhausted step after exhausted step.

In a powerful move, Jax would kick open the door to the room housing the hyperbaric chamber. They would lay Thomas' body down on the floor of the room, Micah collapsing onto the floor with him. Jax would haggardly walk to the swinging steel door and pull it open as far as it goes. He would then walk back to Thomas, and see Micah start to stand to help.

"It's all right, Micah, I can get him." Sarah envisions Jax putting his hand on Micah's shoulder, almost forcing him to stay on the ground. Micah's exhausted shoulders would continue their dramatic rise and fall.

Jax would somehow manage to lift Thomas on his own, and carry his body towards the door, gently laying him inside of the chamber. She imagines Micah forcing himself up onto a knee, still inhaling and exhaling deeply, while Jax adjusts Thomas' feet and legs to be fully inside the chamber. Micah would finally stand, and against Jax's will, help him close the steel door, pulling the latch lock down to tightly secure it into place. The moment the steel clanks shut and lock, Micah would collapse back down to his knee, barely holding himself up with just his hand on the ground.

Jax would then rush over to the control panel, and smash the large, red, plastic button.

The hyperbaric chamber's compression system kicks into gear, and the entire steel machine rumbles slightly. From the deck, Sarah can feel the rumble beneath them. It is working. Sarah imagines Jax looking through the small, but thick, reenforced glass window, and seeing Thomas' body laying on the floor of the tank. He likely thinks to himself that Thomas looks dead, before forcing the thought out of his head entirely. Sarah knows for Jax, dead is not an option.

Micah, now having allowed himself to rest back on his hips, his back propped up against the room's paneled wall, would watch Jax come collapse down next to him. Sarah visualizes the two frightened and exhausted men breathing deep, almost in rhythm. She imagines Jax placing his arm around Micah, a silent acknowledgement of the devastating but triumphant feat they had just accomplished. After a beat, Jax would bring his arm back, and Micah would take his hand, placing it on the back of Jax's head. Paternal, and comforting, Micah would hold it there for a few fleeting moments. A welcomed eternity of quiet, and comfort.

"He'll ... he will be ... all right ..." Micah would struggle to speak between deep inhales and equally deep exhales. "He'll ... be ... all right." Sarah imagines the two men sharing a brief moment of serenity together, perfectly content being so close, and physically touching. They were two men who just experienced a terrible event, and they would be happy to offer genuine comfort to each other for a moment. That moment, however, would be rudely interrupted by the frightening sound of a tiny...

*Click.*

The small, but obviously sound would immediately get both of their attention, and the two would simultaneously look up to see a digital timer appear on the control panel as it would begin its slow, but inevitable countdown.

90:00.

89:59.

89:58.

89:57.

89:56.

# CHAPTER 16
# MICAH

I will be the first to admit that Jax and I stayed in that small room for much longer than we should have. Despite the absolute, and honestly terrifying, chaos we just put ourselves through, there was something calming about the quiet rumbling of the hyperbaric chamber, and cool air filling the room. Neither of us had any desire to leave at all, much less immediately after finally being given a chance to really breath. Still, we obviously understand and know that Sarah and Marie were likely sitting in the same spot on the deck as they were when we carried Thomas' shocking and awful body past them. The least we could do is rejoin them on the deck and give them the update they deserve to receive.

I pat my hand on the back of Jax's head and nod slightly. An understood *it's time to go* gesture, if you will.

"Let's get back up, yeah?" Still breathing heavy, Jax does not respond with any words or even sounds, he just nods his head silently, and looks towards the floor of the room.

Slowly, and painfully, I leverage my weight onto my leg to hoist myself up until my other leg jumps in to help me stand back upright. Even though I know I do not particularly have the strength to help him, I extend my hand to Jax. He takes it, but being aware of my exhausted frame, he does not pull much. I can tell he appreciates the gesture. I do not know if

I can completely explain it, but since we started this expedition, I have felt a strange paternal instinct towards Jax. We are not all that far apart in age, but out conversations have consistently felt different from the exchanges between Thomas and I, in a good way, a genuine way. Jax is not trying to prove anything to me by being here, he is simply here. He is genuinely just excited to help us accomplish our goal. Everything about his demeanor, and composure during this particular experience has only reinforced this idea, which I wholeheartedly believe. The two of us inspect the tank one last time, before we decide to leave the room, and head towards the staircase leading back up to the boat's deck. The place we left Sarah and Marie.

Maybe they were anticipating, or maybe they heard our heavy feet pounding against each stair of the narrow staircase, but either way, Sarah and Marie are already staring directly at the door as we appear in it. I immediately lock eyes with Sarah and watch her as tears still stream down her face. The courageous cry you cannot help but perform only when trying to hold yourself together for someone else's sake; Marie's. The type of cry where the single tear streams solemnly down your cheek uninterrupted without you acknowledging it exists whatsoever. I keep her gaze, attempting to do my best to try and tell her with my eyes *everything is all right,* but we both know my eyes are just telling stories.

Neither Sarah nor Marie stand as we continue to make our way over to them. Sarah's arms still tightly wrapped around Marie, though not holding her down anymore. It was their own small source of comfort, I suppose. The same Jax and I had shared not two minutes ago. Marie looks to Jax, trying to analyze his facial expression, then realizing she is unable to, she looks to me. I suppose my face was equally ambiguous because not a moment after I avert my eyes from Marie's, she swallows hard, and looks back to Jax.

"Thomas…" Marie says, as she somehow manages to muster the courage to finally speak. "Is he … Is Thomas?" We continue our slow pace until we finally make it over to Sarah and Marie, and just stand there before them, quietly at their feet before Jax kneels down to Marie's eye level and hugs her, holding on hard. She immediately hugs him back, expecting the news of tragedy from his mouth at any moment. Jax does not miss a beat and jumps on the end of her sentence. He refuses to let her think what she undoubtedly is thinking.

"He's in the chamber. He'll be fine. He will be fine, I promise." Jax hopes. They stay in a necessary embrace while Marie lets her tears rightfully roll again, quieter now. Sarah climbs to her feet, and throws her arms around me.

"I'm so sorry." She says. I am not sure why she would be, but I do not need to address that frivolous concern right now.

"It's all right. We're all right, Sarah."

With all of us independently embracing, we collectively exhale a sigh of relief. Well, most of us do, anyway. Marie pulls her wet face off of Jax's chest and would have left wet spots on his shirt had he not still been covered in sea water and that layer of whatever was covering Thomas' body. She looks directly at me.

"What now?" Her voice not shaking or wavering like I would have expected, and not yet capable of an anger I assume will be coming soon; she speaks calmly, and plainly. I realize I had not thought to actually explain the decompression chamber process to everyone in our pseudo, makeshift orientation, because I genuinely never thought we would need to use it. I think I have only explained the process to Thomas, and even that might be a stretch. My memory failing me when I need it most.

"I… uh… well," *great fucking start, Micah.* "We placed Thomas'…" I immediately feel Sarah's eyes burn through every layer of my face before I can finish a sentence I would have regretted for the rest of my life. "We placed Thomas," correcting myself, "in the tank and set it for ninety minutes, right Jax?" Jax nods to Marie in agreement. "Now, we wait. The tank will basically… uh… re-pressurize Thomas' body to the pressure at surface level."

"It works, Marie, we used it in the Navy for scenarios exactly like this." Jax interrupts in a perfect way, again jumping at the exact end of the sentence. I am not sure, however, if he is telling her the truth or not. He has no reason to lie, and I know he has the experience, but I cannot shake the idea that he is just trying to *comfort* Marie, by any means necessary. Even if it means a white lie now in hopes of being found correct. Then again, after seeing Thomas' body the way we saw it, I also do not blame him for lying for a single, goddamn second.

"But as for that timer," I continue, "there's not much we can do but wait it out. There's, well, there's nothing we can do but wait it out. The tank can't be opened, early or anything like that. So, we have to wait for it to finish, and then it's over. Then it's all over." Marie nods, seeming to understand, and hoping this whole ordeal is one step closer to it all being finished.

The four of us stand there for a moment, awkwardly not saying anything or looking at each other. In the film version of this stupid mess of a day, here is where the editor will cut immediately to the next scene, sparring the audience of this exact moment. The moment where I, for once, do not have the right thing to say, and where Sarah, for once, is not able to offer corroborated strength. Right now, in this moment, however, there is no movie. No fancy, award-winning editor is manipulating this timeline, and we know we are stuck with each other, understanding every second lost is a second we are hoping that we are all somehow simultaneously trapped in each other's lucid nightmare.

After a few more painfully uncomfortable moments, I walk away. I would give anything for that fancy, tension slicing edit.

I make it over to the boat's edge and stare out into the endless sea before I close my eyes and breath. My eyes burn. The water is calm, and limitless. The cold, ocean breeze burns my face, and I can almost taste the salt. My lungs still working overtime, and my heart still pounding in my wrist. I hear someone walking up from behind me, so I open my eyes, and turn to see who it is. Jax stands just a few feet away from me, his hands pressed into in his pockets.

"I'm going to get Marie bundled up with a blanket from my cabin, then I'm going to probably take a shower." I nod, acknowledging that he does not need my permission for any of it. "I know none of us are probably hungry, but we do need to eat something, so I can work on preparing some food for all of us as well."

"That sounds great, Jax. Thank you. I really appreciate it."

"Sarah's put on a cuppa too, if you want some."

"Thank you. I'll probably get some in a couple of minutes." Jax smiles just slightly out of the left side of his mouth. Again, we stand facing each other in silence for just a moment too long before he turns and rushes away. Then, as if none of it happened at all, I am alone on the deck of this massive boat. I turn back to the ocean and do nothing. For just a brief moment, all is well. For a brief, passing moment there is no chaos, no fright, no stress. Just this boat, and the ocean; the wind rustling my hair and the waves crashing gently against themselves. The salt in the air, and the cold, burning wind on my face. For a moment, there is peace.

Not much time passes before I hear who I assume is Sarah walking across the deck towards me. Only, it is dark now, and in an instant, I realize I have to have been standing here for close to an hour. The footsteps get closer, I turn and see my beautiful wife walking up to me with a cup of coffee for herself, and an extra one I pray is for me.

She walks straight to my side, and hands the spare cup to me.

"Careful, it's hot." She cautions. She always gives me the exact same warning when she hands me a cup of coffee; *Careful, it's hot.* She is thoughtful in those ways, taking into account the one time she did not give me that warning, and I burnt the top of my mouth on a Christmas Bold roast I had decided to drink black a few years prior. Since then, however, it is always, "Careful, it's hot." *She is so good.*

"Thank you," I say. I blow my breath into the cup, pushing the scent of freshly brewed drip coffee into my face. It does feel hot. "How are you doing?" I ask, still afraid to. I take a tiny sip from the steaming cup, and I still feel the slight tinge of the liquid burning my tongue. I keep it in, without reacting, and swallow carefully.

"Shaken," she answers.

"We're almost done, love."

"Micah... we need to shut it down." The grace in her tone I expected, the words she spoke I did not. We both stare out into the ocean, both of us presumably afraid to make eye contact. I take another smaller, more careful sip from my cup. Sarah's simply resting in her grip, warming her palms.

"What do you mean?" I ask another question I am afraid of getting the answer to.

"I mean everything. This has become too dangerous. We aren't prepared for this." I recognize the courage it is taking for her to say these things to me, but it does not stop the rush of blood to my face, filling my forehead, causing me to feel its temperature steadily rise.

"Not prepared?" I tread carefully, through my anger in her proposition, and continue on. "I've worked my entire career, in some capacity, to see this through. We're here. We made it."

"And we've almost gotten two people killed." Her words are quick to cut through mine. Still yet to connect eyes and keeping our voices down as to not cause a scene, we continue our dialogue. "I just don't want anyone else to get hurt." I know she is right. These circumstances have gotten dangerous. It has become reckless even, maybe, but goddamnit, we are here, and we have a fucking job to do.

"Thomas will be fine. A little pissed, I'm sure, but he'll be fine." I can feel the heat in my face start to take hold of my tongue, and sort words for me. I know that feeling is usually a notification I need to end a conversation before I lose the ability to filter my choice in phrasing and cause a larger issue.

"I know, I just… I just feel like something's not right."

I finally break the thousand-foot, lack of a stare, and turn to face her. I see her hesitate at first, no doubt afraid she has hurt me somehow, but then immediately give in, and face me back. We meet each other with a look of comfort and understanding; a welcome emotion. I put my free hand on her shoulder and kiss her forehead softly.

"We are all right, Sarah. Everything is all right. I'm right here." I pull her into me and feel her press her forehead into my chest. After a few moments of comfort, I feel Sarah pull away. Not in a way suggesting the discontent she no doubt felt, and just expressed, but curiously.

"What happened anyway?" She keeps herself close to me but pulls her head away just far enough to ask the question without my chest muffling her words.

"I don't know. His system went dark, and then he just… shot… straight to the surface. I've never seen anything like that before."

"Like what?" She pressed on.

"I've never seen a person move that fast through water before. He was moving way too fast… like something was pushing him back up." I can tell Sarah hears the concern I am trying to hide in my voice, because she moves a hand up to my shoulder, before placing it on the back of my neck.

The only way to describe the feeling I was then immediately consumed by was panic. The feeling you get in your stomach moments before you feel the heart give way to the initial shock of an earthquake. It is not nausea, it is not fear, it is confusion, but it is palpable. Instinctually, I grab Sarah's shoulders and I push her an arm's length away, not letting go. *Something's not right,* my mind echoing my wife's words.

Not sure where to direct my focus, I take a single step off of the deck, and onto the small stepping platform just outside the outer, steel hull of the boat's edge. I can see and hear the water splashing against the boat, and my feet, and I feel the fear in Sarah's eyes as she stares at me, not saying a word. That panic grows.

"Micah..." Sarah says.

Jax and Marie, having come back onto the deck, look over at the sound of Sarah's tone.

"Everything all right?" Jax asks, concerned.

"Micah, what is it?" *I don't know, Sarah, I don't fucking know, but it's something.*

I look at the deck, then to the storage tanks, then to the hoses connected to the tanks. No water flowing through like before, no water flows at all. I take a few steps over to it and run my hands along the tubing. Zero water flows into the tanks from below.

"The pump stopped."

"When?" Sarah rhetorically asks, knowing I do not have an answer.

"I don't know, it was fine before, I just noticed right now."

"Maybe the hose got kinked somewhere down, I can suit up and..." Jax offers.

"No, it's all right. I can go check it out." I connect eyes with Jax, and I see the fear dripping from them like tears from a small child after just falling off his bike. Truthfully, none of us want to go back in right now, but something is causing the pump to no longer work, and I need to find out what.

"I took my time drilling. The first screw buckled a bit, but just a little. It was secure." Jax frantically runs through his mind every moment of putting it together, afraid this error was now his doing.

"Jax, you're fine. This is not your fault at all. I'm sure it's just caught on itself. It'll be fine." I walk past Jax and pat him on the shoulder.

After a few tense moments of silence while I get ready, I zip up the final piece of the diving gear and start walking back towards the boat's edge. Everyone on board a nervous wreck, including me, but I have to find out what the problem is. Sarah, more concerned than the rest, walks over to me, and kneels down, grabbing my face, causing me to stop for a moment and look at her.

"You do not need to do this. Micah, look at me, there is enough water in the tanks to take back and get a proper team, and proper funding."

"Stop it, Sarah." The words come out colder than I had intended. "Please."

"Let's just get Thomas out, and go home. We did it. We don't need to do it again."

"Yes, we did it. We're here, and it's working. So, let's keep it working and bring home a tank instead of a cup." I say harshly, and as Sarah responds, I realize in my mind I am quoting that old, Shakespearean trope declaring, "She may be small, but she is fierce."

"A cup is all we need." Each one of her words pierces like a knife.

We stay in a dead lock stare for a moment before I look down. I kiss her forehead quickly, stand and zip up the final zipper.

"I'll be back in twenty-five minutes." I walk to the boat's edge without acknowledging anyone else on board, and without actually saying goodbye. When I get to the edge, I do not look back to see that Sarah is still kneeling in the same position she was when I walked away. I do not turn back to see Jax and Marie staring at me, disgusted with my lack of acknowledging Sarah's concern. I do not turn back to see my decisions beginning to take their toll among the people I should care about the most right now. I do not turn back at all.

Then I jump into the ocean.

# CHAPTER 17
## MICAH

The water is freezing now, and the sun has set. The current temperature above and below the surface is far colder than before. I am well below the surface of the ocean before the bubbles disappear above me. For only a fleeting moment, I feel the course of shame rip through my body. In my mind, I can see Sarah standing alone on the wooden deck of the boat in silence, watching the last of the bubbles fade, justifiably embarrassed by my behavior. I can see Jax with his arm around Marie try and think of something comforting to say, as they all individually search for the empty words I never gave them a chance to think of before selfishly jumping into the water. After a moment, though, the guilt is completely gone, and stringent focus returns to the forefront my mind. I created this opportunity. I coordinated and organized this entire endeavor. I will not be deterred from this singular goal. I came here for a reason, and I will see this reason through. Whatever it takes.

As the heat of my angry blood flushing across my face and through my body begins to dissipate, and I continue quickly sinking deeper and deeper, the freezing cold chill of the water becomes more obvious and prominent. I still feel my face burning with the final dregs of an undertone of rage I have not felt in years. The type of anger with a tendency of manifesting in the boldfaced lies we constantly tell ourselves.

How could Sarah suggest we just pack up and leave? Does she not care *at all* about the reasons we came in the first place? Doesn't she care about my goals? *Doesn't she care about me?* Bubbles burst from my mask as I exhale deep, and then draw in a new, long flow of oxygen. I should slow my pace, or I am afraid I might get lightheaded, either from the oxygen, the rapid depth, or how fucking annoyed I feel right now.

*Then again,* I think as I begin the terrible game of potentially overcompensating and course correcting myself, *maybe she's right.* Maybe I am the one who has been completely self-absorbed, and unnecessarily willing to let everyone else put themselves in complete and absolute harm's way for the sake of my own glory. Maybe I have placed too much stock and value in the outcome of my own success, and I have become willing to sacrifice everyone else's in the process. She is right. Within that selfishness is exactly how I have been operating, and shame on me for it. I grapple with my shortcomings as I simultaneously realize that I am too far down now to stop, so I press onward.

It is truly remarkable how isolating your mind can feel when you are alone, diving over one-hundred feet below the ocean's surface, with no sound other than the in-hale and exhale your oxygen producing, mechanical breathing apparatus. I continue my steady plummet down towards the mouth of the blue hole, and then it comes into view. Barely visible, I am only sure I know it is there because a distinct area of the ocean comes into focus and is significantly darker than the rest of my view. This shadow in the crust of the earth has to be it.

Without any hesitation, I reach my hand to my head, and click on my interactive opticals and head lamps. Two individual beams of light burst from my head, cutting through the blackness of the deep. I keep my pace and slip right through the mouth of the blue hole without slowing. I have no reason to stop on this dive. I have no gear; I have no real goal. I just need to get down to the pump, and find out why it stopped, or find out what stopped it...

The thought had not occurred to me until right now. What if the pump did not malfunction, or catch on its own tubing? What if... what if something in the ocean caused this error? I try to put the thought out of my mind, but I cannot let go of how completely plausible it is. The ocean is full of creatures living at the depth our pump is at, not to mention the rumble of the suction mechanism could have absolutely disturbed things peacefully resting. I say a quick prayer to whoever is listening that legendary monsters like the Cthulhu are not real. I beg that this moment not the beginning of the next Godzilla film franchise. *Please, just not today.*

I am suddenly brought back from the scary thought, and back from the awful depths of things I typically wash from mind, when I hear Sarah's voice in my ear. For a moment I assume it is my subconscious berating myself for behaving like such a child. I realize it is just her voice speaking into the microphone in the control room area on board the Tethys.

"You're approaching about two-hundred feet." Slightly comforted by the knowledge that she is not still just standing at the boat's edge, staring into the water hoping I will come back and apologize for my abrupt descent, I press forward. She is fine. Angry, I am sure, but fine. I am fine. Angry, I am sure, but fine. We are fine.

My interactive head gear begins to display all of those familiar symbols. The depth, pressure, and the molecular composition of the water in my line of sight. The numbers tick and increase quickly as I do not let up on my pace down. Two-hundred and thirty-six feet, with pressure at 119.7 and various molecular combinations. The light from one of my head lamps bounces back into my sight, reflecting off of a metal something, and I realize it is the chain from the storage tank and filtration systems tubing. I hesitate only long enough to take it in my hand, and I continue following it down, careful not to get too close to the chain links. This deep-sea diving suit has, without a doubt, some of the most incredible and progressive technological gear I have ever worked with. Even still, there are a lot of small, thin tubes connecting my helmet to my oxygen. I do not know if I have the emotional bandwidth to deal with another avoidable mistake right now.

Each link in the tubing's protective chain clinks against my palm as I continue my dive. I try to keep my eyes away from it, because every time I turn towards the chain, the bright lamps shining from my head reflect strongly against the metal and directly into my eyes, making me squint. Much of my dive so far is consisting of me following the chain in my hand and staring at the wall as I continue down. This time I kick my feet to help gravity work overtime.

The smooth rock of the blue hole's wall becomes bumpy, then rugged, and unstable in appearance. The rough surface of the rock wall begins to grow more and more stricken with holes, like a block of Swiss cheese. I start to notice the deeper I dive, the more that strange, black tar covers the holes. The holes continue getting larger, and the tar substance continues to get thicker and thicker with every foot I descend. *What is this stuff?*

"Two-hundred and seventy feet, about thirty-six to go." I can hear the frustration in Sarah's voice. The anger and the frustration pierces her tough exterior, and eases through the static of the communications system. I am guessing it was around two-hundred and fifty feet, but that guilt crept back into the forefront of my mind. I should not have stormed off, and into the water the way I did. I should have taken a breath and explained myself better in *why* I was diving again, why solving this problem is so important. *Damnit,* I think. I can be so rash sometimes. I need to get a grip on my lack of emotional restraint and find a better way of handling this feeling. I am absolutely at fault, and she should not have to put up with it. She does not deserve to be treated that way. *She is so good.*

My momentary distraction of simultaneous gratitude and guilt is immediately interrupted as the thin tube connecting my mask and oxygen tank gets caught on one of the metal links of the chain I tried to not get too close to. It rips my entire face mask off. Bubbles burst everywhere, and my heart rate is immediately back on board the boat. Exactly what I was trying to avoid happening. *I'm going to die.* I grab the chain with my hand, and feel my momentum fling my body down. Careful not to break my hand on the chain, or dislocate my shoulder, I hold still until my body settles in place. The massive burst of unrelenting bubbles certainly sent horrified shivers down the spines of everyone on board. None of us can handle anymore error. I hear Sarah's angry tone become genuine concern, and very real terror.

"Micah! What happened?" I hear her shout into the microphone. I can hear Marie and Jax voicing their frightened concern in the background as well, but I cannot focus on it now. Their shouts and fear registers as nothing more than distracting noise as I try to stay as calm as possible, my only oxygen source pumping life giving air into the ocean.

With my eyes tightly clinched closed, and my lips pressed together/ holding my breath, I reach with both of my hands, and start untangling the thin tubing connected to my mask from the metal links of the security chain. When I was younger and watching a movie where a character had to hold their breath underwater, I would always try to hold my breath along with them. Mainly just to see if I could hold mine as long as they held theirs. It was just a movie, however, and I never could. Our life is not a movie. I let out some of the breath I was holding, sending even more bubbles into the water around me, distracting me and tickling my face.

I can feel my skin getting hot with the realization that my deflating lungs are running out of air. Burning with the feeling of bursting blood vessels, I stay as calm as possible until I am able to successfully untangle the tubing, and finally reattach it to my breathing mask. I pull the mask back around my face, securing it in place. I keep my eyes closed tight, with my breathing goggles obviously still full of water.

I open a small, utility pouch attached to my hip, and pull out a thin suction gadget we have for situations exactly like the one I find myself in. It looks like a small, nasal syringe, and fits perfectly underneath my goggles and breathing mask. With it, once my mask is securely back on my head, I am able to carefully suction out the majority of the water in my face. I can feel the water level pass my eyes, and I am finally able to open them, my face still burning with the last of my saved air leaving my lungs. The last bit of breath collapses my chest with the weight of the ocean and situation.

Finally, I am able to breathe again. I take a deep, exhausted breath.

On my display screen in the control room, Sarah and the others read my small message of, *"All good."* I imagine her exhaling, relieved and maybe even slightly smiling. In actuality, Sarah is likely immediately back to business.

"You're at two-hundred and ninety-six feet, Micah, so about ten more." She is still upset, I can hear it, but we both now fully understand how silly our argument actually was. I know she is so incredibly supportive of me, these goals, and this project. She knows exactly how hard I have worked, and how close I feel we are to this trip being a success. Our conversation and my reaction still need to be addressed, obviously, but we both understand however harsh or insensitive our words may have been, they ultimately do not matter at all anymore.

With the immediate danger curbed, all is seemingly once again well. I continue my way down. My pace is slower now, obviously, and all of my senses are intensely heightened. More cautiously, I take my time as I continue towards my destination. We are not angry anymore, I can tell. The palpable weight of frustration has disappeared from the air, metaphorically in my case. I hear no anger in Sarah's tone as she updates me with my depth in correlation the point of the pump. The warmth in the blood leaves my face, once again circulating throughout my body as normal.

The outline of something faint in the distance catches my eye, and I know I am approaching my targeted depth. I can feel myself fixating on it, unsure of what it is. It is still just too far to make out, but I can tell whatever it is, it is large, and it is not moving. Terrified and anxious, my nightmare of some sort of sea creature interrupting the flow of the pump comes back into my mind. If I somehow willed that fear into existence I will literally never forgive myself. I'll likely be dead, but I will still never forgive myself. Slowly, I focus my sight on the object in my eye line, and I can feel my mind trying to piece together each bit of the information it is absorbing. *What is that?*

It is a large, blank object, immobile, and basically exactly where the pump should be. Only visible by the outline, and the fact it has a deeper visible density than the black nothing of the water surrounding it. I again feel my pulse begin to rise, the warm blood flooding back into my cheeks. While my brain begins deciphering what I am actually looking at, Sarah begins to put the pieces together as well. Our brains, in synch though over three-hundred feet of ocean apart. I unfortunately hear her solve the puzzle first.

"Micah, what is that?" A chilling fear in her voice. A fear I rarely hear in Sarah's words. A fear I never want to hear come from her sweet tone again. A fear I am feeling myself as my mind begins to put the pieces together. The moment the object begins to come into full view, I know it is too late. I hear Sarah in my ears again. "Oh… oh, my God…" The fear is real. *Look away, Micah.* I cannot move my face. I cannot look away, and I know the repercussions of my inability to avert my eyes means everyone else on board is also seeing what I am seeing.

I hear Sarah scream at the top of her lungs back on board, "Jax, get her away from here! Marie, no!" I feel my limbs lock. My entire body goes absolutely and unwittingly numb and I am frozen into place, floating in the blue hole, three-hundred and seven feet beneath the surface. "Micah, get out of there! Get out of there!" It is only at that moment I finally realize what I am looking at.

Thomas' naked and mangled body crushed between the pump and the blue hole's wall.

Impossible.

The steel of the pump bent and broken, partially ripped from the wall, and completely destroyed, burst through Thomas' chest. Almost ripped open by mutilated steel, his rib cage spread, exposing what is left of organs in his torso. His eyes ripped away from their sockets, his tongue swollen and protruding from his mouth. His body pale, and bloated. Understanding the extent of this pure, awful carnage and destruction, I finally scream. Bubbles burst from my mask and fill the water around me.

The screams continuing in my ears seem to slightly fade, as I enter the proverbial eye of this terrible hurricane. I look at my friend, what is left of him anyway, and for a moment, everything is quiet. His limbs, lifelessly float, ebbing and flowing with the slight current of the water at this depth. I feel nothing. The anger and frustration turn into peace and acceptance, and the fear has all but faded. I look at the body of my friend. The body impossibly molested by some unseen circumstance, trapped between wrecked steel, and unmovable earth. The logistics of the body position does not even make sense.

The quiet, calm eye of the storm of this moment passes as Sarah's terrified screams burn back into my ears.

"Micah, get the fuck out of there! Get out!" The fear in her voice brings the reality of the moment back into view. "Jax, get her away from here!" *Oh, God, what is happening? Why can't I move?* My wife needs me on board, and I am several hundred feet away from the surface of the sea. How can I just be floating here, staring at this carnage? *Move, Micah, fucking move.*

Her screams pierce through my earpieces again, and I snap myself out of this terrible trance. I need to get out of this water. I need to get back on board. My face burns once again with the feeling I felt when I was running out of air, but my lungs now breath freely. I feel my pulse pounding in my wrist, and I feel my balls in my stomach. I strongly wave myself away in the water, forcing my body from this mess as quickly as I can.

I glide my arms in a swimming motion and move my body out of the blue hole at a comfortable speed. I have to be careful, not to come up to quick, or I will end up sharing that tank with... *oh, my god...*

The decompression chamber...

If Thomas' body is mangled and crushed between the steel hydraulic pump and the rough rock wall surface of the blue hole, and it absolutely is, then who the fuck is in the decompression chamber? *Who did I carry out of the water with my own two hands?* I cannot think about this new and horrifying mystery right now. I have to focus on not rising too quickly, while trying to get out of this water as fast as I can. I am overwhelmed with the feeling I am a child being chased up the staircase, and I cannot climb fast enough.

The screams through my earpiece consistent, though admittedly I cannot make out the words anymore. I can only make out the terror. I can make out Sarah's voice as she tries to maintain control of a situation she has no chance of controlling. The fear in her voice remains, but the strength in her resolve also makes its stance obvious. Regardless, Sarah's attempts fall short, as I listen to Marie understandably lose control. Every piece of reality we had been holding onto was thrown out of the window in the last several minutes.

After floating and maintaining a safe pace back to the surface, I finally break the water. I rip off my mask, suck in a long breath of freezing cold air and it burns my lungs. I scream into the empty sky, littered with bright and brilliant stars.

Then I remember the rock in the plastic bin.

# CHAPTER 18
## SARAH

Instinctively, she pulls the power cord from the small input on the back of the display screen. The image of Thomas' body disappears, but it remains burned into all of their eyes. Unlike the image of Thomas' mangled mess of a body, Marie's screams do not disappear whatsoever, and rightfully so. She has just visually experienced something no one should ever have to endure. They had all just been staring, only moments before, at her husband's lifeless, and mutilated body. Sarah stood absolutely still for just a moment trying relentlessly to focus on her breathing, inhaling and exhaling. If she can focus on this one thing until Micah gets back, they can resolve this situation together. Like they always do, she knows they can figure this mess out together. While Jax restrains Marie a few feet behind her, she stays as long as she can between her ears.

The heavy trepidation she feels at the thought of turning around was extremely palpable, let alone the idea of looking Marie in the face. She clinches her eyes tightly, holding them closed, and forces the muscles in her torso and legs to turn her body around. Before she has a chance to open her eyes, and see the chaos around her, she is saved by the sound of Micah's scream as he finally reaches the surface of the water. *Thank God,* she thinks. *Thank God he is back.*

Overwhelmed with a wave of relief, she exhales deeply. She completely lets go of the tension she was holding in throughout her body, and a slight dribble of spit falls from her mouth. She wants to walk… run to him, but she cannot bring herself to move. A sense of terror locks her legs in place, and she feels the blood building in her forehead. She fixes her eyes on the boat's edge, and she watches Micah as he uses all of his strength to pull himself onto the deck.

Micah falls, his arms collapsing into themselves, exhausted. His body hits the wooden planks of the deck hard, and he gasps for air. Slowly, and after a few deep breaths and a million panicked nerves, Micah somehow finds the strength to force himself onto all fours. With his first conscious and intentional move, he looks to find Sarah, seeing her standing in her own gridlock by the desk in the control room. He can almost immediately see the panic in her eyes. Securing himself with his hands, Micah finally forces himself up onto his feet. Marie aggressively fights against Jax trying to get out of his grasp. She swings her arms violently against him, but Jax holds her tightly, afraid to let her go. Marie screams in protest, and harshly shoots her angry gaze to Micah. Micah does not break eyes with Sarah.

She recognizes the guilt and shame in his eyes. She keeps her face as soft as possible, even trying to force a small smile. Her attempts are unsuccessful, but she holds herself together. She wants Micah to know she is all right. She *needs* him to know she is all right. She is all right.

"What did you do!" Marie screams, still unsuccessfully fighting against Jax's grip. "What did you do!" Miraculously, she somehow manages to break away from Jax's locked arms, and immediately sprints over towards Micah. She crashes her body into his, and slams her fists into his chest, still screaming. Micah lets Marie pound his chest for a few moments, barely mustering the strength to hold his hands up in a weak attempt to stop and calm her.

"Marie…" Micah says softly. He is finally able to grab her arms and prevents her from hitting him more. Marie still screaming, her voice cracks with the amount of rage it is supporting.

"What did you do!" She screams again, her voice hoarse with anger.

"Marie, please listen…" He grabs her arms tightly, and she quickly stops, tears still streaming down her face causing her eyes to grow red and swell slightly. Micah and Marie finally lock eyes, and Sarah hears him speak clearly and intensely. "Stop it."

The look in Micah's eyes catches everyone off-guard and forces them all to pay attention. There is an extreme desperation is in Micah's glare, and everyone can see it, recognizing it in themselves. "I'm going to let go of your arms now." Marie, still staring into his eyes, has all but stopped crying, and exhales. Her face wet with tears and sweat. Sarah can see that Micah's knuckles have gone white. He is gripping Marie's arms hard, but Sarah chooses to ignore the pain he may be causing her in this moment. He lets go, and Marie rubs her arms.

A necessary but uncomfortable silence comes over all of them. The moment is spiraling out of control, and no one seems to be at the helm. Finally finding the courage to say something, Jax breaks the tense moment.

"What the hell was that down there?" Jax, free of the burden of holding back Marie, immediately is aware that he does not know what to do with his arms. A nervous habit for people in uncomfortable situations.

"It was Thomas," Micah responds soberly, standing like a statue. He still looks to Marie, ready to protect himself from her strikes if she decides to try to hit him again.

"No..." Marie's response is sharp, and intentional. Anticipating her attempt to hit Micah again, Jax chooses to interject again, hopefully taking her focus off of Micah.

"It's not possible. It's not... We put him in that fucking tank, man! I sealed the door myself." Jax's words are genuine, and the concern in his voice is unmistakable. Sarah says nothing, only listening, still figuring out if she has regained control of her limbs, or if they still have her locked into place.

"Jax..." Micah says. Jax tries to calm himself down as he paces back and forth, putting his hands through his hair.

"No... no, no, no... it's not possible..." Jax pleads.

"Jax!" Micah screams quick, and again gets everyone's attention. Sarah recognizes the ice in Micah's tone. His temper is very obviously wearing thin, and she realizes that he has not been given a chance to rationalize this circumstance either. He is the only one who actually saw in person what they are all panicking about, and now he is the only one being forced into owning the resolution. Sarah recognizes it is not quite fair, Micah is still in the dark. He only knows as much as any of them know. They are all in the same boat, swearing they are competing captains in completely different fleets. Micah's shout causes Jax to totally freeze, and they all stand in a dead lock of tension. Tears welling in all of their eyes.

Only able to bear a few fleeting moments of the uncomfortable stand-off, Micah coldly takes a step to walk past everyone towards the control room area. His determined pace interrupted by another shout of Marie's voice.

"My husband is in that tank!"

Micah pauses for a moment, shouting at them without turning to face them. Micah addresses the frantic women standing behind him.

"Your husband is dead!"

The anger building within Micah catches even himself by surprise. Sarah is confident he did not mean to raise his voice so dramatically. Every passing moment had her praying he would not, whatever the cost. "Marie... I'm sorry," Micah continues as he walks farther past the group, "but whatever we put in that chamber... it isn't Thomas." Sarah cannot believe what she is hearing. Twelve hours before everything was mostly fine. Now, they seem to have stumbled into an absolutely terrible and unexplainable worst-case scenario.

"How do you know?" Marie starts to rush towards Micah again, but Jax jumps in and restrains her. "How do you know?" She is again overwhelmed with rage and tears freely roll down her face once more. "What did you do!"

Jax grabs Marie again, wrapping his arms around her. He keeps Marie's distance from Micah, as Micah beelines past Sarah towards the control room area. As he passes her, he gently brushes his hand across her lower back. It is important to Sarah that Micah knows she feels safe, despite the fact neither of them feel safe at this moment. She interprets his gentle touch as an intention, but wordless, gesture; an invitation to follow him. She wants to follow him. She wants to wrap her arms around him until he tells her she is dreaming, and she wakes up in their bed at home.

Finally, her muscles release their lock on her legs, and she is immediately behind him, following him at his pace as he continues towards the control room. After searching, she is able to find some words, even if they are not the ones she was exactly looking for. She begins to speak, but softly to keep her question between the two of them.

"If it wasn't Thomas you put in the tank…" she delicately asks, still sort of searching for the words even as she speaks them, "then what was it?" Her soft tone stops Micah's fierce focus. He stops walking and reaches his hand behind him towards where he feels her standing. She notices he hesitates before he answers.

"I… I don't know." Sarah takes his hand, and he drops his head. She can feel his pulse in his palm, through the sweat and the heat from the flow of his blood. "Whatever it was that did that to him."

"How do you know?" Micah does not turn to face his wife. He does not look her in the eyes. He stands still, back to her, and breaths. He takes a moment, and she tells herself once again he is still figuring this situation out too. He is searching for the right words himself to say to her.

"You saw what I saw, Sarah." She starts to respond, but her voice is caught in her throat, and she is not sure of what to say, even if she was able to speak freely. Still, she pushes through the insecure pause, and continues.

"I… it all… everything happened so fast, I don't know what I saw." Micah finally turns and looks her in the eyes. He looks almost disappointed at her willingness to turn her back on reality.

"Sarah…" Her heart breaks, and she does not want this circumstance to be happening. Finally, Micah takes a breath, and carefully repeats himself. He speaks cautiously, intentionally, and slowly, to make sure she not only hears him, but she understands the words he *isn't* saying. "You saw what I saw." She knows it is true, and she nods, though admittedly, she is not entirely sure of exactly what she is acknowledging. She trusts him, though. She knows he is right.

"So, what do we do now?" She sees the tears welling in his eyes, and she feels herself give in to the emotion of the moment. Though a tear rolls down her cheek, she knows Micah can recognize and understand the resolve in her strength. She is a rock because a rock is exactly what he needs her to be in this moment. She is holding herself together for his sake, and they both know it. Micah swallows hard, suppressing the wave of anger and fear he feels sweeping through his body, and walks past her without responding. He walks quickly, with a purpose. Again, without hesitation, she just follows him. He tries to hide it, but she catches him wipe a tear from his eyes. It almost completely breaks her.

Micah walks directly up to Jax and Marie, and though he looks directly into Marie's eyes, they all know he is addressing the entire group. They all listen, unable to do anything else at the moment.

"Listen, I don't know what happened." He shakes his head and speaks deliberately. "I don't know any more than any of you." Sarah is right behind him, listening intently, and watching Marie avoid eye contact. Micah, undeterred, stares directly at her, and though he speaks to them all, he is focused on an audience of one. "But I know what I saw. Because you saw it too." At this acknowledgement, Marie's tears flow again, silently now, still avoiding looking to him. "Whatever is in that tank isn't Thomas."

There it is.

The definitive statement they were all subconsciously waiting someone to speak with words. "I'm sorry. I'm really fucking sorry, but the quicker we can all get on the same page about that, the better."

In the course of his short monologue, Marie started and stopped crying multiple times. Fighting back and forth within herself between surprising strength and expected weakness. Giving credit where credit was due, Sarah definitely recognized the courage in Marie necessary for her to even still be standing on her own two feet, however tightly Jax held her arms down.

Sarah knows if the roles were reversed, and she found herself in Marie's shoes, she would have collapsed into a helpless, devastated puddle on the ground long ago. Even with all of her strength, a truly impressive attribute she absolutely prides herself on, the idea of losing Micah without actually being given the chance to lose Micah would ruin her. It would absolutely ruin her. Selfishly she wants to smile, knowing she has not lost Micah, but she quickly pushes the thought from her mind, and focuses on the chaos at hand. She cannot allow herself to wallow in her own fantasy when she is aware of the reality they are living right now.

"How can you be so sure?" Jax appropriately asks another question they were all thinking. Micah responds without breaking his gaze on Marie, who still avoids his eyes.

"What other choice do we have?" Everyone knows he is right, regardless of whether or not they want to acknowledge it as fact.

"We can wait." Marie adds. "We can wait until we know for sure. This isn't a game, this is my *husband*."

"And if you're wrong?" Micah immediately responds, discrediting her idea. "What if your wrong, Marie? That puts us all in danger, and I can't risk that."

Marie does not have a response, and simply remains silent as Micah continues. "We have two choices." Micah continues. "We can wait, and see what happens when that chamber opens, or we can get the fuck off this boat." Micah looks to Jax, and to Sarah, before finally looking back to Marie. "Marie, if that is Thomas, and he is alive in that tank, then we can come back when we know for sure that it's safe. But if that's not Thomas, and he's not..." he stops himself from finishing the sentence. "I'm not sticking around to find out."

Marie's silent tears have understandably come rushing back. She averts her eyes again, looking straight down towards the boat's wooden deck. What else is she supposed to do?

"As long as we can keep that chamber sealed..." Micah says carefully, like he has to search for each individual word as he speaks them.

This statement quickly becomes a revelation to Jax's ear, and he shoots his head up, staring straight at Micah. Sarah notices the look at Micah's face and assumes he is already aware of what Jax is about to say.

"It's on a timer."

"What?" Sarah speaks her first words in what feels like an hour, and they came out of nowhere. She was not planning on participating in this conversation, not thinking she had anything of value to add, but nonetheless, the words came from her mouth.

"The tank... it's on a timer. Once the compression cycle ends, it's opening. Whether we are ready for it or not, it's opening." The weight of Jax's words hits like a bomb dropping on London on a cold night during World War II. The hyperbaric chamber is sealed on a timer. There is nothing they can do about this situation. That tank will not be opening until the timer expires, and after the timer expires… the tank *will* be opening.

Confident in her movement for first time during this exchange, Sarah reaches her hand to Micah and touches his arm. She is afraid, still trying to maintain her strong resolve, but she can feel herself starting to fail.

"We need to call the Coast Guard," she finally says. Micah looks to her but does not react to her words. She knows they are in over their heads, and they do not have the answer to this eminent, and inevitable, problem.

"We're two-hundred miles off the coast. It'll take them hours to get approvals and organized enough to get here. We aren't a priority. We don't have that kind of time."

"What do we do then?" The conversation turns from fear and rage to more thoughtful concern, with a sense of a genuine attempt at solving this problem. They need to figure something out, and fast. They need a plan.

"Jason…" Micah says. Quietly, but loud enough for everyone to hear him. Sarah looks up at him, and he returns the glance.

"Cark?" Sarah asks. Micah nods.

"He arranged our helicopter to the airport. I don't know if it was his or not, but that could make it here in an hour." Sarah nods, pretending for a moment it is only the two of them on the boat, and they are simply planning their trip back home. The peaceful thought keeps her from completely breaking down. Micah grabs her hand and holds it tight, looking at her. He then turns and looks towards Jax.

"How long is the timer set for?" Micah asks. Hoping for an answer he would not receive. Jax thinks for a moment, frustrated with the fact he cannot immediately recall how long he set it for. He remembers there was more than one option, but the numbers are not coming to him.

"I… uh, ninety minutes? I think. But that was… twenty-five, thirty minutes ago."

"Then we're already behind." Micah stands, and Sarah can see the million thoughts racing through his mind. In her own, she begs him to say them. She pleads in her mind for Micah to say what he is thinking. If only she knew what was on his mind, maybe she could help. Maybe she could add to the thoughts and ideas of how they could get out of this mess. Micah does not speak, and instead remains within the confines of his racing mind. He shakes his head, not happy with whatever he just decided on. "That helicopter is our only chance." He finally says.

"Chance of what?" Sarah asks, afraid of the answer she will get.

"Getting off this boat."

"Getting off this bo—"

# CHAPTER 19
# MICAH

With Marie still devastated, and ultimately useless, I decide to take
control of the situation. After all, I am the one who got us into it. I begin
by delegating necessary tasks to Sarah and Jax, tasks able to be started
right now, and finished as quickly as possible. I try to grant them mental
grace, consciously limiting my expectations of their ability to react. This
completely unpredictable and horrific situation is the most jarring thing
any of us have ever experienced, but we need to get off this fucking boat,
and we're running out of the time necessary to do so... unbelievable. I
turn to Jax, asserting myself as the person in charge.

"Start with the communications system," I tell him as he walks over
towards the control room area almost immediately. "Just try to reach
anyone you can." Just as the words leave my lips, I recall the
uncomfortable conversation ultimately resulting in us getting access to
this boat in the first place. Professor What's-His-Name; the "just sayin'
hiya!" He told me the only reason he let us on the boat this week was
because he is in the process of having a brand-new communications
system installed, and that reception with the shore would be shoddy at
best. He told me we would be on the water in *total darkness*, as he
described it. *Fuck*, I thought out loud. "You're going to have trouble, just
keep trying. Don't stop," I add to Jax who is already at work trying to

establish communication with anyone willing and able to listen to a shitty boat two-hundred miles out to sea.

I turn to Sarah, and immediately see the tears pooling underneath her eyes. None of them have fallen yet, she is working overtime holding them at bay. *She is so fucking good.* "Sarah, I need you to start gathering essentials and readying them near the life raft. Worst case scenario, we take that and head towards shore."

"Micah…" she interrupts, "Shore is…"

"I know. It's far. But we can make it."

"I'm scared." The genuine fear in her voice gives me a terrifying gut punch. It is starting to sink in that I have betrayed her. I have betrayed all of us. I give pause to my focus, and I wrap my arms around my wife. I pull her body into mine, and I feel the barrier holding her tears back break a little. Not unlike a weak levy in a port city during a monster hurricane, her resolve breaks, and tears begin silently streaming down her face.

"I know you are. I am too." I hold her for a moment longer, before bringing us both back to reality. "We just don't have time. We have to do this now." My mind generating a hundred-thousand other sentiments I could communicate with her if we did have the time. For now, my internal monologue must suffice. *I'm sorry, Sarah. I'm so fucking sorry.* The thought goes unsaid.

She nods, and I kiss her. Harder than I have since we have arrived. With my hand, I gently slide my thumb across her cheek, wiping away a few more silent, but strong tears. She smiles at me, putting her hand on my face too, but I can tell the smile is forced. She walks into the kitchen area to begin gathering necessary supplies. I call out to her, and she turns back towards me. "Make sure you're only getting important things. Data, food, making sure the storage tanks are ready for transport, things like that." Sarah nods, and continues on her way.

Marie, still standing silently crying on the deck, looks up at me. We make brief eye contact before I start to walk back towards the control room area, and the million tasks still piling up we already do not have the time to complete.

"Micah…" My heart is broken for her, but my patience is breaking too. I cannot adequately imagine the pain she is experiencing right now, but I am not, for one goddamn second, willing to allow anyone else to experience the same. I feel my face burn with the same rage from before, and I physically, consciously, remind myself to calm down.

"Marie, I don't have time, I'm sorry..." Marie interrupts me with a gentle, unexpected tone.

"Tell me how to help."

I was not expecting her to at all have a desire to help, but I am immediately overwhelmed with relief she does. I do not move towards her at all, but instead, I quietly find something to respond with.

"It would be great if you helped Sarah." I know full well that Sarah not only does not need the help, and probably does not prefer it, but it gives Marie something to do and keeps her out of my way. Plus, with the two of them, more essentials can be gathered for what will most likely be an absolutely awful journey into the open ocean towards the shoreline. Marie nods, and quietly walks towards the kitchen area where Sarah is already pulling out necessities from the pantry and cabinetry.

I watch Marie walk away, and feel the emotion beginning to make its way through my body. My muscles ache, and my head is pounding. I feel... hungover. I know it is an awful combination of exhaustion and dehydration, and I just need to drink some water and push through it. I have no other choice.

My face feels flush, and I am immediately hit with a wave of light-headed nausea, it almost knocks me to my feet. It is as if a large, rogue wave crashed into the boat, but I am the only one who felt it. My equilibrium completely betrays me, and my legs give way. My left knee pounds against the deck. *You need some fucking water, man.* Water and maybe a sandwich, Jesus Christ, Micah.

After a moment, the vertigo subsides, and I am able to stand back to my feet. I walk quickly back to the control room area and see Jax pull down a small radio towards his face. He holds down the small, black button with white letters simply stating, "COMMS." Once he holds it down, he speaks loudly, and clearly.

"Tethys to Kodiak, come in. Tethys to Kodiak, do you copy?" He lifts his thumb from the plastic button and clicks on a small speaker to the radio's left. Static permeates through the speaker. He tries again. "Tethys to Kodiak, come in..."

I look back to the kitchen area, see Sarah open a cabinet and begin pulling out its contents. Deciphering between what can and should be brought with them on what she assumes will be a smaller life raft, versus what should be left behind for Thomas, I hope. Behind her, she hears a faint creak of wood, and jerks around. Her heart races, and she gasps frightened. Marie stands in the doorway. I watch as wipes tears from her eyes, and snot from her nose.

"I'm sorry I startled you." I can barely hear Marie speak, but she sounds sheepish. "Micah said I should help you." Sarah nods, and Marie joins her.

I watch Jax attempt the same connection several times before I walk into the room. I remember the business card Jason gave me. I remember the cryptic wording he used, and how he refused to tell me who this number was for, but how he intensely stressed it was for "emergencies *only.*"

"You know," Jason had said in-between sips of coffee, "like absolute, undeniable, worst case scenario shit." Thank you, Jason, I thought. *Thank you.* I knew I had placed the card in this room somewhere, not paying attention to where because I had not in a million years thought we would need it at all, not even a little bit.

Thousands of papers and documents are strewn across every inch of table space in this entire room. We had been printing data every moment under water from our first dive, and there was a lot of it. Single printed pages, stretches of connected pages, all types of pages printed full of data clutter the entire room.

"Tethys for Kodiak... Do you copy? Tethys for Kodiak... Do you come in?" Jax continued his tired attempts at making contact with anyone on shore. The consonants in his sentence hit my head hard, piercing through my thoughts. Is he intentionally pronouncing them that hard? *Christ, man,* I think, *ease up.*

I try to focus on my search on this tiny piece of potentially lifesaving paper, with a hand-scribbled number on the back. I would liken it to finding a needle in a haystack, but it is more realistically finding a small sliver of paper within a giant room full of paper.

"*T*-ethys for *K*-odia-*K*. Do you *C*-opy?"

A sharp pain rips across my head, and almost sends me again to my knees. I brace myself against the table and focus my sight onto the papers that clutter it. I grab a handful of the pages and toss them aside. Well, I throw them aside, and it catches Jax's attention. He looks towards me, before continuing his efforts.

"What are you looking for?" Jax asks, as he adjust a small radio signal device next to the microphone he has been speaking into.

"I know I put his card in here."

"Keep looking, you'll find it." Jax is immediately back at the microphone, practically screaming into the small piece of equipment. His volume is blinding. "Tethys to Kodiak, can anybody hear me?" Another sharp pain rips through my head and knocks me down to my knees. I grab my head and clinch my teeth until the pain subsides.

"Goddamnit, man," I erupt at Jax, and he jerks his face towards me. He sees me collapsed onto the wooden floor, gripping my head, he cautiously takes a step to me. "Do you have to scream? There's no fucking signal, Jax. Give it up, we have to find a different way." Jax does not say anything, but I feel his eyes locked onto me.

I force myself to stand back to my knees, and keep my hand pressed into my eyes. The headache came quick and was not leaving. Jax still says nothing, but he is staring at me. I can feel his eyes burning into my skin. I immediately feel terrible about my explosion, and I rub the deep tissue within my eye sockets.

"I'm sorry, I just... I have this awful migraine at like, the worst possible time. I'm sorry, really. It's just... you know." I finally take my hand away from my face, and I look at Jax. The colorful explosion in my immediate line of sight is like what appears after you apply any sort of pressure to your eyes directly. Slowly, the colors and sparks begin to fade, and for the first time in this entire conversation, I see the very real fear in Jax's eyes. Not the fear from before, the fear of feeling suddenly trapped on board. This fear was something else, something new.

Without breaking eye contact, I see Jax reach for a towel on the table next to him. He gently picks it up and tosses it to me. Confused, I catch it, and wait for him to say something. He does not speak, he just continues to stare, terrified, into my eyes. In an attempt to break the awkward silence, I begin to continue my explanation.

"We have that large life raft. Worst case, I'm thinking we can put that together and get back to shore ourselves. The boat is anchored where we are now, so it's not going anywhere." I am suddenly aware Jax has not blinked. He is barely breathing. He simply stares at me, overwhelmed with that unending, genuine fear. The realization generates in me a frightened panic. "What?" I frantically ask. "Jax, what it is?" I am more afraid of what he might say than anything. He does not say a word. Slowly, he points his finger to my face.

Then I feel it.

A small drip of something splashes against my hand. Like a tiny dribble of condensation slipping off or falling from a water bottle on an August afternoon in Texas. The liquid hits my finger. I look down, and see my hand covered in blood.

The panic, the nausea, the fear, it all comes rushing back. *Oh my god…* I think, confused. My hand absolutely covered, as if I dipped it into a pale of deep, red paint. I look down at my blood-soaked hand just in time to see another drop falls from my face and splash against my hand, now holding the towel. At that moment, I realize the blood is coming from my face.

I press my other hand against my cheek, but my cheek is not the source. Not my forehead, not my nose… I cannot find where I am bleeding from. Then I blink. For the first time, I feel the wet layer of something in my eye. A feeling I had been chalking up to sweat and tears this entire time. I wipe my finger underneath my eye, feeling for an abrasion or laceration, or anything similar but I do not feel anything. I do not feel anything except the cool, wet liquid pooling underneath my left eye. I pull my hand away from my face and look down to see bright red blood. I feel it begin running down my cheek, and I look back up to again see the horror in Jax's expression. Gently, but quickly, I press the towel against my face.

"You might want to go look at that, yeah?" Jax says nervously. I can only imagine what he is thinking right now. I want to respond calmly, and continue our conversation about finding Jason's card, trying to get ahold of the number scribbled on the back, and getting everyone safely off of this boat, but I cannot. Instead, I stand for a moment in deafening silence.

Unsure of what exactly to do, I decisively nod and quickly but calmly walk out of the room. I need to go to the bathroom and see what is happening.

I pass the kitchen as quietly as possible, so I do not get the attention of Sarah or Marie. I cannot handle either of them seeing me in this state right now, not after everything we all just went through. Sneak past the opened kitchen door, I glance in, and see the two women still quietly organizing supplies into a box. They do not seem to be talking at all, likely a decision unintentionally executed by Sarah.

I effectively evade the two women, and quietly walk into the small bathroom. I shut the door behind me and stand in silence for a moment without turning on the light. I slowly remove the towel from my face, and reluctantly bring my hand to my eye. I gently feel my lower eye lid, feeling for any sort of flow of blood. It seems to have stopped. I hesitate to bring my hand towards the bathroom light switch, afraid of what I will see in the mirror; afraid to see myself.

*Get it together, Micah, you're fine.* I do not have the luxury of *not* being fine. They are all depending on me. I close my eyes and flip the light on. My eyes are flooded with red, more so than normal when you turn a light on with your eyes shut. Typically, that orange glow covers your sight until you lift your eyes open, but this shade of red is dark, deep. It is blood red.

Slowly, I persuade myself to open my eyes, and I see myself in the mirror. What I see can only be described as a nightmare. Blood covers my lower face, and the front of my shirt, flowing freely again from my left eye. Flowing at a rate suggesting a large, open wound, but upon further inspection, I see it coming from inside of my lower eye lid. The blood drips down my cheek and falls into the porcelain sink. I look at the sink as consistent red drops of blood splatter against the white, otherwise clean surface.

I bring myself to look back into the mirror. My eye is covered in red. It is bloodshot from top to bottom with the only exception being my pupil. While it should be a small black dot in the middle of my eye, my pupil is looks enlarged, covering a wide portion of the surface of my eye, and black. Pitch black, large, and haunting. Something is wrong.

A wave of fear rushes over me, and I slam the faucet handle on, as clean water pours from the spout. I put both hands underneath the flow of water and watch as I clean the blood off of my hands. Making a bowl with my palms, I splash water onto my face. The water flushes the blood away, as a new single stream of blood tears fall from my eye. Palm bowl, water, splash, clean. Again, and again, and I feel myself start to cry. *What the fuck is happening to me?*

Blood now covers the sink in splotches, and I find myself alternating between splashing it off of my face, then splashing it off the sink, hoping I can get all of the evidence to flush down the drain. I look back into the mirror and lean in to get a closer look. A move I am less than happy to do. With my index finger, I slightly pull my eye lid down, and try to find a rational source for the blood. I do not see anything abnormal except for the level of bloodshot my eye is, and the exaggerated size of my pupil. I move my hand away, and blink.

Looking into my eye again, I notice my pupil has gotten slightly bigger. In the amount of time it took me to move my hand away and blink, my pupil's size seems to have increased... *How is that possible? It's not...* I again lean in and look at my growing pupil. I gently pull my eye lids apart and look into my eye.

In the dense black nothing, I see something move. It was subtle, but it was there. There is something inside of my eye.

"Jesus Christ," I ask myself. "What the fuck is happening?" I try not to focus on questions I not only cannot answer, but also do not want the answer too. *Focus, Micah.*

More blood splashes in the sink. I cup more water into my face. I again rinse the sink. More blood... more water... more rinsing... I look back up to the sink, finding myself asking more and more questions, while knowing I am finding fewer and fewer answers.

I remember Thomas' body three-hundred feet below.

I remember the rock in the plastic bin.

# CHAPTER 20
# MICAH

I do not think about what I just watched in the mirror. I am not sure I can bare thinking about it with still so much unknown, and my team still in danger. I clean up as much of the bloodbath as possible, and quietly leave the bathroom. With no real destination in mind, I sneak once again past the kitchen area. It is empty. *Shit,* I think. I realize the women are now somewhere on deck, and I need to stay out of sight until I get a grasp on this situation. I quickly turn the corner, and I am face to face with the staircase leading down to the room with the hyperbaric chamber.

Step by labored step, I make my way down the staircase. I make it to the narrow hallway without making too much noise on the squeaky stairs. Walking down the hallway, I make it to the door and pause for a moment. I have no idea what I am walking into, I just know what has led up to this moment. In my mind, I rationalize my being here under the guise of all of us needing to know how much time we have left. I take a breath and push the door open.

The fluorescent lights seem somehow brighter than they had been before, piercing my head again with the same burst of annoying, and almost unbearable pain. I walk further into the room, and the pain forces me to lean against the tank. The gentle rumble and hum of the decompression system hard at work makes my hands tremble on the steel. The pain dissipates, and I am able to regain control of my stance. I circle around, walking towards what I guess would be considered the front of the chamber. A small window gives visibility into the inside of the tank, but I cannot see through it anymore. A thin layer of… something clouds the view.

*Is that blood?* It seems thicker than blood, but it has the same red, rust look of old blood. It is thick, like motor oil, with a dull red tint. Whatever it is, it is disgusting, and it sends a quick shiver through my spine. I move my face away from it, and walk further along the outside of the large, steel tank. The small interactive display screen shines as brightly as it did when the timer began. The minutes tick away without a care in the world.

58:19.

58:18.

58:17.

Fifty-eight minutes is not enough time, and that truth sinks in devastatingly fast. I walk back over to the small window and try to see inside. I am praying I see Thomas, regaining his consciousness. Slowly waking back up, and seeing me through the window, so a wave of relief would overwhelm me. I could smile, and give him an encouraging thumbs up, and loudly say, "You're going to be fine, Thomas! Everything is going to be fine!" I would rush back up the stairs and wrap my arms around Sarah and Marie and let them know the amazing news. Thomas is awake, and he is all right! Everything is all right.

Instead, I squint my eyes to try and see through the new, thicker layer of what may actually be blood covering the inside of the small window. Barely visible through the liquid, I can see the large, dark object laying on the floor of the tank. It seems to still be where Jax left Thomas' body, and it seems to still be lifeless. Keeping my eyes fixed on the object, still lost in my fantasy of "everything is all right," the object jerks one of its limbs.

I jump back, frightened, convinced my mind is paying tricks on me. It is taking advantage of my fear and using it against me. *Nothing moved, Micah.* Do not be silly. I move my face back into the frame of the window, my heart racing so fast I can feel each pounding beat in my throat. I look back towards the tank's floor, back towards that large, and what I assumed was, lifeless object. It is moving? I lean in closer, trying to squint my eyes even further to clear the image in my mind. It… *is* moving… No, no fucking way. It is impossible. Thomas' body, or whatever the hell we put in that tank, was not conscious, and most likely not alive. *There is no fucking way it...* the object jerks again. It is definitely moving. I lean in again, further, acknowledging my masochistic curiosity. I get my face closer and closer to the screen, watching the large, dark object regain its zest for life... *maybe it is Thomas.* We are not so lucky. My heart sinks, and the realization of what this means settles as a pit in my stomach. I lean in a little closer, almost touching my forehead against the glass, and I hear it. A sound causing my entire body to seize in fear. A sound I was praying I would not hear for at least a little while longer...

"Micah?" Sarah gently asks with a tone of concern I have not heard from her in years. At the sound of her timid voice, every hair on the back of my neck stands straight up on edge. I continue to face the tank, and I know she is standing at the base of the stairs in the narrow hallway. "What are you doing down here?"

I'm frozen in place. My legs locked; my arms pinned to my side. I am paralyzed at the thought of Sarah seeing me right now. I cannot let her see me in such poor condition, but I also know I cannot continue to avoid it. Every terrible scenario rushes through my mind about how she might react if she sees me. Will she scream? Will she run away in fear? Or what might be worse, will she try to help me and get too close? What if this infection, or whatever it is, is something contagious she could be susceptible to? Regardless of everything, I cannot let her see me, not yet. Or maybe I can. Because I just turned around to face her.

"We have to find another way. There's not enough time." I speak the words plainly, with little inflection tipping away my hand towards any specific emotion. They fall flat, and I look up to see Sarah's eyes. Terror has taken over her face as she realizes she is, in fact, looking at her husband, what is left of me anyway. Without regard to her own safety, and without hesitating at the repulsion she no doubt feels, she rushes to me.

"Micah, oh God, what happened?" She hovers her hands around my face, careful not to touch me if I am in pain. I can see her hands shaking in fear of what she does not understand. *That makes two of us.*

"I don't... I don't know." My words fade away. I do not know what else to say. I have no idea what is happening to me. I have no idea what is happening to any of us right now. I have no idea what to do next, and I have no idea how to get us out of this mess. I do not even know what this fucking mess is.

But I might.

"We have to get you to a doctor…" Her mind still thinking in rational terms. She grabs the towel from my hand and starts gently wiping the blood away from my face. She does it with such ease, careful not to cause me any further pain. *She is so goddamn good.* I find myself lost in her grace for a moment, before coming back to reality, and letting the weight of the circumstance crush me again. I grab her arm hard, and it momentarily locks her in frozen place.

"Sarah… stop it… We need to get off this boat." I hear the soft tick of the digital timer continue to force us closer to whatever fate lies ahead.

57:03.

57:02.

57:01.

Tick, tick, tick…

"We're running out of time. Our communications are down." I start to explain the gravity of this terrible situation to her. "Even if by some fucking miracle we got a hold of Jason right now, there's still a gap, the timer… there's a gap between the timer ending and help arriving. There's a gap in time, and we're on the losing end of it."

Sarah's expression remains blank. She is listening, and I know she hears the words I am saying, but I need to know she actually *hears* me. "Sarah… Do you understand me? Tell me you understand." She lowers her head slightly, and nods. She understands. God, we both look so fucking defeated. "Whatever is inside of this tank is coming out."

A silent expression takes over her face. I wonder what she is thinking, but she does not let me wonder for very long. She nods and takes my hand, squeezing it hard. Through her choked back tears, she speaks to me with all the courage she can muster.

"How did any of this happen?" My heart breaks.

"I don't know." I want so badly to pull her into me and throw my arms around her. To hold her tightly and assure her of the coming happy ending. I want to, but I know I cannot. I also do not want her to come in contact with the absolutely blood-soaked clothes now on my body. Sarah takes a step towards the door, and I am expecting her to leave the room completely. To leave me here alone in my solitude, waiting for what comes next. She does not. Instead, she looks to the tank's timer, and sets her watch to match the countdown. She then pulls my hand still in hers, and we walk back through the door and into the narrow hallway once again.

"We need to get you cleaned up." She is so strong. *She is so good.* I do not say a thing, I just let her pull me at her will. Up the stairs, past the kitchen again, and back into the bathroom I was just in.

She turns on the faucet, and I start splashing the water on my face again.

"Jesus, Micah, what happened? Tell me what happened." She is gentle with me, careful not to expose herself too much to whatever I am dealing with. She helps me as much as she can, though. Wiping excess blood with towels or cloth, helping wash my face and hands.

"I was looking for the card that Jason gave us; the one with the number written on the back for emergencies. I didn't even realize it had happened. Jax pointed it out." This revelation gives Sarah a slight pause.

"Jax saw you this way?" She asks concerned. I nod. "It's probably best Marie doesn't. I feel like it would be… too much." I nod again. Sarah grabs a small hand towel off of a rack on the wall, and carefully blots the blood and water off of my face. She puts just a slight amount of pressure on my face with the cloth. "It seems to be stopping, sort of." She continues patting the cloth against my face. I just close my eyes, and breath. I do not deserve this kindness, a fact I am beginning to viscerally understand. A million things to say race through my mind. I can only muster a simple sentence.

"Thank you, Sarah." She does not say anything back. We both know she does not need to.

"Does it hurt?" She asks after a few tender moments in quiet.

"No, it just feels like a really sharp headache. Like an intense migraine." She tears a strip of the cloth off of the towel, and starts to wrap it around my head, as a makeshift bandage.

"If she asks, you hit your head on the counter and it started bleeding, no big deal." She ties a knot with the rag, careful not to tighten the wrap around my head too tight.

"Thank you." I say. She smiles slightly out of the side of her mouth. Upset, but moving forward.

"I need you healthy." She says. As she speaks, I hear a tremble in her voice, and see tears begin pulling under her eyes.

With most of the blood cleaned off my face, and the consistent flow temporarily subdued, Sarah feels comfortable enough to kiss me. More importantly, I feel comfortable enough to let her.

"I love you." Her voice cracks slightly as the words come out. A solitary tear rolls down her cheek again.

"I love you too," I respond, with all the emotional strength I have left. In a quick move, she exhales and grabs my hand. Wiping tears from her eyes, she shakes the water off of her hand, and pulls me towards her and the door.

"We should get back to Jax and Marie. Figure this out." I do not need to actually respond. With Sarah's help, we immediately start making our way to the door.

Jax is back in the control room still trying to contact someone on shore as we quietly walk back onto the deck. I watch as Jax tirelessly, and desperately, speaks into the microphone, holding down that same small, black, plastic button.

"Tethys to Kodiak, do you copy?" Frustrated, he strongly pushes the microphone away. "Fuck it all." He shouts, angry and mentally exhausted. He pushes forward back into the microphone, "Fucking anyone? Anything? Can anyone hear me?" His voice roars across the deck of the boat.

He hears nothing but static in response. Jax lowers his head in defeat. In a miraculous turn, the static slightly hiccups. Not enough for Jax to know he has made contact, but enough of a hiccup to immediately capture his attention. He shoots his head to the speaker next to the small microphone. He wonders if someone is there trying to contact them back. He jumps back to the microphone, not waiting to find out, and shouts into the small device again, all of his energy restored.

"Kodiak? This is Jackson Pond, aboard The Tethys. Can anyone hear me?"

Static... hiccup...

A massive wave of relief rushes over Jax as he hears the sound of another voice break through the intermittent static. The voice of someone in one of the control towers on shore at Kodiak Airport, two hundred plus miles away.

"Kodiak to-" then static... "-hear you-" then more static... "-understand-" more frustrating static... "-over." Taking the victory where he can, Jax springs back into steadfast action. He presses the button again hard.

"Tethys to Kodiak!" His loud voice bellows across the deck again. He is unabashedly shouting now. Marie walks back into the deck, following the booming voice, and rushes over to his side. Jax sees her, and without giving it a second thought, puts her to work. "Coordinates! Help me find our coordinates!"

"Jax, did you get some…"

"Marie, now! Help me!" He interrupts, and Marie immediately joins him in his frantic search. Jax leaves Marie to search herself and jumps back into shouting excitedly into the microphone. "Tethys to Kodiak, do you copy?" Static… then… as clear as the morning sun…

"Tethys, we copy. Go ahead."

In a sweeping, desperate breath, all is quiet; the eye of the hurricane. The crisp, clean voice sends a shock down both their spines. Jax freezes for a moment, as they stare at each other.

"Well, say something!" Marie shouts. In a normal situation, she would have shouted those words through laughter. She does not laugh now. Jax turns his focus back to the microphone, Marie turns hers back to her search.

"Uhh… distress! Uhh… fuck. Seelonce distress!" Jax struggles to find the correct sequence of words. Something he feels should come naturally and immediately given his training and experience. "Fuck… what is it… Mayday! Mayday! Oh, for, Christ's sake, we fucking need help!" With a welcomed shout from Marie, she catches Jax's attention.

"Got them!" She lifts a thin slip of paper with their coordinates printed clearly. She rushes the page over to Jax, who rips the paper from her hands, and with a quivering voice recites them into the microphone praying the connection is still strong.

"Mayday! Latitude: 58.54532, longitude: -146.53375, do you copy?" Silence sits on the other end of the line. Silence for what feels like an eternity. The static breaks back into play, and simultaneously ruins the mood and energy in the control room.

"...hear you...location...what...help you..." Their connection breaks. Static blares through the room, cutting the air like a knife through fresh, strawberry jam.

"Fuck!" Jax shouts in frustration, and continues his efforts, trying to regain the contact they had literally just made. "Tethys to Kodiak, do you copy? Mayday, Mayday! Latitude: 58.54532, longitude: -146.53375. Do you copy, over!" Marie silently walks up behind Jax and places her hand on his shoulder. Her action should signal a willingness to give up, but Jax refuses to take that lead. "Do you copy!" He shouts in one last ditch effort. A final roll of his proverbial dice.

Static permeates through the open air of the control room, nothing but static. Finally, Jax lowers his head in defeat. He relinquishes his pressure on the button, looks away from the speaker, and turns towards Marie. They collapse into each other, each one practically holding the other up. Then there is another slight hiccup in the static.

"Copy, Tethys." ...No way, I think, Sarah and I still watching from the shadows.

Jax and Mare both burst into excited tears, and shouts of joy; victory.

They both continue their overwhelmed celebration, as Sarah delicately clears her throat and we finally take a few steps back into the control area. The slightly blood-soaked bandage still carefully tightened around my head.

"What's going on?" Sarah asks rhetorically, using the moment to also let them know that we are there.

"Jax got to Kodiak! He gave them our coordinates and..." She is interrupt by the man himself.

"They're sending help." Jax says dryly, but still bursting with relief and excitement. Marie runs to Sarah and throws her arms around her. They both cry, however, these tears are based in joy. Joy, and a strong sense of comfort and solace.

Jax looks directly at me, and at the bandage Sarah crafted for me. The bleeding has for the most part subsided, but a small, damp patch of red has made its way through the cloth and is visible where my eye is placed underneath. Jax gives me a stern, solemn look, and with the voice of someone who has seen too many appalling sights in his life to be phased by a little blood, he extends his hand and speaks to me.

"You all right, then?" I shake his hand in return.

"I will be. Good fucking work, Jax." I say, proud, as a wave of relief allows me to finally breath. Maybe we will be all right.

I remember the rock in the plastic bin.

# CHAPTER 21
# SARAH

They were all gathered on the deck now, unsure really of what was supposed to happen next. They were able to contact Kodiak Airport who will be getting a rescue helicopter in the air any moment now, and they had gathered supplies which somehow now seems a waste of their time. Micah recruits Jax to help him disconnect the storage tanks full of water from the filtration system. He asks Sarah and Marie to move the supplies they gathered towards the edge of the boat's deck. Despite contacting the airport, and help, Micah seems determined to be off of the boat before the tank opens regardless of when help arrives.

Sarah and Marie compile all of the items they deemed necessary for the duration of the time they will spend on the life raft before their help arrives. Food rations, water bottles, extra clothes, things of that nature.

"We need to load the life raft with as much as we can without capsizing it. We need to be on it, and well beyond this boat by the time that tank opens, because we'll still have time before the helicopter gets here. We can't still be on board." Sarah recognizes that familiar controlled tone in his voice. Captain of the ship, and owner of the fallout. He sounds less afraid now, she thinks, but she knows he is. What she cannot tell, however, is whether the fear is of whatever is in the decompression chamber, or what is causing his bloody mess of a face.

Sarah checks her watch, and sees the seconds relentlessly disappear.

24:36… tick.

24:35… tick.

24:34… tick.

Micah removes a brightly colored cushion cover from one of the benches lining the wall of the boat. He sets the cushion to the side, revealing a tightly wrapped bundle of vinyl; the large, industrial life raft. Sarah and Marie continue gathering and organizing the supplies they have plundered from the different areas of the boat, as Jax helps Micah lift the large vinyl bundle across the deck. The sturdy life raft was designed and built to successfully support up to thirty individual adults, yet it compacts down small enough to be stored underneath the fashionable cushion sitting on the bench lining the edge of the boat's hull. They lift it, but struggle to carry it across the deck. Sarah knows it has got to be horribly heavy, because even veins protrude from Jax's neck. Jax may be straining, but Micah is completely struggling.

"Almost…" Jax speaks, encouraging them both, "there…" Sarah watches Micah. He is broken, and yet he is still somehow giving this objective everything he has for all of their sakes. She watches sweat drip from his forehead, and his shoulders dramatically rise and fall with his strained breathing. She sees his joints and his knuckles, white from exerting all his strength to lift and carry this bundle with Jax. She sees a thin stream of blood begin pouring out of Micah's nostril. Her brain finally begins forming the thought to articulate what she is seeing when Micah's grip slips, and he screams.

The large bundle on Micah's end hits the deck and causes Jax to drop it too. Micah falls down on all fours, hitting his knees hard against the wooden floor. Blood again pours heavily from his face, and splashes as it hits the wooden deck in a pool around him.

"Micah!" Sarah screams, as she races to help him back up onto his feet. She is immediately at his side.

"No, no, no! Oh, God… Are you all right?" She asks and starts to help him stand back up. Struggling to help him, she shoots a glare to Jax, who still just stands and stares at the two of them in their struggle. "Are you just going to stand there?" Micah lifts his head to look at Jax, and finally gets back onto his feet. Sarah helps him and they walk away towards the bathroom once again. Horrified, Marie walks to Jax, and quietly speaks to him. Sarah is still close enough to hear their conversation as she helps Micah away.

"What happened?" Marie nervously, and almost silently asks him.

"Something isn't right." Jax dryly replies. It is obvious, and Sarah knows they can both tell something is very wrong. People do not bleed from their eyes if everything is all right.

Sarah and Micah make it back into their bathroom sanctuary, and she holds her arms around Micah as he leans over the sink, screaming. The water runs powerfully down the sink, and Sarah helps clean the blood from Micah's face again.

"Micah, what is happening? What's wrong?" She is stuck between having an ardent desire to rescue her husband from this nightmare, and simultaneously wanting to be anywhere but this bathroom. She is overwhelmed by having to watch Micah in such dire and extreme pain, while being completely unable to do anything about it. She is helpless, and she is stuck.

Then Micah vomits blood and water into the sink.

Sarah jumps back, caught off guard and taken completely by surprise by the move. Micah is equally as shocked by the action, and he dry heaves into the sink after it passes. Terrified, and overwhelmed, Sarah bravely speaks through her freshly falling tears, "I need you to tell me how to help you…" After overcoming the fear he likely felt, Micah lifts his head to look into the mirror. He sees exactly what he was afraid of seeing: his own reflection.

Both of his eyes are now starkly covered in red, splotchy and bloodshot. His pure black pupils oversized, and misshapen. Blood freely flows from his nose, and now both eyes. Exhausted, he leans into the mirror to examine his face. She watches closely, and sees a slight, subtle movement of something in his right eye. A brief moment of panic. Neither of them speak a word, but they both saw it. She is sure they both saw it. He leans into the mirror again.

Something small again shifts in his eye, moving in the black area of his right pupil. Paralyzed by her fear and confusion, Sarah silently watches him lean in closer to the mirror. With his finger, he pulls his eyelid down only just. Blood drips over his hand, and he leans even closer still to the mirror. *What the fuck is that?* She thinks. Sarah watches in horror as Micah lifts his other hand towards his eye. Tenderly, with his index finger and thumb, he presses his fingertips against his black, bloodshot eye. Sarah watches Micah as it looks like he is grabbing at something in his overgrown pupil. She holds her breath, and wants to look away, but cannot bring herself to.

She brings her arms up, and holds her hands to her mouth, keeping in a scream. She watches Micah as he pulls a thin, elastic string out of his right eye.

*What is that?* She thinks.

She watches Micah struggle to pull his hand away from his eye. In absolute horror and disbelief, she watches a long, thin, worm-like creature slide out of Micah's eye. Blood rushes out of the tiny hole. Micah screams, in pain.

Either holding back a scream, or vomit herself, Sarah presses her hands into her mouth harder and harder. Terrified tears stream down her cheeks. Micah finally pulls the little terrible thing completely out, and it writhes in his fingers, wiggling its translucent body unabated. Without hesitating, Micah lets go, and the tiny worm is swept down the drain of the sink with the rushing water flowing from the faucet. He shoots his eyes to meet Sarah's in the mirror, no doubt hoping she missed it all.

Without saying anything, he looks back to his horrible reflection. He again locks eyes with Sarah behind him, still gripping her mouth, still silently weeping, terrified of what she just witnessed. Micah shakes in fear, and breaths heavily. The flow of blood from his eyes and nose slows.

"What's happening to me?" Micah says. Tremors shake his entire, and blood still drips from his eyes and nose.

She does not know what to say. She does not know what to say because she does not know the answer. It is clearer now than ever, however, the answer is something terrible. The answer is something awful that will forever change their lives, and likely not for the better.

Sarah looks down at her wrist, her watch's timer forces them closer to their fate.

17:47... tick.

17:46... tick.

17:45... tick.

Time's relentless lack of care for any of them or their circumstance persists without yielding, waiting for no one.

They quietly make their way back onto the deck, and Sarah sees Jax continue maneuvering the vinyl raft out on to the deck before he ultimately begins inflating it. He is stone cold focused and has expressed no issue in executing this task by himself and in silence. Marie, standing nearby, does not have the same resolve. Finally feeling confident enough to at least speak, instead of consistently cry, she watches Jax work, exercising her newfound courage to actually say something. Sarah and Micah keep their distance, but listen.

"Jax, talk to me, please. Tell me what's going on with Micah?" Her voice wavers, shaking and cracking with a sense of very real unrest.

"His eyes are bleeding, Marie. I don't know, I have no idea at all. Your guess is literally as good as mine." His words are harsh and cut quick. He does not slow up his work, and he does not even look at Marie as he speaks to her.

"But why?" She asks the way a child would ask their parent the same question over and over again. Her arms are wrapped tightly around herself, a small sense of comfort in her confusion and fear. The question falls on deaf ears, and Sarah is sure Jax lets a horde of random thoughts fly through his mind. Sensing his anger begin to build with the stress of putting all of the information together, Sarah watches Jax unintentionally snap, raising his voice to a shout.

"I don't know! I don't know anything that's happening right now, Marie. I don't fucking know!" A tense silence falls over the two, an uncomfortable development in their otherwise very caring friendship. The tense but understandable silence is temporary, as the moment is cut short by the sounds of Sarah and Micah taking a few steps back onto the deck. Jax, now feeling a sense of resolve from his ability to speak unreserved, continues the approach. "Micah, what the fuck is going on, man?" Marie joins in with his curiosity, absolving him from his outburst just moments before.

"We need to know what's happening." Marie echoes Jax's sentiment. Exhausted, Micah responds with the only words he is comfortable responding with.

"I don't know." He looks down and avoids making eye contact with either of them. He no longer stands within arm's reach of Sarah, and she imagines how overwhelmed he must be with the feeling of solitude.

Sarah, having had enough of the hostility she is interpreting from Jax and Marie's combined body language chimes in. Using only her words, she positions herself between them and Micah.

"He's fine." It is as if there is a physical heat attached to her words, and it burns directly into Jax who does not waste a moment in his response. He bursts with frustration and takes an aggressive step towards them.

"He's fine? He's fine?" He says, repeating himself in the condescending way people do to ensure their words are being heard, even when they already know they are. "His fucking eyes are bleeding! He's not…" Jax says, practically yelling, before he is equally, and just as abrasively, interrupted.

"Hey!" Micah yells, actually physically positioning his body between Sarah and the others. "You do not speak to her like that." Each man, lion and lamb in their individual minds, Micah and Jax stare at each other in a standoff. Sarah stands just behind Micah, her heart beats almost entirely out of her chest. Marie throws her hands up to her face and breaks them apart.

"Enough!" She shouts, trying to end the confrontation.

Jax and Micah stay face to face shouting directly into each other, matching each verbal jab tit for tat. Sarah cannot quite make out exactly what they are yelling at each other, but she becomes very aware when she hears Micah yell the word, "Stop" at Jax. When he pronounces the *"p"* his lips pop together, sending a small splatter of blood into Jax's face. Sarah watches Jax stumble back, shocked and scared, and wipes his face. The tiny drop of blood splatters onto Jax's face effectively ending the confrontation, accomplishing what Marie had been trying desperately to do.

Micah is immediately overwhelmed with remorse. He let his anger get the better of him, and he became someone he prides himself on not ever being. It was obviously unintentional, and Sarah knows if Jax had not chosen to be so aggressive, it never would have happened to begin with.

"Jax," Micah starts saying, "I'm so sorry. I'm so…" His voice fades into mortified obscurity. Marie rushes to Jax's side, helping him clean his face off, and Sarah is immediately at Micah's side. An invisible line in the sand is drawn.

Sarah imagines a million thoughts racing through Jax's mind, but as he lifts his head and looks up to Micah, his sight focuses past his friend. He looks at the two large, full water tanks standing tall and ominously behind Micah and Sarah, and one thought in particular seems to land with its audience. Sarah watches as Jax tries to formulate a theory to the question Marie had asked him just moments before. *"But why?"*

"You…" Jax searches for the rest of the words, speaking so quietly Sarah can hardly make out what he says. "You drank the water." Sarah sees Jax raise his hand, and point towards them, only he is still not focusing on them. Lifting his eyes to meet Jax's, Micah also realizes that Jax is pointing beyond them.

"You have it now." Jax says loud enough for everyone to hear. Sarah and Marie both look at the tanks, and then back to each other. Micah and Jax lock eyes and hold each other's stare.

"Shut up, Jax." Sarah again enters the fold, immediately defending Micah, and formally defining the decisive line in the sand. "You don't know what you're talking about." Jax is not deterred at all, he is not slowed down for even a moment. He keeps his eyes locked into Micah's and continues speaking directly to him.

"You have it inside of you, Micah." Each word cuts like a knife. Each word based in the only scenario makes any logistical sense to Jax.

"Shut up!" Sarah shouts, feeling her own rage swell inside of her.

"He's right." Micah says, still locking eyes with Jax. "I'm the only one that drank the water." Sarah feels her strength immediately dissolve into terrible concern.

"Micah, what are you saying?"

"Thomas… whatever is in that tank… It's in me too. It is." Sarah's body sways slightly back and forth, not able to compartmentalize her nervous energy.

"Micah, quit it." She essentially pleads with him.

"He's right, Sarah." Micah now looks at his wife and reaches his hands out to grab her shoulders. His words strong and definitive.

"You sound ridiculous," Sarah says. "You're just having an allergic reaction to something." She tries to rationalize the symptoms into something more palatable. She gently presses her hands to his face, holding it. Micah closes his eyes, then looks down.

"An allergic reaction? To what?" Jax interrupts with a hostile edge to his tone. "We've had the same meals for a bloody week." Marie tries to calm Jax, and have him lower his voice, understanding the revelation happening in front of them.

"Jax, come on." Marie says. She puts her hand on his shoulder, hoping it will slow down the building of his obvious frustration. Her touch, however, has little to no effect.

"What?" Jax, erupts at Marie again, undeterred by her attempts to calm him, and pushes harder into Sarah and Micah. "He's putting us all in danger." With these words, Sarah has had enough. She erupts at Jax, causing him to retract his aggression slightly.

"Shut the fuck up, Jax!"

Finally, after considering the realistic possibility of this new idea, Micah speaks out to them all. His voice is powerful, and loud. It immediately causes everyone else to shut up and listen.

"He's *right.*" Micah gives in. He exhales, and mentally pieces his words together before he speaks. "He's right." When she hears Micah validate Jax's theory, it finally becomes real for Sarah. Her aura immediately turns from one of aggressive defense, to one of care and worry.

"How do I help you?" She asks, pathetic in her delivery.

"I don't know. We wait."

"How much time do we have, though?" Marie asks. Sarah at her watch, as Micah responds.

"Not enough," Micah says, more upset than before. "Kodiak is sending a helicopter. We just need to stick together, and we'll get out of here." Sarah notices that Micah says these words directly to Jax, who nods in return. Jax's demeanor very subtly changes, and he begins to understand the gravity of the words Micah speaks. Sarah, hearing the conceit in Micah's voice puts her hands on his face, still bleeding.

"Micah…" He does not let Sarah finish her sentence. He takes her by the hand and starts to pull her away. "Come with me."

They start to walk away together, and Micah stops. He turns back to see Jax and Marie standing, just watching he and Sarah walk away from them. He locks eyes again with Jax, before he calls back out to them.

"Jax, get that raft ready, all right?" His voice shakes. Bloody tears pool in the bottom of his eyes and begin rolling down his cheeks. Sarah notices, but says nothing. She looks to Jax, who does not break his stare with Micah. Jax silently nods but does not move.

Jax watches as Micah leads Sarah away again, before he continues filling the large vinyl raft with air. Sarah hears Jax ask Marie for help, having to try multiple times to get her attention before she is able to look away from Micah and Sarah walking away, and focus on the task at hand.

Micah turns to walk away again. Still holding Sarah by the hand, she follows him across the deck.

# Chapter 22
# Sarah

With a strong sense of urgency, Micah walks back into the control room area, gripping Sarah's hand in his.

"What you do mean 'what's in the tank?' Micah, what's going on?" She jerks her hand out of his, causing him to stop and look at her. He is a mess, but his focus is sharp.

"Sarah, listen… You saw the same thing I did. Whatever came up first… we know it wasn't Thomas. Whatever is in that tank… isn't Thomas. I'm the only one who drank the water. He and I are the only ones that came in contact with…"

"With what?" She asks, terrified of but desperate for a more clear and certain response.

"Whatever it is that killed him. Whatever is sitting in that tank, waiting for that latch to open."

Micah sees her begin to cry, or continue to cry at this point, and instead of moving towards her and consoling his wife, he turns away from her and continues his search.

"I don't understand." Sarah says, beginning to lose control of her resounding composure. The one thing she has hung her hat on all evening. After frantically throwing papers to the side, Micah finally finds what he is looking for. The card Jason gave him before they left with the phone number scribbled in black ink on the plain back side. Micah turns to her, and rushes to stand near her, face to face.

"Promise me," he says, handing her the card. "Promise me that as soon as you get to shore you will call this number."

"What about," she begins to ask, struggling to speak through her tears.

"Promise me," Micah persists, interrupting her. Sarah continues begging her mind to find more words to say.

"What about all of this, Micah? Everything we've worked towards." She says, desperately trying to keep their conversation going. Micah simply shakes his head.

"It's over. The water isn't safe. Without that... it's done. Everything is done." He holds her shoulders in his hands. His grip feels weaker than before, but not for lack of effort.

"You don't know that the water did this to you. You don't know that's why you're..."

"Tell them what happened." Micah says, not giving her the chance to finish her thought. "Don't let anyone come aboard this ship." Sarah's concern turns to panic, which turns to genuine fear.

"What are you talking about?"

"Don't let anyone take that water off this boat. Don't let anyone come back. Don't let anyone pick up where we left off. Don't let anyone." Micah's persistence scares her more. It is as if he has more information still but is unwilling to share with her. The rational tone in how he is speaking, she thinks, is what nightmares are made of.

"Micah, please..." she pleads. Cutting her off again, Micah raises his voice. He is careful not to scream, but he needs to make sure she is hearing and understanding him clearly.

"You're not safe here!" She stops trying to respond. His attempt to speak calmly falls flat before him. He startles her with his shout and corrects himself. "Please, you just... you have to trust me. You are not safe here, Sarah. No one is safe here. Do you understand me?" Sarah does not waver. She does not crumble. She understands, but she does not want to.

"What about you?" She asks. Micah does not have a response strong enough to combat the words he assumes she will begin speaking. "You're going to play hero? What about *you*, Micah?" Carefully, and intentionally, Micah looks into Sarah's eyes. He again takes her hands in his and holds back as much emotion as possible as he begins to speak, directly addressing her question and concern.

"If I'm in that room when… whatever it is comes out of that tank… I can at least try to hold it off long enough for you and Marie, and Jax, to get off this boat. Until help arrives. You'll be safe, Sarah."

"I am not leaving you," she barks through her tears, fear becoming rage. "I am *not* leaving you!"

"That is not an option." Micah immediately retorts. A new, steady stream of blood begins dribbling out of his nose. It still frightens Sarah, but she braves the moment, and stands her ground.

"I'm not leaving you."

"You don't have a choice, Sarah. You need to help Jax get that raft into the water and as far away from this boat as you can, before…"

"Micah, I'm not leaving you! I'm not fucking doing it!" She begins to yell at him.

"You have to!" He matches her volume and shuts the conversation down.

He wants to stop raising his voice. He wants to stop yelling at the woman he loves. He wants to wrap his arms around her and again tell her everything will be fine. They both know it will not. Sarah can sense his temper rising, and a strange sense of rage boiling deep in his abdomen.

"I'm lost, Sarah. I'm already lost, and I am so sorry." A flash of that same bright light seers across his mind and knocks him to his knees. Cracking against the wooden deck, Sarah hears a bone in his leg fracture. She knows body is weakening. She kneels down to help him back to his feet, ignoring the painful screams he is letting out, and she sees the next body breaking moment.

Snapping involuntarily to the side, Micah's neck unnaturally contorts. He lets out another roar of pain. It corrects itself, with a small bulge now protruding from the side of his neck.

"You have to go!" Micah screams. "You have to leave, Sarah. Go!"

"Micah…" Her heart is breaking alongside his bones and his body. Again, trapped between wanting to leave and desperately needing to stay.

"Go, goddamnit!" The anger in his voice causing Sarah to take a large step back. Again, she finds her hands at her face, and she struggles to take a full breath. She can again feel her pulse in her wrists and neck. Feeling her fear, and seeing Micah's body betraying him, she begins to understand he is right.

It breaks every ounce of her being, but she knows he is absolutely right. He is lost. He will die on this boat, and if they are still on board when he does, they will die along with him. Fully aware she is only moments away from forever losing the love her life, and as much as it pains her, she knows he is doing what he is doing so he can save hers. New, fresh tears pour from her eyes, mimicking the blood pouring from Micah's. Slowly, she kneels down to his side, and with one sentence, she assures Micah it is fine.

"Let me help you." Sarah helps him back to his feet, Micah still screaming in pain from the crack in his knee and neck. With one of his arms around her, she helps him towards the staircase down to the narrow hallway leading to the room containing the hyperbaric chamber.

Slowly, and carefully, they continue their descent down the stairs. Each time Micah puts pressure on his feet to the ground, it seems a new bolt of pain is shot through his body. Sarah, strongly holding in her emotion, pushes forward helping him every step down the long, thin hallway. She does so, against her own desire to stay at his side, until they stand in the doorway of the room containing the decompression tank.

Fresh blood drips from Micah's ear now, as well, and he stumbles a step forward, positioning himself between Sarah and the tank. Behind him, Sarah can see the digital timer tick away the last few minutes of their life together.

07:11.

07:10.

07:09.

Tick, tick, tick...

Micah also watches the seconds disappear, knowing the weight of what each digital tick means. He turns back to look at Sarah, weeping, standing in the doorway of the small room.

"I am so sorry, Sarah." He begins to cry along with her, as the water from his tears mixes with the blood dripping from his face. He kneels, and she immediately meets him on the ground. His face in her hands, she tries her best to comfort him one last time.

"Shh," she quietly coos, as she grazes her right thumb across his wet, and bloody, cheek.

"I love you," Micah says, his voice shaking with fear.

"I love you so much," She instantly replies.

Micah, mustering the little strength he has left, takes Sarah by both of her shoulders, and begins to stand on his own. His face grimacing with pain, he brings her up to stand with him.

Once they are both on their feet, Micah looks into her eyes. His stare deep with remorse, he gently pushes her away. She steps back about a foot, standing just outside the door frame.

This is it.

They both weep, and Micah takes a step towards the tank, positioning himself just inside the room, beyond the door frame. The timer behind him ticks away, relentlessly, and without care for the devastation they both feel.

06:44.

06:43.

06:42.

Tick, tick, tick...

Through his tears, and terror, and fear, and shame, and guilt, Micah finds the ability to mutter a quiet sentence.

"Shut the door, love." Sarah chokes her weeping back as much as she can, and hesitates before she closes the door.

The large, thick, steel door now solidifies the space between them with Micah inside the room, and Sarah just outside the room standing in the hallway. They maintain their eye contact through a small window in the door. Sarah cries hard. She watches Micah's mouth move, but she cannot hear him through the robust door and the loud wails of her crying. Knowing she cannot hear him speak, Micah gently holds his index finger up to his mouth, encouraging her to quiet down. *It's okay, Sarah,* he tells her with his eyes. The look in his eyes makes Sarah cry even harder, but she does her best to lower the sound of her cries, so she can hear Micah's muffled speech through the small window of the thick, steel door.

Recognizing she is trying to calm herself, Micah again speaks through the pane of glass.

"Lock the door, Sarah."

He watches her, as a fresh wave of large tears pour from her eyes. She shakes her head, and he sees her mouth moving.

"I can't do it. No, I can't." She says.

Micah tries to force a smile through his own tears, and he speaks, his voice muffled by the industrial built door, "Lock the door, Sarah."

She cries hard and continues shaking her head as she raises her hand towards the reinforced lock on her side of the door. Crying impossibly harder, she feels the cool steel under her fingers. Micah, face fluctuating between pain, fear, and encouragement, smiles again. "It's all right, Sarah, you just have to lock the door." Micah again forces a smile and wipes the blood water from his face.

"Please." He says one last time.

Sarah turns the deadbolt latch, and they both hear the steel crank together, securing the door locked tight from the outside of the room. She has locked him in. Relentlessly weeping together, Micah places his bloody hand against the glass window of the large, steel door. Sarah, practically collapsing her body into the door, matches his hand with her own. He rests his forehead on the glass, and again, she mirrors him. Micah lifts his head back and looks at her. He nods, and Sarah forces herself to walk away from the door. Before she reaches the stairs, she turns back to look at her husband.

She sees Micah turn to face the tank. He looks at the timer, continuing to tick without care.

05:17.

05:16.

05:15.

Tick, tick, tick...

Micah, his skin rotting into a deep purple, blotchy appearance, drops to his knees.

Sarah finally turns back, and makes her way back up the stairs to the main deck of the boat, collapsing at the top, weeping hard. After a moment of recovery, she breaths heavy, wipes the tears from her eyes, and stands to her feet. With a new resolve, and with a new focus, she walks to Marie and Jax who are on the deck, unraveling the large life raft.

Jax sees her first, and takes a step towards her, with a blank facial expression. He takes one look at her appearance, her clothes covered in her husband's blood, and her eyes red and puffy with tears. Jax knows without needing to ask what she has just had to do. Hoping to distract her with a task, he calls out to her.

"Come on, Sarah, we need your help." It seems to work, as Sarah walks over the them, emotionless and silent. Jax attaches a large machine he found to the raft and cranks it on. The life raft begins inflating, more quickly than before. The three stand in silence, other than the roar of the machine inflating the raft, and none of them make eye contact. None of them need to. The life raft finishes inflating, and Sarah begins helping Marie lift their supplies onto it. Jax walks over to one of the tanks and starts to disconnect it from its security chains. Sarah sees, and shouts at him, her voice piercing the air around them.

"No!" Jax looks to her. "It's not safe. Leave it." Jax nods and helps them with the rest of the supplies. Marie checks her watch.

"Four minutes, we need to hurry." Sarah, carrying a large bag of food, drops it, and collapses to the ground. Her strength and resolve are broken, and she begins to cry again. She falls on her knees, giving up. Jax hits a latch on the boat, and a large portion of the wall crashes down into the ocean, splashing water high. Marie and Jax push the life raft into the water. Jax looks back to Sarah, still kneeling and weeping.

"Sarah…" He speaks as gently as he can, understanding the turmoil she feels, but also forcefully, understanding himself the lack of time they truly have. "Sarah, we have to go, now."

Sarah imagines her husband inside the room with the hyperbaric chamber, still sitting on his knees. He does not move but focuses on the sound of the ticking timer. Sarah looks at her watch.

03:32.

03:31.

03:30.

Tick, tick, tick…

She imagines Micah leaning back, lifting his face towards the ceiling. He lets his arms fall to his side, and he exhales, seemingly finding a small pocket of peace within this chaos. A vein in Micah's neck begins to swell slightly, and a loud pop cracks in his neck, contorting it again to the side. He screams in pain. A loud, booming scream.

A scream they all hear from the deck.

Marie jerks her head towards the staircase, and they all acknowledge what they just heard.

"Oh, my God…" Marie spits out.

"Sarah," Jax now shouts, "we have to go, now!" He helps Marie onto the raft and pushes it out into the water. He stands at the edge of the boat's deck, and hold his hand out towards Sarah, still kneeling and weeping. "Sarah… come on!" Marie looks to Sarah, and then down to her watch.

02:58.

02:57.

02:56.

Tick, tick, tick…

"Sarah, please!" Marie now begs her to come as well. Jax walks over to Sarah, and grabs her by her arms, lifting her to her feet.

"Come on, now," Sarah immediately fights Jax off, standing to her feet on her own.

"No!" She screams at him. "Stop it!" They stand, now face-to-face.

"I'm sorry. I'm sorry this happened, but we cannot stay here any longer." Jax pleads with Sarah. A strong desperation in his voice. "We are not safe." Jax gently lifts Sarah's chin, so they look each other in the eyes. "We have to…"

"Go." Sarah finishes his sentence for him. Jax pauses, trying to reach the intent of her words through her calm, still flowing tears.

"What are you…"

"Go." She interrupts again. "It's all right, Jax." She forces a smile through her tears. "I can't leave him."

"You have to, Sarah."

"No, I can't do it. I won't do it." She resists, putting her foot down.

"I'm not leaving you behind."

"It's my choice. I'm choosing. It's all right, I promise." Then, almost as a whisper, she reiterates, "I just… I can't leave him."

The two stand facing each other in another emotional stand-off. Sarah wipes away a tear as it falls, and she smears a slight bit of Micah's blood from her hand across her cheek. "It's okay. Go."

"Sarah…" Jax is not sure if he should take her at her word.

"Go. Find help. Get off this boat." She nods continuously, not taking his retorts kindly. She hands him the card Micah had given her. "Go, Jax. Please, just go." Again, she wipes a tear from her face leaving more of Micah's blood on her cheek. After a moment of uncomfortable but understanding silence, Marie shouts at them both. "Call this number. Don't let anyone pick up where we left off."

"We have to go!" Marie calls out to them both.

Jax and Sarah embrace. They hold onto each other. Then, Jax turns, and calmly walks over to the boat's edge. Marie, seeing Sarah hold her ground where she was, looks Jax.

"What's going on?" Sarah hears Marie ask Jax, confused and concerned. Jax does not respond. He simply dives off of the boat, and into the ocean. He swims over to the life raft and pulls himself onto it.

He and Marie look to the boat, and see Sarah standing there, in solitary strength. She holds her fingers to her mouth and kisses them before holding them in the air towards them. She watches as Jax begins paddling in the water, and the raft moves farther away from the boat, further away from the chaos.

She takes a breath and closes her eyes. She feels the cold breeze against her hot skin. She hears the water clash against itself, and against the steel side of the ship. She opens her eyes and turns to face the water tanks. She walks to them and opens the spout on both. One at a time, she cranks them open, and the water begins spilling freely onto the deck of the boat. After a moment, she turns to face the small staircase. She walks towards it and begins making her way down.

Feeling the rumble of the tank at her feet and hearing the loud hum of the decompression system still at work, she approaches the bottom of the stairs. She firmly places her feet off of the stairs, and into the long and narrow hallway. She takes a step.

In a moment of clarity, she remembers the fundraiser that had started this all. She remembers Micah standing next to the podium in that large conference room. She remembers it being filled with the group of rich, would-be patrons. She remembers Micah staring out at them, taking a breath, and smiling. She remembers the words he closed his presentation with.

"I want to leave you with this." Micah calmly and confidently said to the large crowd. "In the entirety of 'The Descent of Man,' Charles Darwin mentions his theory of 'Survival of the Fittest' just twice. Love, however, he mentions ninety-five times."

Sarah stands in the hallway, and looks at the large, steel door. The small window once clear, and the last thing between her and her husband, is now blocked by the same thick, red, blood like substance that was covering the inside of the tank window. She hears a strange, piercing sound coming from the other side of the door. She clinches her eyes shut, and again remembers Micah standing quietly at the podium.

"We live in the most privileged nation on Earth. We have the resources, the science, the technology, everything. But we need to be doing more for each other." She remembers you could hear a pin drop; the large ballroom was so silent. "We need to help one another. We need to look out for one another. We need to *love* one another."

Tears stream down Sarah's face as she slowly takes another step towards the steel door. Closer to the door, she deciphers the strange, piercing sound is a scream. Not Micah's scream, and not Thomas' scream, but a scream. She lifts her hand, and places it on the glass of the small window in the large, steel door. Again, she remembers Micah.

He continued his closing remarks, speaking directly to the crowd in the large ballroom.

"Then, and only then, will we be able to truly make a difference in this world."

Sarah holds her hand against the window. Sarah weeps, and presses her forehead against the window as well. Tears stream down her face. A shadow passes by the window and catches her attention, but she does not look up or into the room. She does not need to. She cries harder. Inside the room, the digital timer ticks away without a care.

00:03.

00:02.

00:01.

Tick, tick, tick...

*Click.*

The metal latch pops open.

# THE END

# ACKNOWLEDGEMENTS

First and foremost, I'd like to thank my family for their unending support.

I would specifically like to thank Mallary McKinzie for knowing what's best for me, even when I don't; the Thirst Project, for doing the hard work that's changing the world; and Stephanie Morris, for putting up with my inability to distinguish "further" from "farther." I still can't.

Thank you to Bryan Price, Daniel Oliver, Brian Johnson and Callie Prendiville Johnson, Brett Simmons, Tim Losee, Wesley Freitas, Kathrynn Cobbs, Rachael Poupis, Ramona Czernekova, Kaya Herman, and thank you to Reagan Rothe and the entire team at Black Rose Writing.

Finally, thank you to Kelsey Hansen for being a constant source of encouragement.

# ABOUT THE AUTHOR

Trey Everett is a Texas-born author and screenwriter. While his family had no professional creative ties, he was drawn to the arts. For college, he moved to Southern California and attended the American Academy of Dramatic Arts, studying film & television. After many years of flirting with success, he settled back into his original passion; storytelling. Now based in Los Angeles, he focuses on carefully and meticulously crafting stories he is most compelled to tell.

# Note from the Author

Word-of-mouth is crucial for any author to succeed. If you enjoyed *Beneath the Surface*, please leave a review online—anywhere you are able. Even if it's just a sentence or two. It would make all the difference and would be very much appreciated.

Thanks!
Trey Everett